## Hal blinked.

A few moments ag̶...  blended very well into the grey shadows of the night; now she was brilliant with colour. A Spanish grandmother would explain that shade of hair colour, and the ripe mouth. Her figure, too, undisguised by her ill-fitting gown, was seductively proportioned and her skin, so creamily pale, also declared her ancestry. But how to explain those eyes—the colour of autumn-touched beech leaves—or the clipped English voice?

**Laura Cassidy** followed careers in both publishing and advertising before becoming a freelance writer, when her first son was born. She has since had numerous short stories and articles published, as well as novels. She began writing for Historical Romances™ after discovering sixteenth-century romantic poetry, and very much enjoys the research involved in writing in the historical genre. She lives with her husband, who is a creative consultant, and their two sons, near London.

# Chapter Fifteen

Rachel looked astounded. Hal's warm smile flashed again. He let go of Rachel and went to his mother, putting an arm around her. She straightened her back, slipped a hand into her belt and took out a ring. Hal looked down on it. It was an old-fashioned double ring, a ruby cut in the shape of a crude heart and a large diamond, the two linked by bands of pale Italian gold—Harry had given it to her on a Devon seashore a lifetime ago. Hal had seen it many times before, for Bess always carried it about her person. She lifted one of his hands and dropped it into his palm.

'Then let us proceed,' Elizabeth said.

Hal took his mother to George, who set her in a chair beside him, and took her hand. 'Bravo, Mother.' She gave him a bitter look.

'Madrilene's granddaughter, wearing my betrothal ring!' she said in a stifled voice.

'Then why did you give it to Hal? We have baubles and to spare in this house, any one of them would have done for the purpose.'

Bess sighed. 'I promised your father last year that Hal would have it. Oh—I hope you are not offended that Judith should not wear it?'

'Why should I be? Hal was Father's favourite child, so 'tis right and proper.'

'I didn't know you knew that,' she said slowly.

'Well, I did and have never minded. And I don't mind about the ring—after all, Hal got precious little else.'

'Why do you think that was?'

'Because Hal is very like Father, and—also like Father—must fight a little to get his place in the world. A rich young man, as physically favoured as he is, would be a magnet for every unscrupulous woman in England were he proportionately rich.'

'Yes, indeed, women like Katherine Monterey,' Bess said thoughtfully. 'And yet I think she knew he didn't care enough for her. However…' she brightened '…he thought he did and that was only a short time ago. Perhaps this is just another fancy.'

'Don't pin your hopes on that,' George said. 'Only look at the two of them now.'

The parlour was well lighted with many candles, but all that light seemed concentrated on the two standing before the Queen. They both radiated a glow. When the proceedings were concluded, Hal led Rachel to the door.

'One moment, sir,' Elizabeth said mildly, 'there is the question of a little unfinished business.'

Hal came back reluctantly. The elation of the ceremony of the past few minutes had wiped the reason for it from his mind and he could see it was the same for Rachel. She was examining the wonderful feeling of having Lady Bess, Hal's mother, her inherited enemy, standing up for her and even giving her own precious betrothal ring to seal an occasion she could surely have no stomach for. Now, would it all be spoiled as Katherine gave her spiteful evidence? But, never mind, Bess Latimar had stood for her!

Hal was less convinced of his mother's volte-face. He had seen at court the curious freemasonry amongst women when one of their number was attacked by an overbearing male—in this case, the obnoxious Thomas Carstairs—seen them close ranks with their bitterest enemy: for a short while, at least. Well, Bess could make Rachel's life miserable in the domestic field, but Elizabeth, with her obsession in a particular area, could lose his love her life. He knew, with a frisson of premonition, that it was up to him to win this battle, and every dark fear he had ever had of his own inadequacy rose up to confront him. He would have liked to turn over the responsibility to his brother with his talent for advocacy, but George had shown his detachment when asked about the betrothal. No, he had to do this alone. Inwardly he squared his shoulders to meet the challenge. Very gently he guided Rachel back to her chair, she sat folding her hands in her lap. She looked up at him and his heart contracted. My darling one, he thought, how beautiful she was…and how trusting. God send I do not fail her. Hal sent forth this urgent prayer to his Maker whom he had not addressed in any serious way since his childhood. He turned back to the others with a purposeful air.

'Now, how do we proceed?'

Thomas Carstairs got up. He looked to Elizabeth. 'I must protest, Your Majesty,' he said sternly, 'the unorthodoxy of this whole matter.'

'Yes, yes,' Elizabeth said irritably. 'We have discussed that already, but I have agreed it should go ahead. Pray get on, Sir Thomas.'

Carstairs looked at Hal. In the flickering yellow light the two men measured each other. One a fanatical self-server in the new regime, the other a spoiled member of the old guard, not tried or tested. Nevertheless, Sir Thomas dropped his eyes first.

Hal looked to his brother. 'George? How do we go on?'

George rose without haste. He bowed to Carstairs. 'You read the charges afresh, sir, call your witnesses and state your case. After which I will call my witnesses and state mine…'

Sir Thomas fumbled in his sleeve for the paper Hal had returned to him. Finding it, he read the words in a sonorous voice. It sounded quite damning, even Hal had to admit. 'And now,' Thomas continued, 'I call the Lady Katherine Monterey to the—er—room.'

Hal opened the door and called, 'Lucy, please

ask Lady Katherine to come to the parlour.' He closed it again and Rachel had a crazy desire to laugh. How surprised Katherine would be to have to answer now for all the sly comments she had made into interested ears. And before the Queen, too!

The door opened and Piers put his head around it. 'Are you wanting Katherine?' he asked enquiringly. 'Oh, I beg your pardon, Your Majesty,' he said quickly as Hal pulled the door wider and he saw the others in the room. He looked around, mystified.

'This, as you may not know as yet, is the Lady Katherine's intended,' Hal said cheerfully.

With rising colour Sir Thomas said testily, 'We have enough betrothed or intended gentlemen in this room already!'

Piers came further into the room. 'I don't believe I know you, sir,' he said to Carstairs. George made the introductions just as Katherine appeared. Bess's dressmaker had been delivering a new gown to her bedchamber and she was wearing it—her favourite shade of green, sewn with tiny pearls, the wide ruff around her neck studded with matching seed pearls. She curtsied to the Queen.

George said smoothly, 'We are holding a somewhat impromptu court here, Katherine—with Her Majesty's consent.'

'But…what is it all about?' Katherine asked uncertainly.

'The charges you have made against Rachel,' Hal said, moving closer to her.

'The charges I made? But surely there is some mistake?' She raised her eyes to his, but he was immune to their appeal. 'Rachel has already been questioned and released.'

'There is no mistake,' he said softly. 'Rachel was only released—by the Queen's kindness—on the understanding she would answer at a later time. This is that time.'

'Well, I scarcely…' Katherine looked at him again, then Piers, who lifted a chair and put it beside her.

'Sit down, sweetheart,' he said solicitously, 'it will not take long, I am sure.'

'Continue, Sir Thomas,' Elizabeth said, settling herself more comfortably in her chair.

Carstairs began. He read the nucleus of the charges once more, and who had said what, and in what connection, and George saw what Hal had immediately seen: the charges were serious, yes, but they were based solely upon what Katherine Monterey had said. Thomas droned on, then said, 'So if you will now rise to answer my questions, Lady Rachel.'

Rachel got up with trembling legs. I am a raree show for this company, she thought resentfully, and they might as well have their coin's worth. She walked to the centre of the parlour and stood facing Elizabeth. 'I am ready, sir,' she said, lifting her chin.

Darling, don't lose your temper, Hal begged silently.

Madrilene, thought Bess, I have seen you wearing exactly that expression.

I have never noticed before how lovely Rachel is, mused Piers.

'Very well,' Sir Thomas said. 'It is reported that you have frequently sought the company of a known traitor, one recently executed for conspiring against the English throne. Master Walter Corlin.'

Rachel considered. That nice little man in the library at Greenwich, she thought sadly. Walter Corlin, who had lightened so many of her hours as they discussed the poetry and prose of some of the world's greatest creative writers in the dim and dusty library. 'I helped Master Corlin, who was chief librarian to the court, to catalogue the treasures therein,' she admitted.

'He was of the Papist persuasion, as you will know.'

'I do now. At the time we never discussed such things.'

'Yet you yourself are of that persuasion,' Thomas said silkily. 'But you never...discussed such things?'

'No. Why should we? When we had so much else to talk of—' For a moment, Rachel saw in her mind's eye the sunlight slanting through the narrow panes of the library on to the silk-bound books containing the words of a long-dead scholar—the timeless words so beautifully constructed on old parchments—and remembered the joy she and her companion had found in those words. She pressed her hands together and looked at the Queen. 'Madam—your father collected most of the volumes Master Corlin and I were so entranced with. He must have been a singular man.'

'Indeed,' agreed Elizabeth frostily.

Carstairs smiled scornfully. 'So you merely discussed books? How very unlikely.'

'I do not lie, sir,' Rachel said with dignity.

'Well, if you will not even admit to that, lady, there seems little point in asking if you plotted against your sovereign.'

Rachel's eyes darkened. 'Who dares accuse me of that?'

'Dares! Dares?' Sir Thomas came very close to her.

George rose and said quietly, 'I must ask you to keep your distance from the accused, Sir Thomas.'

Carstairs swung round. 'Why?'

'Because if you do not, I will remove your head from your shoulders without benefit of axe,' Hal said, a vibration in his chest.

'Madam, I must protest!' Sir Thomas said angrily.

'I think Her Majesty will agree that no lady may be intimidated in any court she presides over,' Hal said quickly, leaving Elizabeth no choice but to nod her agreement. 'And that no gentleman could be expected to standby whilst it happens,' he added for good measure.

Sir Thomas sighed. 'You may question the accused now, my lord Earl,' he said to George, who got up again and smiled at Rachel.

'You have already told us you discussed no religion outlawed in England with Master Corlin?' he said. Clever, thought Hal, because documented evidence of many religions were contained in the books at Greenwich, and George did not want this particular fact to be raised at a later time.

'That is so,' said Rachel firmly.

'And you do not deny that you are Catholic in your upbringing?' he enquired casually, managing to make it sound none of her volition, as of course it was not.

'I do not,' Rachel agreed gravely. 'My family's roots were in the old religion.' As were everyone else's in this room, the rest of the company thought involuntarily.

'But,' George went on, 'if you did not discuss this religion, it is not possible you plotted against England with Master Corlin in his bid to revive it. So, I think I have no more questions for you at this time. Now, Sir Thomas, I believe you will wish to call your witness.' He sat down. Hal took Rachel gently back to her chair.

'I call Lady Katherine Monterey,' Carstairs said in ringing tones. Katherine looked up at him.

'I am here, my lord,' she said. Thomas consulted his notes.

'It is said here you frequently saw the Lady Rachel contravening the law. It is said you observed her touching the crucifix around her neck and calling upon her god to help her.'

Katherine said demurely, 'That is so. At Abbey Hall, my family home, Rachel often did that.'

'So! And, at the court of Our Gracious Lady, Elizabeth Tudor of England, 'twas the same?'

'Oh, yes,' Katherine said, ''twas the same. She often called upon her god to witness something or other. Many times touched the cross on her neck when upset or discomforted. It was a source of great distress to me, you will understand.'

'It must have been,' Sir Thomas said heavily. 'So, being a good Englishwoman and patriot, you made it your business to bring this state of affairs to the notice of those vigilant in the protection of your country.'

'Well, er…' Katherine was not anxious to admit to that '…I may have shown my concern and others felt the need to act.'

'On your behalf?' This silly girl, thought Sir Thomas irritably, obviously did not realise she was the chief reason this farcical court was in session.

'On behalf of all staunch Protestants,' Katherine corrected him, still refusing to commit herself. Sir Thomas decided to let it go; nothing was to be gained by pressing this lady, so determined to sit on the fence. He bowed and George rose.

'But, Katherine,' he said gently, 'was it not on your evidence alone that the Lady Rachel was arrested and taken to the Tower?'

'Well…I don't know, really.'

'That it was your evidence, or that she was taken to the Tower?'

'Of course I know she was imprisoned,' Katherine said crossly. 'Your own brother had her released from there! Although why he should do so, I have no idea.'

'Perhaps he has a regard for truth and justice,' suggested George.

'Pray get on with the questions,' the Queen said reprovingly. 'I believe the arguments for the case should be presented at the end of the evidence.'

George bowed. 'I thank you, madam. Very well, I will now ask Lady Rachel—no, do not get up, lady—tell me what form the cause of the distress Lady Katherine spoke of took? As you remember.'

Rachel looked blank. 'This is a serious question,' he reminded her carefully. She raised one slim hand and touched her breast, under the bodice of which lay her little crucifix. The gesture was not lost on Sir Thomas, who looked significantly at Elizabeth, who looked back down her aristocratic nose.

'The words you might have used,' George said kindly, 'in moments of discomposure.'

'Er…' Rachel, who in moments of the discomposure George referred to, tended to revert to thinking in the Spanish of her childhood, murmured, *'Madre de Dios!* How can I remember what I said and when?'

Sir Thomas rose again. *'Madre de Dios?* Mother of God? A very Popish exclamation, surely.'

George said placidly, 'Your Spanish accent is

poor, Sir Thomas, as might be expected of a good Englishman. Lady Rachel's, however, is excellent as might be expected of someone raised in that country. Don't we all use expressions remembered from our childhood? I know I do.' He went on, 'You hail from Suffolk, do you not, sir? I have, myself, heard you pronounce the word "wholly" to rhyme with "wooly"—as are the coats of your good East Anglian sheep.' One of the guards snickered; Sir Thomas gave George a thunderous look.

'This is a court of law, my lord Earl, not to be reduced to a comedy.'

'I was simply illustrating the point,' George returned mildly, 'that we all in moments of stress revert to words and phrases and gestures learned when we learned all our mannerisms and language.'

'I think we understand that,' Elizabeth said brusquely. 'What I am waiting to hear is what Lady Rachel said or did which makes her traitorous.'

'Aren't we all?' murmured Hal, receiving in his turn a venomous look from Katherine.

'So…moving on,' George said, consulting his notes, 'you were, after the evidence of this lady—' he indicated Katherine '—brought before the Court of the High Commission which, as we all know, deals with those who do not accept the rules of the new order, as decreed by the Supreme Governor—' he indicated the Queen '—of the Protestant religion in England today.'

'I was,' Rachel said breathlessly, 'and thereafter confined in the Tower.' She shivered.

'Where you remained at Her Majesty's pleasure, until released? Now, I think I would like Henry Latimar to take the—er—stand so I may continue the story.'

Rachel blinked. She had risen during George's interrogation. Events were moving too fast for her, and too wordily, to take in. But she allowed herself to be taken away by Hal to a chair by the window, next to Bess and Piers. She sank down, casting a sideways glance at her companions. Piers gave her an encouraging look, Bess remained carven-faced, watching as Hal took his stance before the Queen.

'Now, Hal,' George said informally, 'you went to Her Majesty upon hearing of Rachel's incarceration and asked her to release the accused into your custody. How did you persuade her?' His confiding tone injected a relaxing and cosy note into the proceedings.

Hal said, 'I informed Her Majesty that the... accused was a relative of a family closely connected with my own. I advised her the Lady Rachel had recently survived a serious illness, and she—in her wisdom—agreed the lady be taken by me away from that horrible place and be brought to more congenial surroundings to be cared for by my kin.' He bowed gracefully in his mother's direction.

''Twas not that way at all, Hal!' Elizabeth said irritably. 'You know perfectly well you bullied me into releasing yon Spanish girl!'

'She is not Spanish, but English,' Hal returned equably. 'And also—' he looked about the room at faces which showed various expressions of amaze-ment that their sovereign should express herself in this way '—I prefer my explanation. So much more dignified…'

'Yes, well…' Elizabeth collected herself. 'Carry on.'

'Having brought the lady back here,' George said, as if there had been no interruption, 'you were therefore able to observe her conduct and draw your conclusions as to her guilt or innocence of the charges levelled against her. What were your con-clusions?'

Sir Thomas said angrily, 'Madam, I must object: how can my lord Latimar possibly be qualified to reach any such conclusions?'

'I have eyes, sir,' Hal said, 'and excellent hear-ing. Far more relevant to my mind is the other con-clusion I reached—that I was in love with the Lady Rachel and had probably been in that state since our first meeting, but did not realise it until she was under my eye.'

Sir Thomas, and his blood pressure, rose with another sigh. 'Has this some bearing on these pro-ceedings?'

'Well, perhaps not,' Hal said cheerfully. 'Then, to answer your former point—I did not need further proof of Rachel's innocence, because I knew that before. Otherwise, I would not have gone to Her Majesty in the first instance.'

Under cover of this declaration Rachel stared at Hal. Their recent solemn vows had not made the

kind of impact his last words had. And before the
Queen and his mother! What further proof did she
need of his love? She turned the ornate betrothal
ring on her finger. It was really to happen…Hal
Latimar would marry her and no one, not the
Queen, the High Commission, or his mother, would
tell him nay. This was why she had come to this
alien place. Cold and grey, with coldhearted people,
Madrilene had declared, but her granddaughter had
found, eventually, the reverse. The reverse in the
shape of golden Hal Latimar, handsome and indulged, but with the courage to outface a Queen
and a matriarch to get her. Rachel sat up straighter
and prepared to do battle for her future in the way
her beloved had done.

Shortly, however, it appeared that the battle
might never be fought further than already. The
Queen was growing bored; what had begun as a
malicious amusement—directed at both Latimar
and the Spanish girl—had not produced comedy but
romantic drama. Besides—'twas true what Hal said,
if she had not believed Rachel innocent of all treason charges she would never have let the girl leave
the Tower. Elizabeth was indeed fanatical in her
distrust and hatred of the Catholic faction in England, largely because of her conviction that they
wished to supplant her with her Scottish cousin,
Mary. While the Stuart Queen lived, Elizabeth
knew, there could be no real peace amongst the two
English religions. But she could not seriously think
Rachel Monterey's crimes, which amounted to no

more than a tendency to remember her Spanish childhood when under pressure, were a threat to the throne or herself. Also, the Latimars had been supporting the Tudor dynasty since its inception. Such continuing loyalty was not political or dependent on personal gain, it was just…there. As Bess had suspected, she had signed the document for two reasons, neither rational. She had wanted to torment Madrilene's granddaughter, and also test the Latimars. She had done both and was satisfied. She broke in on Hal's impassioned eulogy on Rachel's virtues, saying, 'Yes, yes. But I think we are done here now, Sir Hal. I find there is no case to answer and discharge the defendant forthwith.'

'Madam…!' Sir Thomas spluttered. 'Madam, I have not yet delivered my concluding deliberations!'

'We will take them as read,' Elizabeth said, rising stiffly. 'George, my dear, I would like to rest a little in the hall now, and perhaps listen to some congenial music. Have you your lute?'

George took her arm, saying gently, 'I have indeed, Your Majesty, and Judith and my two daughters are already in the hall to swell our musical evening. Pray come with me.' He took her to the door, where she gave him a sharp look.

'A celebration, eh? I suppose you had no doubt of the outcome of all this?'

'I cannot deny it. For, as my brother declared earlier—your wisdom is unique.'

'Hmm.' The Queen paused a moment to say over

her shoulder to Thomas Carstairs, 'Will you join us, Sir Thomas?'

'I thank you, no, madam. With your permission I will take my men and leave.' The guards shuffled to the door. They had no idea what had happened in the parlour this day, but knew their master to be in a furious temper. It boded ill for them on the way back to Hampton. Thomas came to Bess and said politely, 'Thank you for your hospitality, my lady.'

'Oh, but surely you will not leave without refreshment?' Bess said, her housewifely pride offended.

The guards looked hopeful, but Sir Thomas said stiffly, 'I regret I cannot spare the time.' He spun around on Rachel, still sitting in her chair trying to believe the bad moment had finally passed. 'And you, lady, were lucky today. Should you come before my court in the future, the outcome will assuredly be different.'

'I think it unlikely that my wife will come before any court convened in the future by you, sir,' Hal said with deadly clarity. 'And I feel I must tell you now that I am considering asking the Queen to demand you issue an apology for putting the Lady Rachel through the ordeal she has just been victim to.'

Sir Thomas was speechless with rage. 'Now, gentlemen—' Piers was beside them '—I think we wish no more hard words. The matter is decided by the greatest authority in this land and we must all accept it.'

Sir Thomas subsided. Signalling to his men, he left the room.

Piers went and pulled Katherine to her feet. 'Come, love, we will join the merry assembly in the hall.' He hustled her out of the parlour and closed the door decisively behind him.

'Well…' Hal half laughed. 'What a disagreeable man Carstairs is.'

'He has his duty to perform, I suppose,' Bess said. 'Now, I must—' Hal caught her arm.

'Before you rush to the kitchen to ensure one of your good meals is set before us in due course, I would like a moment.' He filled a glass for each, then sat down. 'We must discuss wedding plans, must we not?'

On one wall of the parlour was hung a portrait of the late Harry Latimar, painted long ago. Bess raised her eyes to it. 'I think,' she said pointedly, 'there can be no celebration of any kind for some time, Hal.'

Hal followed her eyes. 'I said…plans, Mother, not the date for the wedding. Naturally, I would not consider my own happiness during the expected time of mourning.'

Bess took a mouthful of wine. She rarely drank these days, it was no pleasure when she could not share it with Harry, and the hearty liquor gave her courage. 'I think we should wait longer than that. It is possible to change one's mind, after all.'

Hal sat back in his chair. 'I will not change my mind over this.'

Bess looked at Rachel. She had not tasted her drink. 'Nor I, my lady,' she said quietly.

'So,' Hal went on, 'as to the future—Rachel will live here until our marriage, as is fitting.'

'Fitting!' Bess repeated bitterly. 'What is fitting about that?'

'It is my home,' Hal reminded her gently.

'It is my home, too,' Bess said coldly.

'Indeed. And I would wish that both the women I love most in the world understand each other and can live together in peace.'

'I shall never understand your attachment to this girl!' Bess said angrily. 'Could you expect me to?'

'Because her grandmother was once your rival?' enquired Hal casually. 'Come, Mother, I expect more of you.'

'Do you? Well, you don't know what happened, Hal.'

'Indeed I do.'

Bess looked outraged. 'I suppose you told him,' she said to Rachel.

'Why not?' Hal said easily. 'It is all in the family, after all, and not at all to your detriment.'

'No, indeed, not to *my* detriment,' Bess said scathingly.

'Perhaps not entirely to Madrilene's either,' Hal said thoughtfully. 'No, don't explode, Mother. Let us think for a moment... Here is this young girl, cast into the English court. All her life she had been given everything she wants—except wise guidance from her parents...older brother or sister...anyone.' He sampled his wine a moment. 'I, too, went to court when I was eighteen. But I was armed with good advice. Even so, I had too much of everything, just like Madrilene.'

There was a silence, then Bess said, 'You're grown up, Hal.'

'Having someone to care for, less fortunate than oneself, has that effect.'

'If she did not look so like—' Bess said distractedly.

So like my grandmother, thought Rachel. But can I help that?

'We Latimars are singularly alike physically,' Hal said, still in a thoughtful tone. 'But not in personality, I believe. Yet, all my life I have suffered from being compared to my father, my brother and my sister. It is not a happy state to be in.'

'You have not suffered!' Bess exclaimed. 'How can it hurt to be compared to three such exemplary people?'

'It does hurt, actually,' Hal said, fixing her with his straight, blue look. 'I think I may be good enough without being judged in the light of others' admiration for my family. And, continuing that thought—there are those who remember Madrilene de Santos without the cloven feet you attribute to her.'

Bess rose with dignity. 'I think there is no more to say, Hal,' she said, turning away.

'I very much dislike having to contradict you, Mother,' he said, rising politely. 'But this...thing must be settled, and I think it must be without delay.'

# *Chapter Sixteen*

The clash between the two, who loved each other, distressed Rachel greatly. She rose, too, tears welling up into her dark eyes. 'I don't want to come between you,' she choked, 'but 'tis as Hal says, my lady, I cannot help looking like my grandmother and—I am proud of it, to tell the truth!'

The two Latimars looked at her. 'So you should be.' Hal put a hand on her arm. 'Sit down, sweetheart. If you are to be a member of this family, you must get used to defending your ground in civilised fashion.' Under his eyes she sat back in her chair. She looked up at Bess.

'I am sorry,' she said haltingly, 'that my grandmother caused you so much grief all those years ago. But I know her side as well as yours. Naturally she had no right to set her eyes on your husband, but she was that way, you know. She was a passionate, straightforward creature who saw what she wanted and exerted all effort to attain it. But she knew…she told me, she always knew 'twas a losing battle. For Lord Harry loved you... Can you not imagine what her life was when she lost that battle? It ruined her...nipped all that joyous passion in the bud. She was never the same again. You were triumphant in that particular game, Lady Bess, and do not—even now—realise it.' Rachel gulped, but went on, 'At court a gentleman who had known her asked what had happened to the gay and beautiful girl he once knew. My cousin answered him. She died, Katherine said, in penury, crippled by her gambling debts. True...all too true. My dear brave-hearted grandmother once chanced all she had on a single throw and lost. That set the pattern for the rest of her life. Again and again she repeated that pattern, and always lost...although from that time she restricted her gambling to the cards and the dice. She cheated my grandfather, and he knew it... It is time, I think for you to be a little generous to her memory and, also, to me.'

Bravo, darling! Hal exclaimed inwardly.

Very much affected by this frank speech, Bess said slowly, 'Yes, well, perhaps we should have had this conversation before...Rachel.'

'I would never have had the courage, if Hal had not forced it,' Rachel said candidly.

Bess glanced at her son. 'Courage appears to be contagious between you two.' She turned back to Rachel. 'I am most sincerely sorry your grand-mother was so unhappy after leaving here,' she said with an effort. 'I am capable of no criticism of my beloved husband, but...sometimes Harry conveyed a false impression. Madrilene misunderstood the situation—I shall try not to make the same mistake.' It was as far as Bess could go to admit that she knew, really, the episode between Harry and Madrilene had been almost totally one-sided. She went on with energy, 'Now I must see all is in order in my kitchen. Er…shall you wish to join me, Rachel? You will want to be at home here.'

'Another time, Mother.' Hal accompanied her to the door. 'But thanks are due for the offer.' He bent to kiss her and murmur, 'And thank you for the olive branch.'

She sighed and patted his cheek. 'Would it have made any difference if I had not offered it?'

He smiled without replying and closed the door gently behind her.

Rachel blinked. 'She now seems prepared to accept me! I can hardly believe it…I wonder why.'

'Perhaps she wanted to be sure first we were united in this. I know I did.'

'And now you are sure.' It was a statement, not a question. She and Hal had come a long way in the last hour in the parlour.

He came to sit beside her. The sun, sinking in fiery splendour behind them, gave her black head a coppery glow. He admired this for a moment, then said, 'It was not you I was unsure of, but myself. I do have an unpleasant habit of never finishing anything I begin.'

She turned her eyes on him. He noticed they were the light shining colour of newly run honey, all trace of the haunted darkness had left them. 'You mean Katherine? But she was not right for you.'

He picked up one of her hands and studied it. Her hands had the same creamy pallor as her face, but were strong fingered and supple. Good hands for a horse, for the mistress of a house like Maiden Court, and—for caressing a man. He raised it to his lips and said against the palm, 'I am not speaking of Katherine. I have never in my entire life seen anything through to its end. Always I have left the task unfinished for fear of—failure. Although others attributed my lack to boredom, or a fickle nature, or—certainly the excuses made for me have been legion.'

'Until I came.'

'Yes, until you came,' he agreed. 'Then, 'twas stay the course or put you at risk. When you were sick, when you were in the Tower, and again today when I wanted to put away forever any chance you might be accused again. Of course, I had some help today. From my brother.'

'Oh, no!' she said vehemently. 'I was watching the Queen's face throughout the testimony. It was your words which decided her. She could not believe that anyone you thought innocent could be guilty. I was so proud of you!'

He half laughed. 'You were proud of me? I was proud of you when you confronted my mother a few minutes ago. We are indeed brave to take on two such formidable ladies, and be victorious!'

'Your mother, too, faced a ghost today, and overcame it,' Rachel said consideringly. 'My poor grandmother; she will not even have a faint claim to her love after what I said to your lady mother.' Hal put an arm around her and she smiled up into his eyes. ''Tis funny how wrongly we categorise each other. For example, the way you described me once—as looking as if I expected the world to take a stick to me? I never felt that, not really. I was always—in my heart—sure of my own worth.'

His grip tightened on her. 'I know. When I said that, I was only telling of my own fears.'

The singing from the hall had reached a conclusion now. There was a burst of applause. Hal said regretfully, 'I suppose we must join the others now, darling. Her Majesty does not like to not be the centre of attention in any gathering. Later, we must all hang on her every word, and there will be toasts to her health.'

'Quite right, too,' Rachel said. 'And I will raise my glass as enthusiastically as anyone.'

'But first,' Hal said softly, 'let us make our own.'

'Oh, yes,' she said delightedly. 'What shall it be? Health, wealth and happiness to us all?' Hal got up.

'Yes, of course. But also—especially for you, my darling, my own, my love.' Ceremoniously he touched his glass to Rachel's. 'To…Madrilene's granddaughter!'

\*　\*　\*　\*　\*

# MILLS & BOON®

*Makes any time special*™

## Mills & Boon publish 29 new titles every month. Select from...

Modern Romance™      Tender Romance™

Sensual Romance™

Medical Romance™   Historical Romance™

MAT2

## FREE!
## 2 Books
### and a surprise gift!

We would like to take this opportunity to thank you for reading this Mills & Boon® book by offering you the chance to take TWO more specially selected titles from the Historical Romance™ series absolutely FREE! We're also making this offer to introduce you to the benefits of the Reader Service™ —

- ★ FREE home delivery
- ★ FREE gifts and competitions
- ★ FREE monthly Newsletter
- ★ Books available before they're in the shops
- ★ Exclusive Reader Service discounts

Accepting these FREE books and gift places you under no obligation to buy; you may cancel at any time, even after receiving your free shipment. Simply complete your details below and return the entire page to the address below. *You don't even need a stamp!*

**YES!** Please send me 2 free Historical Romance books and a surprise gift. I understand that unless you hear from me, I will receive 4 superb new titles every month for just £2.99 each, postage and packing free. I am under no obligation to purchase any books and may cancel my subscription at any time. The free books and gift will be mine to keep in any case.

H0ZEB

Ms/Mrs/Miss/Mr ...........................................................Initials..........................................
BLOCK CAPITALS PLEASE

Surname.................................................................................................................................

Address..................................................................................................................................

..............................................................................................................................................

....................................................................................Postcode ........................................

**Send this whole page to:**
**UK: The Reader Service, FREEPOST CN81, Croydon, CR9 3WZ**
**EIRE: The Reader Service, PO Box 4546, Kilcock, County Kildare (stamp required)**

Offer not valid to current Reader Service subscribers to this series. We reserve the right to refuse an application and applicants must be aged 18 years or over. Only one application per household. Terms and prices subject to change without notice. Offer expires 28th February 2001. As a result of this application, you may receive further offers from Harlequin Mills & Boon Limited and other carefully selected companies. If you would prefer not to share in this opportunity please write to The Data Manager at the address above.

Mills & Boon® is a registered trademark owned by Harlequin Mills & Boon Limited.
Historical Romance™ is being used as a trademark.

# MADRILENE'S GRANDDAUGHTER

Laura Cassidy

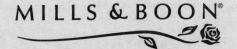

*First published in Great Britain 2000*
*Harlequin Mills & Boon Limited,*
*Eton House, 18-24 Paradise Road, Richmond, Surrey TW9 1SR*

© Laura Cassidy 2000

ISBN 0 263 82313 X

*Set in Times Roman 10½ on 12½ pt.*
*04-0008-67341*

*Printed and bound in Spain*
*by Litografia Rosés S.A., Barcelona*

# Chapter One

In the fourth decade of their marriage, Bess and Harry Latimar decided they would mark this by gathering together all of their family for a grand celebration. It was worth so marking for it was unusual, even miraculous, that they should both have lived to such an old age and also that so many of their years had been spent within the confines of a happy and successful marriage. As was their custom, they discussed the idea in the small parlour of their manor house, after the last meal of the day and before a blazing fire.

'It must be only an intimate family affair,' Bess said thoughtfully. Their house, Maiden Court, was famed for its hospitality, but—these days—she felt lavish entertaining took its toll on the master and mistress.

'Mmm.' Harry was listening, of course, but he was also admiring the way the firelight shifted over his wife's face, ignoring the lines of age and choosing to linger on the lovely bones, the pointed shadow of her eyelashes on her cheeks and her shining hair, once an unusual shade of silver gilt and now the true silver of old age. Bess ticked off each family member on her fingers:

'George and Judith, and their two children and grandchildren.' She paused, thinking yet again how unlike a great-grandmother she felt. 'Then Anne and Jack must come from Northumberland with any of their offspring they can gather together. Hal, too, must be persuaded from Greenwich. Do you think the plan feasible, dearest?'

'Well, George and his brood have only to walk the short distance from the Lodge, so there will be no problem there.' Fifteen years ago, when it had become apparent that George and Judith's two children, who had made their home in their parents' house, were intent on raising a large family, Maiden Court Lodge, built on the Latimar estate, had been considerably extended to accommodate them. 'But it may be difficult for Jack to get away, and his son, and I know Anne won't come without them.' His son-in-law, Jack Hamilton, ten years since created an Earl to acknowledge his services to the English crown in commanding a defensive fortress on the Scottish border, was gradually relinquishing the reins of Ravensglass to his firstborn, but retained a strong sense of responsibility for his position. 'But Hal will come from Greenwich if I have to personally go and haul the young vagabond home. After having settled his gambling debts yet again, no doubt.'

Bess smiled at this. After four years of marriage to Harry she had triumphantly produced twins, Anne and George, and then—to her great grief—no more live babies until Hal had been born eighteen years later. He was in his twenty-first year now, both a delight and a trial to his parents. A delight because, in the Latimar tradition, he was intelligent and handsome, excelling in both intellectual and physical pursuits; he surpassed any other young courtier in the games the ageing Elizabeth Tudor still so delighted in. A trial because he had inherited his fair share of his father's attraction for the opposite sex and more than his fair share of Harry's passion for gambling. In his day Harry Latimar had been the most reckless gambler in King Henry Tudor's court. George, his heir, had never been a problem in this way, nor his sister Anne, so perhaps the taint—or extraordinary talent—had been concentrated in the youngest member of the family. Certainly from the time Hal could deal a deck of cards or roll a pair of dice he had been obsessed with any game of chance.

Catching Bess's smile, Harry smiled in return. Bess always had a soft spot for a young gambler—after all, she had married one. She might not, he thought, be quite so sympathetic towards Hal's other obsession—that of women. Apart from saving his younger son from penury every now and again, Harry had, in the last few years, been called upon to placate many an outraged father of a pretty daughter. These fathers would have been quite satisfied if the Latimar boy wanted a permanent liaison with their girls. Such an old established family, favoured by successive monarchs, would have been a welcome link. But Hal never had marriage in mind. No female ever held his interest for more than a few short months.

Harry closed his eyes and leaned his head back against the chair rest. The years had dealt very kindly with Latimar, but he was in his seventies now, still spare and upright, white-skinned and there was very little silver in his thick black hair. But lately he had had distressing symptoms—a sensation in his breast he could only describe as a hundred horses' hooves galloping, occasional dizzy turns, and frequent lassitude.

Bess, vigilant as always over her beloved husband, asked immediately, 'Are you tired, love?'

'I am,' he admitted. 'It is after midnight, you know,' he added hastily. 'Now, had you thought when this party might take place?'

'Well, 'tis April now. Allowing for the roads to be fit to travel should Anne and her family come, and before the harvest is upon us here, I thought… June?'

Harry rose stiffly, and stretched. 'June…' he said thoughtfully. 'That reminds me—' despite giving the impression to those around him of casual disregard, he was actually a thoughtful and organized man '—I recall that is the month I promised John Monterey to introduce his granddaughter to Elizabeth's court.'

Bess sat up. 'Oh! I had quite forgot… What exactly are the arrangements?' John Monterey was an old friend from Harry's youth. At least, not exactly a friend, for John had been the wealthy and aristocratic heir of a great family and Latimar—in those days—had been spectacularly poor and disadvantaged apart from the interest and patronage of the young King Henry.

The Earl of Monterey had been blessed with two sons, Ralph and Thomas. Both, curiously, had been suitors for Anne, Latimar's daughter's hand, but that had come to nothing once she fell in love with Jack Hamilton. Thomas had been killed by an outbreak of plague when he was but five and twenty, Ralph had married and produced a daughter, before he, too, was dead from a duellist's bullet. John had taken his little granddaughter to live with him at his vast estate near the capital called Abbey Hall. A year ago, knowing himself too old to present the girl in the way she should be introduced to the world, given her heritage and wealth, John had applied to Harry and Bess Latimar. They had agreed that they would use their influence with the Queen to further the girl's career. And considerable it was, as Monterey had known. For the Latimars had been beloved of all the Tudors—Henry, Edward, Mary and Elizabeth, as well as their consorts. So it had been decided; Kat—Katherine Monterey—would be taken under the Latimar wing in June of the coming year.

'Just that we have the girl here for an extended

visit, to live as part of the family and in due course take her to court. I must visit John to finalise everything…'

Bess stood now and put an arm about her husband. They leaned against each other at the hearth; lover-like, they smiled and turned about to look at the room. On their right on the wall, facing the window, there was a portrait of a man in grey standing behind a table on which lay a hand of playing cards. It was Harry's likeness in the picture, and the cards displayed the hand with which he had won the house he had now been master of for almost half a century. When his older children had been toddlers he had, thrown off course during an estrangement from Bess, been forced to offer his Maiden Court to the moneylenders to cover staggering gambling debts. Henry Tudor had redeemed the note, gifted it to Bess and she had contrived a card game between her husband and herself whereby she had most conveniently lost it back to him.

Seeing Harry's eyes on the picture now, Bess said soothingly, 'Now don't worry about Hal. He is a little wild, I'll agree, but his heart is right. Of course I would be happier if he spent more time at home—he does run with a very sophisticated crowd.' Hal's friends at the royal court were of the slightly raffish society Queen Elizabeth liked to surround herself with. All young, all wealthy, good looking and talented in one way or another, but without any apparent purpose in their lives. Elizabeth, although middle-aged now, encouraged them in their extravagances, frequently angering her more worthy friends and advisors.

Harry began to extinguish the candles. He grunted. He loved his children, and theirs, but Bess he loved most of all. If she wanted a family party, she should have it. If she wanted to think her younger son was not a young wastrel but a good-hearted gentleman, then let her think so. Right now Harry wanted the comfort of his feather bed and the further comfort of his wife's fond arms about him. 'I am sure you are right, you usually are. But no more talk of him or any of our brood just now. Let us get to bed.'

At the moment his parents were climbing the stairs of Maiden Court, Hal Latimar was sitting in on the preliminary stages of a card game likely to last the night and perhaps continue into the next day. The Queen and the older members of her retinue had retired. Hal had danced for a while in the great chamber, drunk for a while at the refreshment tables, and then been lured to Oxford's apartments for a game. He looked around at the others who played this cool spring night. Ned Oxford, of course, slightly the worse for wear because he had a weak head for liquor and had indulged freely earlier. The ladies Ruthwen and Maidstone; both beautiful and superbly dressed, but past their first youth and with a reputation in common for being light as regards morals: Hal was familiar with these three.

Also taking part in the proceedings was Piers Roxburgh—slim, dark, wryly witty and inclined to pick a fight if events did not go his way—and a new addition to the court, Philip Sidney, a soldier poet who was possessed of a fine and great name and had recently added lustre to it by being appointed to the Queen's parliament. Roxburgh was Hal's best friend, Sidney he hardly knew at all.

The play began and surreptitiously Hal yawned behind his hand. There would be no surprises tonight, he thought, and no excitement either. After a half-dozen hands, Sidney, on his left, asked quietly, 'How do you do it?'

'What?' enquired Hal, tossing down a card and picking up his winnings.

'Manipulate the play.'

Hal's fine blue eyes narrowed. 'You accuse me of cheating, sir?'

Philip made a deprecatory gesture. 'No, indeed! 'Twas in the nature of an interested enquiry. For instance, I see you have managed it so your friend, Roxburgh, has won a goodly sum, that Oxford and the two ladies have lost consistently, and I have broken even, as it were. I am simply curious to know how you do it.'

Hal looked attentively at his neighbour. 'If you have noticed my manoeuvres, I am obviously not as adept as I thought I was.'

'Oh, but you are! I only...noticed because it is the curse of any writer to be more observant than his fellows. I have also noticed you are bored by such skill, and so might ask you instead: *why* do you do it?'

Hal half smiled. 'Why? Well, because Piers is out of funds at present and needs a little revenue. Ned has plenty of cash and can afford to lose. Meg Ruthwen and Jane Maidstone have elderly husbands tucked away in their rural mansions and—I can only assume—pay their ladies well to keep away. And you—you I do not know at all, so must not decide financial matters for.'

There was now a break in play. Servants refilled the wine jugs, rebuilt the fire and those around the table rose to stretch their legs. Philip Sidney followed Hal to the window which he had opened to reveal the thick dark. 'You are George Latimar's brother, are you not?'

Hal sat on the window seat, the breeze through the opening lifting his blond hair from the nape of his neck. 'I am,' he agreed.

'I know George,' Philip said, sitting down himself. 'You're not in the least like him.'

'I know,' Hal said equably. 'He is better than me in every way.'

'He is a lot older than you.'

'I was an afterthought. A Benjamin sent to try my parents in their twilight years.' Hal was answering almost automatically. For years he had been compared to his intellectual and politically adept brother. Or his pretty and talented sister. Or his parents, who both held such a special place in the circles he moved in. When he had been younger he had fought against such comparisons, but to no avail—his very name assured him of a place in the important scheme of things. It also denied him the chance to achieve such a place on his own merits. He was too intelligent not to have reasoned long ago that one did not strive for what was freely given. So now he was frankly bored by the kind of probing any newcomer to court subjected him to.

'I've met your father, too, and your sister Anne,' Philip continued.

'Have you made a study of the Latimar family?' enquired Hal ironically.

'Perhaps I have. I am interested in all things truly English.'

'Are we truly English? Is there such a race? Made up as we are of so much invaders' blood?'

'So you are an historian!' Philip said delightedly. 'I knew no Latimar could be merely a light-hearted courtier concerned only with trivia.'

Hal groaned inwardly. Here it was again. The assumption that no Latimar could be an average human being. He was truly bored with it. He attempted to put an end to this particular interrogation. 'I am no historian. I take back what I just said—yes, I am English and wish no other title.'

From her place by the fire, Jane Maidstone had fixed her eyes full on him. She had been chasing him for a full month now and always seemed to be at any gathering he was part of. She was attractive and no shrinking virgin, but Hal had resisted her thus far. Not because he was in the habit of refusing such open invitation but because...why? Because for some time lately he had had the strangest feeling. That there was something tremendous coming right to him out of the unknown. If asked, he would have found it impossible to explain this feeling, but it was affecting his every action at the moment. He felt strongly that a dalliance with Jane Maidstone, however pleasant, would distract and divert whatever it was. All nonsense of course! But so... insistent. Yesterday, he had begged leave to be absent from the court and taken a wild, half-broken horse from the stables and ridden out into the wind on an impulse to rid himself of the unaccountable feeling.

Instead of outrunning it, it had stayed with him for every league. He knew his family had a curious tradition of being 'fey'. His mother, a reluctant inheritor of this gift, believed it had entered the Latimar family through her father's Celtic mother, who had come out of Ireland to wed her father. One of each succeeding generation had had the uncanny facility to see or feel that which was denied ordinary mortals. Pausing to water his unruly horse yesterday, Hal had been glad to remember that his brother George carried the honours in this particular field. And thank God for that! George was a balanced personality, well able to deal with such unfathomable matters. He, himself, Hal felt would be the reverse. All the same, the extraordinary premonition of stirring events to come stayed with him.

These thoughts had taken no more than a fleeting second in real time and Philip was smiling and replying. 'No sensible man would want other than to hear you say that. Latimars have been a part of the fabric of the English royal court for so long, have they not?'

Hal glanced over his shoulder into the black night. The clouds were low, the moon obscured and no star visible. But, between the sheltering trees, he could just make out the glitter of the Thames. 'Taking no official status…' Philip was pursuing his train of thought '…but always significant in the life of the reigning monarch. A friend to them. It is quite a heritage for you, is it not?'

Hal moved uneasily. He had nothing against the man sitting next him; he was as agreeable and charming as any he had met, and presumably was just passing the night in conversation. He could not possibly know how tired Hal was of hearing of his great heritage. How each time he had this discussion of old times, dead times—dead men and women—he longed to shout: But I am not just a Latimar! I am Henry Francis Latimar, quite another soul altogether from my father, my brother and any other member of my family. I am a person in my own right and capable of writing my own message in history's shifting sands. But was he? These endless comparisons—how they took the heart from a man. Tonight Philip's words scraped a painful place on his soul. Once he had heard his brother say: What happens has been decided long ago. We may dispute it, we may try to change it, but…it will happen just the same. Terrible notion! Hal had thought then, for why trouble to rise each morning and confront the day?

He was silent for so long that Philip glanced sideways in consternation. 'Have I offended you?' he asked. 'It was not my intention.'

Hal got up abruptly, mentally shaking off old ghosts. The group in the room was now reseated at the table. 'Not at all, my dear fellow. Shall we rejoin the others?'

'I think not. I am a country cousin, you know, and used to early nights.' Philip Sidney was anxious not to have alienated young Latimar, for he thought him an engaging young man. Attractive, of course, with his stunning fair looks, and witty tongue, but interesting, too. What had he read in the handsome face of his companion a few moments before? he wondered. As a student of human nature, as went with a poetic soul, Philip would have given much to know which particular nerve he had touched with his desultory comments. That flash of puzzlement and disillusion sat ill upon a boy who so obviously had everything. For, if anyone in this green realm could be said to have everything, surely Hal Latimar aspired to that title? However…Philip bowed and walked away.

Hal watched him go. Faces came and went at court, all of them mildly intriguing—for a while. He shrugged. Sidney was probably more talented and worthy than many, but—sooner or later—the changing pattern of any of the royal residences precluded fast friendships. Except for Piers Roxburgh. Hal's eyes rested affectionately on the dark face opposite. He and Piers had served their pageship together: two grubby little boys in the teeming world of Petrie Castle, where Hal had been sent in the Latimar tradition to learn the knightly arts and courtly skills. At seven years old, Hal, already taller than average, blond and handsome and with the solid weight of an estate behind him, plus the knowledge that whatever situation he found himself in he excelled, had greatly enjoyed himself. Not so poor Piers, who had been born the illegitimate son of the heir to a proud family. His father was married to a barren wife and Piers had been the fruit of a union with one of the servants in the family castle home. Piers had never known his mother, had only met his father twice, was singularly poor and completely unacknowledged. A bitter inheritance indeed for anyone with his proud blood.

It was a mysterious attraction—that between golden Hal and sullen Piers, but curiously enduring. So much so that, when Hal received his summons to Maiden Court to celebrate his parents' anniversary, he naturally took his best friend with him.

# *Chapter Two*

Maiden Court, the family home of the Latimar family, was ablaze with light in the dusk of the evening which saw the first night of the three-day celebrations planned for Bess and Harry's long marriage. It was a beautiful place, without the grandeur which might be expected of such owners, and virtually unchanged since the Norman conqueror had caused it to rise from the hotly contested land he had been given as reward for his valour in battle. He had been named William after his commander and the estate had remained in the Christowe family for many years, until one of the young Franco-English heirs had misguidedly sat down to play cards with Harry Latimar.

Harry had brought his new bride, Bess, to it; it had then entered into its golden age, for Bess had been both lady and farmer's daughter. Her strong instinct for the soil had encouraged her to bring the land back to fulfilment; her more delicate strain, vested in her by her aristocratic father, had enabled

her to make it a true gentleman of England's home.
Over the past three decades Maiden Court had become renowned for being the most flourishing and
lucrative estate within a radius of one hundred
miles, and also a place English nobles enjoyed visiting to take their ease. Gay King Hal had spent
many hours beneath its accommodating roof, as had
his successive Queens, and his sickly heir, Edward.
Mary Tudor had expressed the opinion that Maiden
Court, with its peaceful verdant acres, 'offers me
peace in my troubled life', and her sister, Elizabeth,
obviously felt the same for scarcely a half-year
passed during her reign when she did not visit.

Hal, pausing on the slope overlooking the manor
and gazing down on the mellow house, every window yellow with candle light, smiled sideways at
his companion, saying, 'I have been riding back
from some place or other for ten years and never
fail to be moved by the first sight of my home.'

Piers shifted in his saddle. 'There is no place like
home, or so they say,' he murmured sardonically.
'Naturally, I do not speak from experience.' He
knew it was unforgivable to make such a bitter
comment, but—just sometimes—he was overcome
by envy. It was irrational, he knew, for he probably
had been given in his short life every reasonable
entitlement. But, a dedicated gambler, he often felt
the odds to be so damned uneven. Why should one
man have so much, another so little? It was not a
question which could ever be answered, or presumably there would be less miserable beggars at the

gates of Greenwich or Windsor or Richmond. And
he had to admit he was more advantaged than they.
After all, his reluctant father need not have made
so casual a gesture as ensuring his bastard son was
educated and trained and sent out into the world as
a qualified soldier. And yet, occasionally, Piers was
resentful. Resentful of Hal Latimar who had it all:
good breeding, good looks, plenty of money and
not a care for any of it. Not a thought other than
where the next card or dice game would be held,
or the next cock fight or bear-baiting bout would
take place. And if these excitements palled, there
was always the prospect of an assignation with a
pretty woman, usually falling over her silken skirts
in her haste to succeed in snaring Latimar where so
many of her sisters had failed.

Hal put a swift hand on his arm. 'You know,' he
said, 'you are always welcome in my home.'

Piers returned the smile ruefully. It was impossible really to resent his generous friend for long.
'I know, but your mother's letter said this was to
be a purely family affair—I may be out of place on
this occasion.'

Hal shook his reins and began to descend the
rise. Over his shoulder he replied, 'Nonsense! If
anyone suggests any such thing, we shall take our
leave immediately.'

In fact, Bess was a little put out that Hal had
brought his friend, not because she did not like
Piers, but because she knew Hal well enough to
know he rarely made the journey home without

company because this company was a kind of protective armour against any complaints which might be directed towards him. She was aware her husband wanted to speak to his son of the debts he so frequently incurred and of his irresponsible behaviour in general. This coming autumn Hal would come into his majority, would be granted—if he wished—an establishment of his own and considerable monies would be settled on him. Thereafter he would be his own master. Meanwhile, he must live within his generous allowance. Nevertheless, she embraced both boys fondly and hurried them into the house.

'Are the rest of the clan not gathered yet?' Hal asked as he looked about the hall, acknowledging its unspoken welcome and accepting a glass of wine.

'Sadly Anne and the rest of the Hamiltons cannot get away, but George and his family are expected before nightfall and we are soon to entertain visitors… Tonight will be an adult party, tomorrow we will do it all over again with the little ones present.'

'It sounds terrifying,' Hal commented, turning towards the stairs as Harry Latimar descended. Regretfully, Hal noticed the slow movements, the breathless pauses, the general deterioration of his father since last they met. With his characteristically graceful stride he crossed the floor and leaped up the stairs to embrace the other man who gratefully took his arm for the remaining steps. Safely in his chair by the hearth, a glass of his own in his hands, Harry gave the charming smile his younger son had inherited to both young men. 'Dear Hal, how well you look, and Piers, my boy! Come, both shake my hand and forgive my decrepitude.' Piers and Hal leaned affectionately over the back of his chair, laughing and joking. But soon Hal straightened up and his eyes sought his mother's across the hall. She made a wry little grimace and turned back to the table.

At that moment horses' hooves and voices could be heard in the yard outside. The door opened and a young woman stepped inside, throwing back the hood of her cloak. Bess hurried forward. 'Katherine, my dear, welcome to Maiden Court!' The girl acknowledged the greeting with a little smile and offered her cheek.

Hal, conscious that his father was struggling to rise and that Piers was helping him, remained rooted to the spot. He was dazzled. Surely this latest addition to the hall had brought every last ray of the setting sun in with her. Katherine Monterey was astonishingly fair. No, not fair, but golden. Golden-haired, golden-eyed; her vivid face cream and rose and gold. She shimmered against the dark panelling of the old hall. Time paused for Hal as she smilingly and sympathetically waited for Harry Latimar to reach her. She then stood on tiptoe to kiss him, took his arm and that of his lady and, thus linked, came further into the room. Behind these three George was ushering his family in, but Hal had no eyes for anyone but the apparition approaching. He moved at last and Harry introduced him gravely. Katherine smiled mischievously.

'Well…the only member of the family I have not yet met. How do you do, sir? I have heard a great deal about you.' She laughed, a marvellous musical expression of enjoyment, then glanced behind her. 'Rachel—where is Rachel?' Unnoticed, a small dark girl was standing shyly amongst the chattering visitors. 'May I introduce the Lady Rachel Monterey? A very distant cousin who is lately come to England to be my—er—companion.'

The girl came forward tentatively and dropped a graceful curtsy. Rising, she said in a soft timorous voice, 'Good evening my lord, my lady and sir.'

Katherine grasped her hand and turned her about to present her to the others. Hal bowed and his uninterested, but assessing, eyes swept over her.

Rachel Monterey was delicately made, unfashionably full-bosomed, but otherwise very small and slender. Her downpouring of shining blue-black hair appeared too heavy for her elegantly moulded head on its slim white neck. Her face was a pale triangle, distinguished by a small straight nose, a determinedly firm chin and a pair of extravagantly lashed dark eyes overlarge with an expression both wary and proud. She had been born in Spain of an English father and a mother who had both English and Spanish blood in her veins. Her father she knew only from a little miniature painted before he died, her mother from a great portrait which had hung in her maternal Andalucian home, painted the year before she died when her little daughter was but eight years old. Rachel had been raised by her grandmother who hated all things English.

Two years ago, when Rachel was fifteen, the grandmother—her only relative in Spain—had died and she was suddenly alone. A strict Catholic, she had applied to the local priest for advice and the good man had been dismayed to find that when all the estate debts were paid there was nothing left for Rachel. The servants in the *casa* were fiercely protective of their little *señorita* and one remembered that her mother had once spoken of her husband being related to a great and aristocratic family in England. Enquiries were made and it was established that Rachel did indeed possess powerful paternal links. Various letters were dispatched and received and eventually she had left the warmth and light and colour of Spain for the cold grey coast of Dover. She had been met there by one of John Monterey's envoys and so transported to Abbey Hall near London.

John, although he acknowledged the connection with Rachel's father and was anxious to do his duty, was very old now, very sick and felt he had shot his last bolt in this world in arranging for his dead son's daughter to take her place in society. In her one interview with her great-uncle, Rachel had had the impression that the poor man was simply awaiting death, content to allow his well-run estate to run down and his granddaughter to reign supreme in his manor.

Through Katherine, Rachel had been made aware of her status—that of poor relation, a well-born beggar who should be overwhelmingly grateful for each poor scrap tossed her way. She had learned this lesson well over the last year and arrived at Maiden Court at the end of this brilliant June day knowing her place.

Accordingly, as Katherine was welcomed and made much of by the Latimars, Rachel withdrew respectfully to the fire hearth and sat down. She was glad to do so for her boots were her cousin's cast-offs and both too short and too wide. She had ridden the miles from Abbey Hall on another cast-off: poor shambling Primrose had been Katherine's first real mount and was now pensionable. Every stitch of clothing on Rachel's body and in her battered trunk was also second-hand, either too shabby or outdated to interest their first owner. Never mind, Rachel thought, looking around this new place with interest. The great thing is I am clothed and fed and housed.

On the journey here she had witnessed sights to make her shudder. Beggars, ragged and starving and desperate. The girls had been sent to Maiden Court with three sturdy grooms and they had thrown coins to these scarecrows and frowned over their misery. The Lady Katherine had shrugged her shoulders and frowned in a different way. She disliked such evidence of suffering because it offended her eye, not her heart. I am no better than those beggars, Rachel had thought miserably, wishing she had something to give them, no better than these pathetic examples of abandoned humanity and much less deserving of pity for at least I have a place in the world, however insignificant. She was vastly surprised, therefore, to feel a gentle hand on her arm now in this stronghold of plenty when Lady Bess Latimar came to ask her how she did, and to offer her wine.

'You are a Monterey cousin?' Bess enquired, sitting in the other chair at the hearth.

'Very distant,' Rachel agreed mutedly. 'Scarcely related at all. I had always lived in Spain, but when my grandmother died the Earl took me in. It was very kind of him,' she added dutifully.

Bess, sensitive always to others, thought she understood the painful vibration she had received on first meeting Rachel. 'It is not easy to lose a loved one, or to be uprooted to another country; the two combined must have been very painful.' Rachel stared into her glass without speaking. 'In so little time,' Bess went on, 'you have done wonderfully to master a new language so thoroughly.'

'My…mother had an English lady as companion. She stayed with us and we always spoke English when together. She was glad to do so because she missed her home so much.' And how my grandmother had always hated that, Rachel thought wryly.

Bess settled herself more comfortably in her chair. She was a good listener, and would be interested to hear this girl's story. She said, 'You have very unusual looks. Were both your parents English?'

'They were, but my maternal grandmother was Spanish. When my father died my mother lived with her and Spain became her home. I was born there and it was very…dear to me. An unpopular sentiment in this country and in these times, I know.' Spain and all things Spanish were viewed with a distrust bordering on the obsessive by the English. Its religion was outlawed and its converts and devotees subject by law to charges of high treason. Rachel's slim fingers touched the outline of the gold cross slipped within her bodice.

Bess had seen the movement. 'You are Catholic?'

Rachel lowered her wide eyes. 'Not officially, naturally—out of respect to the family who kindly gave me a haven. But when I arrived the Earl of Monterey asked me the same question and then said no one should insist I attend the Abbey Hall prayers.' This was a considerable concession actually, for those who did not practise the Protestant faith were viewed with extreme suspicion, as were those who condoned such a lack.

'You do not call the Earl…Grandfather…or Great-uncle?' Bess asked.

'Oh, no! Katherine said that would be most inappropriate.'

On her arrival at Abbey Hall, confused and terrified and taken immediately to confront an elderly gentleman, so sick and grey-looking against the mountainous white pillows, Rachel had run to the bed, eager to embrace her new family with the whole of her warm nature. Looking at her, even John—so weary and tired of trying to face each day—had brightened before such entrancing life. Katherine, who had been present, had soon put a stop to that, keeping her cousin away from John and his few visitors.

'Oh, but surely—' Bess began, then caught herself up. It was not her concern, naturally. She knew Monterey very well—her daughter Anne had once been courted by his older son, who had been a poor heir to such a fine man, and she and Harry had retained friendly relations since. She looked thoughtfully over at Katherine, holding court with Hal and Piers hanging on her every word, and George's two sons-in-law annoying their wives by doing the same. Bess returned her eyes to Rachel. Poor little girl! No parents, no brothers or sisters and forbidden even to call her scant-remaining relative fondly. Her sympathy was communicated to Rachel, who took a breath.

'Please don't feel sorry for me, my lady. I am so lucky, really. On the road here I saw so many far more badly placed. I wish I could have done something for them...'

Brave, too, Bess thought. An admirable sentiment for a girl who had little enough. She sighed and smiled and rose to go into the kitchens to ensure the splendid meal under preparation was progressing well.

As was her habit, Bess ordered the places of those around her table. In the merry confusion, Rachel scarcely noticed who her supper companions were until she was seated with an empty plate before her and a glass of wine to hand. Nervously she sipped the wine and saw that she was to the right of George Latimar and to the left of his brother Hal. George, in his easy pleasant way, helped her to food, saying, 'So many Latimars must be quite intimidating for you, my dear.'

Rachel looked at the delicious food. Abbey Hall made the greatest effort when entertaining, but that was rarely these days with its master ill, and usually the housekeeping was fairly mediocre for Katherine was a poor manager and Rachel—who could have helped, for she was an excellent housewife—was never asked for her advice. Everything on the board tonight fulfilled the dual role of pleasing the eye as well as the appetite, she thought. Beautifully cooked spiced meats, green asparagus gleaming with butter, tiny orange fingers of new carrots and fat river fish, baked whole, their scales removed and replaced with costly slivers of almond. There was even—as a separate course—a deep glass dish of salad, its contents glistening with oil and lemon juice: a delicacy Rachel hadn't seen since leaving Spain where she and her grandmother had often gone out into the warm gardens to gather the leaves and tiny jewel-red tomatoes... 'Oh, yes,' she murmured, swallowing with a throat closed by homesickness.

'My mother tells me you have been at Abbey Hall for nearly a year now. One of the Earl's sons— Tom—was a great friend to me in my youth. 'Tis a beautiful place, I remember, with splendid gardens, once the talk of the countryside.'

'Yes, sir,' Rachel said, thinking of the remains of what had obviously been a showpiece of horticultural beauty, now run to ruin without care and attention from its mistress. Too cold! Too rainy! Too boring… Such was Katherine's opinion of any outdoor activity. A silence fell.

'Are you not hungry? My mother prides herself on her fine food,' George tried again. Rachel lifted her eyes to his face, noticing, even as she blinked away the memory of a mass of vivid blooms which had jostled each other in splendour around her bedroom window every summer of her life before she was banished from her home, how like his father he was and, in turn, his mother. Looking about the table, she saw Latimar features produced again and again: the unusual height in both men and women, the extreme slenderness, the fine eyes—of whatever colour—and the clear pale skin. And, especially, the peculiar vivacity of manner. They all had these traits, in some degree or another, but by some strange alchemy it had been distilled in Hal Latimar. He was, Rachel mused absently, the most perfect human being she had ever encountered.

'Well…' George was smiling at both her perusal and sudden thoughtfulness '…do you approve of us?'

She smiled tentatively in return. 'You are a very good-looking family.'

He inclined his head. 'Thank you. Tomorrow you will inspect the next generation. I am a grandfather, you know, and scarcely believe it.' At ease now, Rachel began to eat, relaxing and offering a comment here and there. At length George turned to his mother on his other side and Rachel glanced sideways at Hal.

Hal had spent the meal so far staring at Katherine. Part of the effect she was having upon him was the extraordinary excitement he felt because it was so long since he had been so immediately attracted to a woman: she was very different from the women he was used to—so vital and fresh, as well as so beautiful. Throughout the meal she had shared her favours between Piers Roxburgh and Harry Latimar. Piers seemed as struck with her as his best friend, and Harry, with a lifetime's association with the great and glamorous behind him, was plainly enjoying her company. 'I beg your pardon?' Hal turned courteously to Rachel as she spoke.

'I was just remarking how very fond your family seem to be of each other. I have seldom heard so much laughter and happy conversation.'

'Oh, yes, we are all good friends. We do not see much of my sister and her husband, but letters are exchanged on a regular basis and George and his family are near enough to be a part of our life here.' He again allowed his gaze to centre on Katherine and Rachel fell silent. For a brief time, while she

was speaking with George, she had felt interesting
and worth noticing. Now she was back to feeling
the tolerated onlooker. The outsider of any group.

After the meal there was a general move towards
the parlour and Rachel came to Bess's side and
asked leave to retire. ''Tis a family party,' she murmured. 'I have no place there.' Bess was swift to
hear the desolation in her voice, and gave her a
thoughtful glance. Rachel's looks, the set of her
head and firm chin, somehow did not match the
uncertainty of her manner. There is good blood
there, Bess mused, and she reminds me... A memory from the distant past tugged at her.

'My lady?' Rachel was bearing the scrutiny
meekly enough, but her expressive eyes darkened.
She is judging me, she thought, as all in her position must do when confronted by someone like me.

'You may go to your rest, of course,' Bess said,
'but I would be pleased if you would stay for the
rest of the festivities.'

'In that case...' Rachel's smile flashed out.

The impression of having known her, or someone
very like her once, grew stronger in Bess, although
she could not think who it was. It would return to
her—these days her memory was not what it was.
Meanwhile, she led the way into the parlour where
she and Harry received gifts and more good wishes.
Later the family caught up with the news.

George and Hal sat on the long settle. Hal had
been a baby when George married his love, Judith;
in his growing years his older brother had been rais-

ing his family and frequently away in Elizabeth Tudor's court. As George began to spend less time in the royal residences, Hal had completed his training, received his silver spurs and duly been taken up by the Queen. He and George saw little of each other, but were very good friends.

'So, little brother,' George said now. 'How is it with you? You look fit.' It was an understatement, he thought wryly, for he had never seen such an example of fair and handsome youth.

'I am,' agreed Hal. 'You look fine yourself, George. I am sorry not to see Anne here tonight. Is she well, do you think?'

'I know she is.' George and Anne were twins— the one always knew the other's feelings and state. 'I think if she could speak to you now, she would say: I wish I could be at Maiden Court, but my beloved husband and children need me.'

Hal glanced at him; he would not argue with one who knew what he was talking about. 'Yes…well. What think you of our visitors?'

'Katherine Monterey and her handmaiden? I think Katherine a very beautiful girl.'

Hal turned to him. 'So do I! She is lovely, is she not? And also sweet.'

George considered. He knew Katherine, of course—as the niece of one of the greatest friends of his youth, Tom Monterey, he had taken an interest in her. He knew his parents had been asked to present her when she was old enough. He also had known her father—Ralph—a court favourite and dead these long years. Ralph had sued for Anne Latimar's hand and George had been greatly relieved when the projected match had foundered for he had had no liking for the attractive unscrupulous courtier. Was his only daughter like him, George wondered, or like her grandfather, who had been as fine an example of stalwart English gentleman as could be found? He said, 'Piers seems to share your enthusiasm.' Piers had drawn up a chair close to Katherine's and was holding earnest conversation with her. Hal frowned.

'I think I have made it clear this night, even after knowing her so short a time, my regard for Katherine,' he added stiffly, 'Piers is my friend.'

'Friendship is the first thing cast overboard when a woman gets between two men,' George said mildly. There was a short silence, during which Hal's fair face darkened. Piers was certainly doing all he could to charm Katherine, he thought cynically, with the kind of performance he only usually put on for a lady who might advance his static career. Obviously he had registered the name of Monterey— He rose abruptly. 'Excuse me, brother.' As he moved purposely across the floor, his mother touched his sleeve.

'Hal, my dear, I was speaking to Rachel earlier of our small innovation here at Maiden Court. The Queen's Rest, you know. She expressed a wish to see it, and I thought we would go now. Come with us, won't you?' Hal looked down at her blankly. 'I need a little air,' Bess went on.

For a moment she thought he would refuse, but he smiled and said, 'Very well, Mother. I will ask Piers and Katherine to join us.' He bowed before Katherine and leaned to offer his invitation. She shook her curls and protested how comfortable she was. Hal looked at Piers. 'You will escort us, won't you, Piers?'

'Thank you, but no, my friend. I would not leave such a charming lady unattended.' Katherine gave Hal a mischievous look, then fixed her marvellous eyes once again on Piers. Hal turned on his heel.

## Chapter Three

In the cool night air Rachel dropped behind the others until Bess turned and offered her arm. 'Perhaps we should have brought our cloaks, Rachel. It is not as warm as I expected.'

'Would you like to go back in?' Hal asked immediately. He resented being pressganged for this expedition; who knew what progress Piers—so adept with women—would make in his absence?

Rachel looked at him. If he was reluctant to be out in the moonlight, it certainly admired him. Inside the manor, by soft candlelight, he was almost too handsome: so much coin-bright hair, vividly blue black-lashed eyes and classically modelled face gave the impression of delicacy. In this pure cold light the strong bones of his face, allied to the athletic shape of his body beneath the rich clothes, conveyed uncompromising masculinity. When Bess shook her head decisively in answer to his question, he passed a hand over his hair resignedly.

Rachel had particularly noticed his hands at the

supper table. They were unusual in their length of
sensitive square-tipped fingers and a beautiful example of the human bone structure. She thought,
quite impersonally, that she had never seen quite so
lovely a feature on a man's body before.

The innovation Bess had mentioned to Rachel
and called the Queen's Rest was a little stone house
built on a space of land just before the formal house
gardens became the pasture land. It was solidly
built, its apertures glazed. From the front could be
seen the manor, surrounded by its protective trees,
from the back the open fields of the estate, patch-
worked in this white light. It was furnished very
simply with two wooden, cushioned settles and
warm and faded rugs underfoot.

It had come into being because the Queen enjoyed walking outside in all weathers but was becoming older now and needed to rest after even
short walks. Maiden Court had, for many years,
been somewhere she could go to relax in informal
congenial company. Her long-time love, the Earl of
Leicester, was very attached to George Latimar and
liked to visit his friend—Elizabeth often came with
him. Recently she had said to Bess that she found
it difficult to remain mobile for even short periods,
and so the stone building, known as the Queen's
Rest, had been established.

'Oh, I like it!' Rachel said now, sitting down and
looking back towards the lighted house. Bess sat,
too, but did not reply. After a moment, Rachel's
eyes were drawn to the sweep of rolling country-

side. She did not see it, however, for her mind's
eye produced the very different view which she remembered from her grandmother's *casa* in Spain.
If I were there now, she thought wistfully, I would
be looking at the tangled groves of olive trees, and
listening to the cicadas which would surely be ac-
tive on this June night. Later would come the traditional Andalucian singing until dawn— 'I beg
your pardon, my lady.' She started as Bess spoke
to her.

'I was saying that it is positioned just right to see
two views, but sheltered from the worst of the
weather.'

'Indeed, my lady,' Rachel agreed.

'Now you have seen it,' Hal, who had propped
his shoulder against the stout doorway, spoke impatiently, 'shall we go back to the house?' Each
moment, he felt, away from Katherine was a wasted
moment. Who knew what advances Piers was making in his absence? As he thought this, he experienced a shock to realise how close he was coming
to being seriously at odds with his best friend. Dan-
gerously so, given Piers's reputation—no insult,
fancied or real, was allowed to pass by Roxburgh.
It must not come to that, Hal resolved…but if it
should, then so be it. Tonight he had met the girl,
the one girl, he wished to marry. No one, not even
Piers, could change his mind on that.

'If I could pay a short visit to the stables,' Rachel
said, getting up.

'The stables?' groaned Hal.

'Why, yes,' Rachel said resolutely. 'I rode here on a very…old, but valiant, mount. I would see she is quite happy before retiring myself.'

As they walked the path to the stable yard, Hal asked, 'If she is so old, Rachel, why is she still in commission?'

'You should ask my cousin that question,' Rachel said quietly. 'Where I am come from, such a horse, with years of faithful service behind it, would be out to pasture. Katherine feels differently.'

In the stables, filled with the warm breath of its occupants, Rachel looked about her with bright eyes as Bess paused to caress those she knew and Hal attended her. Harry Latimar kept a fine selection of blood horses. Rachel progressed along the stalls until she found Primrose, who greeted her with weary delight. As Bess began a conversation with one of the grooms, Hal came to Rachel's side. He looked Primrose over with a frown, sure that the Maiden Court stables had never seen such a shambling wreck before. He said idly, 'You enjoy riding, lady?'

'Yes, I do, or at least I did.' She was sure he was not interested, but added just the same, 'In Spain, in my home, I was set up on my first pony before I could walk. My former countrymen are the best judge of horseflesh in the world.'

'Is that so?' Hal enquired, stifling a yawn. 'But since coming to this country, you do not enjoy the activity as you used to?'

'I have no opportunity to enjoy it, sir,' she said

bleakly. 'You see before you—' she indicated Primrose '—the poor creature I was given for the journey here. She is, in fact, the only horse at my disposal.'

Hal raised his eyebrows before her vehement tone. 'Yes, well, while you are here please feel free to take any nag you wish from our stables and try it. My father, too, is accounted a fair judge of the animals.'

'I know,' Rachel returned unguardedly. 'My grandmother told me that many times.'

'Your grandmother?'

A little flustered under his suddenly interested eyes, Rachel said, 'Yes...my grandmother, who was, in her time, also a connoisseur of all things equine. In fact, the horse that she acquired in England when she knew your father and took back to Spain was so fine an animal it sired a whole generation of colts owned eventually by the great families of Madrid and Castile.'

Hal blinked. A few moments ago this little girl could have blended very well into the grey shadows of the night; now she was brilliant with colour. A Spanish grandmother would explain that shade of hair colour, black with a bluish sheen, and the ripe mouth—rose-red without resort to the French paste. Her figure, too, undisguised by her ill-fitting gown, was seductively proportioned and her skin, so creamily pale, also declared her ancestry. But how explain those eyes—the colour of autumn-touched beech leaves—or the clipped English voice? He said, 'And your parents? Were they Spanish?'

Rachel lifted her chin before his deprecatory tone. 'My father, sir, was an English gentleman, and my mother of Irish descent, whose antecedents claimed Brian Boru as their blood kin.'

'Ah, well, that explains your interest in horses. A combination of Spanish and Irish blood is indeed formidable in that field.'

Rachel flushed brightly. Her tongue had been carried away by the familiar scents and sights in this place, and she had made a fool of herself. Before she could answer a groom appeared in the half light.

'Lady Bess has returned to the manor, sir,' he said to Hal. 'She bids you return when you are ready.'

'I am ready,' Rachel declared. 'More than ready.'

Hal laughed easily, saying, 'Well, if the Lady Rachel is satisfied, then so am I.' He glanced at the groom. 'She is somewhat of an afficionado in the place we are standing now, Wat.'

Rachel, who had been conscious of her flush and trying sternly to repress it, now found herself colouring more deeply. Afficionado! she thought angrily. To use such a word clearly puts me in my place. There followed some private thoughts using the untranslatable language of the Spanish stable-yard where she had spent so many of her formative years. She followed her escort back to the manor, struggling for control, thinking also that it was a year since she had felt so angry—or so painfully alive.

In the hall, where a yawning servant was quenching the candles, they discovered the party had disbanded. George and his wife and family were being accommodated in the house and Bess and Katherine had also retired. Only Harry Latimar waited courteously in his hall to bid them goodnight.

Hal embraced him. 'Go to your bed, Father, you look exhausted.'

'It is the excitement of having so many family members all in my home at once,' Harry said. 'Some of whom,' he added with characteristic irony, 'are seldom to be coerced back.'

Hal smiled. Only his father could issue a rebuke with such grace.

'Will you show the Lady Rachel where she is quartered?' Harry said as he turned to walk slowly up the stairs.

'I will.' Hal and Rachel watched him climb the stairs, then looked at each other. Used to court hours, Hal thought he could not sleep so early. He might as well spin out the time in the company of this odd girl. 'Shall we go into the parlour and take a last glass of wine?' he asked. Rachel felt she had no choice but to accept. Why, she wondered, was she plagued with this feeling of inferiority? It was…humiliating.

The lights had been doused in the main hall, but the parlour still showed a flickering yellow glow from the heaped fire and a wash of moonlight pour-

ing in through the open window. Rachel walked
towards this light, wishing she could go to bed, and
despairing with herself because she did not have the
confidence to say so. She seated herself on the window seat. Hal opened one of the oak cupboards and
took out a flask. He extracted the wooden stopper
and poured a portion of the contents into two
glasses.

'My mother's blackberry cordial,' he said, turning with the glasses in his hands. 'Reputed to be
the best in four counties.' He had always loved this
potent brew—or perhaps he loved the memories it
evoked of endless hot Maiden Court summers, with
their bounty of fruitfulness at the end, and the memory of himself, a small boy accompanying his beloved mother as she gathered the sweet-smelling
berries under a hazy burning English sun. They had
been such happy days, he thought now, he so intent
on eating that which she wished to confine in her
basket. He had often defied her, he recalled, with
aggressive stance and stained mouth, but had never
received a word of rebuke. Instead, Bess had
laughed at his infant fury and cuddled him close,
calling him her little wild man.

As Hal crossed the floor of the parlour to give
Rachel her glass, he found himself wanting to relive
those times—to tell her of them. It was a foolish
notion, he decided, for his mother had been soft and
gentle and this young woman was stern-faced and
hardy. She had had, he guessed, a difficult youth,
and such people were incalculable. He did not sit

beside her, but stood staring out at the moon-silvered gardens. 'So,' he said, when the silence between them had lengthened, 'your grandmother knew my father once?'

'She often spoke of him,' Rachel said softly.

'My father used to have quite a reputation with women. Were they in love, do you think?' His voice, light and dismissive, annoyed her. She lifted her eyes to the portrait on the wall facing her. In love? What an understatement! At least, on her grandmother's part.

Hal ceased looking out at the shadowed gardens and watched her face. 'Well,' he continued, with an amused smile, 'if it was a *grand affaire*, please don't tell my mother.'

'Why should I? Anyway…it was a long time ago. Over and forgotten.' She had noted the smile and was instantly defensive in a way which hurt her to acknowledge.

'Nothing is ever over—or forgotten—with wives, or so I have heard,' Hal replied wryly. He finished his drink and went to the cupboard to replenish his glass. 'What happened with them, I wonder?'

'Oh…my lord Earl preferred your mother, I believe.'

Hal came back to her, frowning. 'So. My mother knew your grandmother, too? When did all this happen? Surely not after my parents were wed?'

'I believe so.' Why had she begun this? Rachel wondered. Only because she had desired his full attention after his disparaging treatment of her in the stable and later in this hushed room. Well, she had his full attention now: his blue eyes were fixed accusingly on her face. Yet, it was truly so long ago. But, surely, strong emotions must have a life of their own and continue to exist long after those who felt them were consigned to the cold grave, or sterile old age? Madrilene de Santos's passion for Harry Latimar, so often expressed, even when she should have been past all physical longing, had been so vital—its very substance and force was tangible even in this quiet room, in this quiet house, where she had never visited. 'I loved him so!' she had so often, and so fervently, declared, 'and he would have loved me, too, if that cold-hearted woman had been prepared to let him go.'

Bess Latimar had been that cold-hearted woman, Rachel thought. Bess, who had most warmly welcomed her rival's granddaughter to her home, Rachel also thought guiltily: and it is her son who stands before me now, defensive for his mother. Perhaps he would always associate her with something which had happened a lifetime ago, and judge Rachel Monterey as he must judge Madrilene. He had mentioned his father's reputation—but we are two different people, Rachel and Hal, and should meet as distinct personalities. Even so, seeing the cynical smile playing over his mouth, she thought, if he has family to defend, so have I! She said indignantly, 'It was not like that!'

'Like what?' Hal was startled once again by her

sudden change from resigned composure to vivid attack.

Rachel got up. She crossed the room with her graceful step and stood before the portrait. Harry Latimar's likeness looked disinterestedly out of the faded canvas. 'I know what you are thinking,' she said. 'But it was not like that. My grandmother was not one of your father's…light o' loves. She was a lady of the first water.'

That curious dignity, thought Hal, looking at her straight back and delicate, yet strong, shoulders. It is so hard to define, but I recognise it. My mother has it, and all my family. But it is more a part of this girl than them, for it has been hard won, and hard to maintain for her… And that expression in her eyes! As if she had just now seen the biggest threat to something dear to her. He reached behind him and closed the window with a sharp thud. 'Well, as you say, it was all a long time ago. Now, you must be tired. If you have finished your drink, you will wish to seek your bed. I will show you where.'

Rachel swallowed. Why was she continually making herself appear foolish before this man? It seemed a long time since anyone had been able to provoke her so. She watched him select and light a candle, trying to decide why he antagonised her.

He came to the door and stood back so she could pass through before him, giving her his negligently charming smile as he did so. At the door of her room, he opened it, placed the candlestick on a table just inside and bade her a courteous good night.

Surprisingly she fell asleep as soon as her head touched the well-stuffed pillow.

In the early morning she awoke and lay for a few moments wondering where she was. Her room at Maiden Court was small, but well appointed; low-ceilinged over a very comfortable bed, richly curtained as was the glazed window. A luxuriously thick rug covered almost all the floor space. Rachel sat up, noticing the polished chests, the shallow bowls of dried herbs and flower petals thereon, the way the sunlight streaming in picked out the delicate embroidery of the wall hangings. A beautiful and tasteful room, she thought with satisfaction, arranged exactly as she herself would have done.

This chamber had one door to the passage and another to a larger apartment which had been given to Katherine. It was too early yet, Rachel judged, for Katherine to begin to call for hot water, for food, for…well, anything the spoiled young woman wanted and which she expected her despised young kinswoman to provide for her.

Rachel lay back a moment, enjoying the unaccustomed luxury and leisure. What had Hal Latimar said last night? Take any nag from our stables and try it! She thought she would do that now.

Suitably dressed, she found the stables. A groom came forward and politely asked if he could help her. Together they examined the satin-skinned an-

imals, and— Oh! the delight of choosing a lively,
lovely creature with breeding and pride in every
line; the joyous freedom of galloping out into the
new day, scarcely dawned but already warm and
fragrant with the scent of summer. To be riding
through leafy country lanes, the fields on either side
so full of healthy crops. Rachel rode for miles, ec-
statically happy, until the position of the sun over-
head reminded her she was a long way from
Maiden Court and should turn back. She rode more
slowly home; her mare was still lively but Rachel
knew better than to return her to her stall in a lather.
As she cantered gently down the slope before the
manor house another rider joined her and she saw
it was Hal Latimar.

'Good day, lady.' He removed his cap as he drew
level with her. 'I see you took me at my word last
night.'

'Indeed.' She smoothed Belle's damp mane. She
was embarrassed by the exchange between them the
previous evening, but saw that no such awkward-
ness existed for him. He sat carelessly on his tall
chestnut, playing with the reins, his eyes fixed on
the flushed roof of his home. The climbing sun
turned his hair to gold. 'You are out early today.'
Somehow she had fancied him one of the breed of
men who lay long abed in the mornings.

He turned to survey her and, as if reading her
thoughts, replied, 'We are early risers, us Latimars—well, apart from my sister who dearly loves
to waste the best part of the day. Shall we ride on

down?' He assisted her to dismount in the yard and took both horses into the stables.

Bess was already in the hall. She had enjoyed the supper last night, but would enjoy today even more for her precious great-grandchildren would be present.

'May I help you with anything?' Rachel asked, shedding her cloak.

'How kind. I would welcome your help cutting some flowers from the garden. I love to have fresh blooms in the house, but fear bending is difficult for me these days. There is a basket and shears by the door.' The two women strolled out into the radiant day.

'It will be hot today,' Bess remarked.

Rachel lifted her eyes to the sky. 'Yes. I enjoy this warm weather, it reminds me of home—my old home, I mean.' Her voice was so wistful.

Bess said in quick sympathy, 'Yes, I suppose you must miss Spain very much.'

'Oh, I do!' Rachel said, adding impulsively, 'You cannot imagine, unless you have seen for yourself, how much colour and light there is there. Even the poorest of dwellings has its brave show of flowers in little pots the owners have made themselves. And the sea is almost as bright a blue as the sky.' She paused as she saw Bess regarding her with a little pucker on her brow. 'I beg your pardon, my lady.' She flushed. 'Of course it is not quite…proper in England to praise anything Spanish.'

Bess began to walk along the path, looking into the flower beds. She touched a fragrant bush of roses. 'Shall we have some of these? They smell so sweet, apart from being beautiful. As to praising one's home—we all should be allowed to do that.'

Rachel bent to snip an armful of the glossy-leaved flowers and, as she leaned close to Bess, her own perfume hung in the air between them. Bess closed her eyes a moment. It was not a scent favoured in England; it was both subtle and invasive and it held memories for her. Of another girl in another time.

'Madrilene...' she murmured.

Rachel started. 'That was my grandmother's name,' she said without pausing to think. 'Madrilene de Santos—very unusual, I believe. Few have heard it.'

'I have heard it,' Bess said shortly. She began to walk swiftly away. Rachel followed uncertainly.

'My lady?' she faltered. 'Have I offended in some way?' Bess stopped and spun around.

'I think I knew your grandmother,' she said abruptly.

Rachel blushed. 'Yes...I know.'

'Ah...you know,' Bess repeated. She looked about her garden unseeing, then said, 'I think I would prefer to gather the flowers alone. Pray return to the house.' That time! she was thinking, that dreadful time! When an unscrupulous girl almost wrecked my good marriage. Now her granddaughter stands on my land as bold as brass and says,

Yes…I know! Ever since Rachel Monterey had entered the hall of Maiden Court, Bess had been constantly reminded of someone else. Reminded! Why, she must have been blind. Rachel could be Madrilene's reincarnation. And she had felt pity for the girl. Pity, bah! Any female with Madrilene de Santos's blood did not need that gentle mercy—her pathetic ways were just a pose as her grandmother had assumed so many. Oh, it was an old, old story, but as fresh to Bess as if it were yesterday.

While Bess had been confined producing her twin son and daughter, Harry Latimar had remained with the royal court when Madrilene de Santos, spoiled and wealthy Spanish ward of King Henry Tudor, had arrived to take her place as one of Catherine Howard's waiting ladies. Immediately her lustrous dark eyes had alighted on Harry and she had waged a deliberate campaign to snatch him for herself. Bess, and Harry, too, had eventually foiled her in this, but—standing now in the tranquillity of her gardens—Bess could still remember the pain of that whole year of her life. And the anger. Gentle and peaceable Bess had always been, but not meek, and to be confronted nearly four decades later with such an unwelcome ghost roused fire in her breast. With a face of stone she made a sweeping gesture. 'Go back into the house, I say!' As Rachel stumbled away, she thought again, I must have been blind. Why, it could be she, my old enemy: all that shining black hair, that walk—as if she carried a crown on her elegant head. She stared after the retreating figure with hatred in her heart.

# *Chapter Four*

On her way back to the manor Rachel thought, Hal Latimar! He had said last night, 'Don't tell my mother', yet he had done so himself at the first opportunity and caused upset to that kind woman and—what?—to herself. Yesterevening she had received kindness and sympathy from Bess; for the first time since landing on England's cold coast she had felt that someone actually cared. Now it was all spoiled. Rachel entered the hall, raging with the injustice of the situation. Whatever her grandmother had done was nothing to do with her, it had been done and decided before she was born. Tears filled her eyes.

'Why, whatever is wrong?' Hal was standing just inside the door.

'You should know!' Rachel returned furiously. Judith, George's wife, joined them, looking into the trug at the roses.

'Why, you did not do so well. Where is my mother-in-law?'

'Still in the gardens,' Rachel said indistinctly. 'She no longer wished me to help her.' Judith looked out.

'I'll go and help her. Find a receptacle for those, will you, Rachel?'

Rachel brushed past Hal. Yes, she would find a receptacle. That she could so, for that was her function—to be nothing more than a servant arranging flowers. Hal followed her.

'What do you mean, I should know?' he asked her at the kitchen door.

'Please stand aside. I must find a…receptacle.'

'My lady mother does not keep her flower bowls and such in the kitchen, but in a cupboard in the parlour. I will show you.'

Grimly she followed him to the parlour and selected a bronze bowl from those he showed her. Hal called for a maid and asked her to fill it with water. Rachel still held the basket gripped in her two hands. He removed it and set it on the floor.

'Now, what is this all about? Why are you so upset?' he asked again.

'You told your lady mother about what we talked of last night,' she accused him.

'I did not. I have just this moment come in from the stables and have not seen her yet this day. Besides—what if I had? Why should it matter so to you?'

'Why?' Rachel turned her eyes, tearful and brilliant, on him. 'Because she was so kind to me last night and now looks upon me with disfavour. Extreme disfavour.'

Through the open door Hal could hear Katherine's distinctive voice and Piers Roxburgh's deeper tones. He had no time to waste with this girl's fancies. Impatiently he said, 'Well, if you walk about life looking as if you expected it to take a stick to your back, you can be sure it will. The real world is not…kind, or…favourable, Rachel. One must hold one's head high and learn to keep one's pride.'

Rachel was outraged. 'I beg your pardon? I hardly think you are the best judge of that!'

Hal considered her for a moment in silence, then said slowly, 'Why? Because you perhaps think, as so many do: there goes Hal Latimar—good looks, good breeding, wealth, competent skills in all the courtly arts and a proud ancestry? Fortunate man! But, my dear girl, where I have chosen to make my way there are dozens better bred, scores better heeled, and hundreds more comely. The one advantage I have over any of them is my heritage of the Tudor monarchs' penchant for Latimars. And that is a card I would disdain to lay.' There was a heartbeat's pause in which she, in turn, considered him, guessing this was a side of the golden Latimar boy he rarely exposed. It was interesting, and so was his first comment to her.

'Do I really look as you described?'

'Indeed you do. When you entered the hall last night you looked for all the world as if you expected to be banished with all speed to the servants' quarters.'

The unshed tears were still present in her eyes. She blinked them away. 'Is that so surprising?' she asked with a catch in her voice. 'It is hard to be me, you know. With no one do I come first now. Or even second or third.'

'Yes, well,' he said uncomfortably, 'I can see it must be difficult to spend so much of your time with someone so incomparably beautiful and talented as your cousin.'

That was not what she had meant at all! Annoyed, she retorted, 'My mother was ten times more lovely and talented, and she treated those who served her with the same respect they granted her.'

'I am sure you intend no criticism,' he said coldly. 'I assume you have some gratitude towards the Lady Katherine,' he said the name with reverence, 'for welcoming you into her home and making you her friend.'

'We are not friends—' Rachel bit back her next words which would have been bitterly lacking in 'gratitude'. Many times in the last year she had thought, Some keep a dog they can kick when the mood takes them, Katherine keeps me for this purpose. There was a rustle of silk at the door and Katherine herself appeared in the doorway. She wore a gown of amber satin, almost an exact match for her eyes, and flashing diamonds at her throat and in her ears. Inappropriate, Rachel thought, for a midday meal where children would be present, but Katherine often displayed poor taste in an area where any true lady would have been adept.

'Hal; so this is where you are hiding yourself,' Katherine said in her attractively husky voice. She moved aside to allow the maid to bring in the bowl and place it on the table, then picked up the basket of roses and began to transfer them. 'Mmm, how sweetly they smell.' Rachel and Hal watched the slender white hands deal with the defenceless blooms with differing thoughts. Every movement she makes is graceful, Hal thought. Every situation is turned to her advantage, Rachel thought.

'Now, where had you thought to put these?' Katherine turned to Rachel. Having come upon her cousin and an attractive young man in intimate conversation, she now sought to put Rachel firmly back into her place.

'I will take them through to the hall,' Rachel said resignedly. She picked up the heavy bowl. Piers, who had come in unobserved, sprang forward and took it from her.

'Allow me, my lady, this is much too heavy for you. Show me where you would like it placed.'

When the two had gone, Katherine laughed and said ruefully, 'Now Piers will think me unkind. Actually, Rachel often makes me feel in that unhappy state. And yet I am sure I do my very best to please her.'

'She is a prickly girl,' he agreed.

'When she arrived, last year, she was quite haughty,' Katherine said, sighing. 'I remember my grandfather remarking that she behaved as one might expect visiting royalty to do.'

A faint warning bell sounded in Hal's head. He had met the Earl only a few times some years ago, but thought it a strange observation for the man he remembered to make. 'It is hard to believe the Lady Rachel could ever have felt secure enough to behave so,' he said thoughtfully.

Katherine, aware she had made a mistake, recouped it deftly. 'Ah, well, I suppose her grandmother made her feel like a little princess—Rachel's parents died many years ago and there were no other children. Brothers and sisters make a difference, I should imagine. As you will know, I think.'

Hal smiled, the moment of uncertainty faded and he took her arm. 'I do indeed. Shall we join the others?'

The meal was a triumph of delectable fare. Bess was a very good housewife; her kitchens were—as was the rest of the manor—spotlessly clean, her staff industrious and happy, too. In season she delighted in bottling and preserving all the fruits of her flourishing estate. Her gentle but firm hand extended to all parts of her little kingdom and both human and animal creatures who called Maiden Court their home received her compassionate care. No animal was ill treated, no man or woman or child need fear a bitter winter, a failed harvest, an illness or disability.

Tonight the laden table, the gleaming surroundings, gave evidence of her talented husbandry. And
all in an atmosphere of willing service, Rachel
thought as she came down the stairs, having
changed from her riding clothes. On returning to
her chamber she had found her only presentable
gown laid over her bed, newly sponged and
pressed. A cheerful maid had tapped on the door
asking if she might 'wash and dress my lady's hair'.
The bed linen had been changed, the bowls of fragrant dried flowers renewed.

Descending to the kitchen and offering to help in
some way, the fat and jolly cook had asked her if
she might like to transfer some of the redcurrant
jelly and mint sauce into little bowls for the table.

'My lady does like them with the mutton. And
you'll find the little pots of horseradish that my lady
sets up for the beef.'

Exploring the larder, Rachel was transfixed by
the rows and rows of jewel-bright sealed glass con-
tainers, all with their labels written in Bess Latimar's careful hand: Quince Jelly, this year of Our
Lord 1582; Damson Jam, this year of Our Lord
1583. Rachel turned out the enviably clear jelly and
the pungent horseradish into little dishes and took
her place at the table where the others were already
assembled.

Two great sirloins of beef dominated the table,
flanked by two pink hams, baked in honey glaze
and spiked with costly cloves. There was fresh
white bread to soak up the juices from the beef, a

dish of new carrots and another of tiny green peas.
There was river fish, baked in their skins, then de-
nuded of them and replaced with slivers of al-
monds, then returned to the hot oven to brown. After the savouries came the sweetmeats; marchpane
and gingerbread and little coffers of pastry filled
with sugared currants and topped with yellow
cream. Finally came sweet and spicy dried apple
rings and walnuts.

The Latimars en masse were merry company and
took a lively interest in the two strangers in their
midst. Katherine was an immediate favourite, so
beautiful and vivacious, and Rachel was perceived
to have a charm all her own, particularly when she
had relaxed enough to chat shyly to her neighbours.
As these neighbours were children she might have
earned Bess's approval, but Bess found herself unable to look at Rachel without seeing another
woman entirely.

Hal's eyes, too, were frequently on Rachel, with
irritation rather than approval. Aggravating woman!
he thought, she had quite unsettled him earlier,
when he especially wanted to feel confident and
able to project that confidence to Katherine Monterey. Why had he spoken so personally in the parlour earlier? Why had he spoken of that closely
caged demon to her—the fear that came to him on
dark nights that he was somehow masquerading as
the model of a successful courtier, successful man,
that all he really was was the lucky inheritor of
generations of favour? He hated to acknowledge

this fear, and it was humiliating to have voiced it to another. He also regretted his unkind comment on her personal demeanour, for he also disliked feeling guilty of unkindness.

After the last morsel had been enjoyed they all left the table to play various games suitable to the young guests. Then came the present-giving and Bess and Harry accepted the gifts from the children, gravely appreciating the effort and thought as much as the content. Lastly there was a spirited display of dancing.

Rachel, watching the proceedings from a wide settle by the hearth, said to Hal, who had most reluctantly had to give Katherine up to Piers and so moved out of the line of dancers, 'They are all so happy, are they not?'

'Mmm.' Hal looked moodily across at Katherine. She and Piers grew more friendly with each passing moment… An ignominious thought crossed his mind: perhaps if Katherine knew how very impoverished Piers was, she would— Hal was instantly ashamed of this thought. Firstly because it assumed that Katherine cared for such distinction, and secondly because it was a disloyalty to his best friend, for there had never been any division between them regarding estate—at least on his part. Rachel glanced at him.

'You're not enjoying yourself. Why? Because of Katherine's performance? It means little, you know, and jealousy only makes you miserable. It's a very

unproductive emotion.' As she said this a premon-
itionary shiver ran down her spine. She had never
been jealous of Katherine for what she had mate-
rially—and 'jealous' was the wrong word for the
pangs she had always felt that her cousin had her
definite place in the world. So why the cold feeling
in this warm room now?

Hal sat down and leaned back, saying in answer
to her words, 'Well, you should know.'

The half-acknowledged thought flashed away and
anger took its place. 'If you are saying I am jealous
of Katherine, then 'tis not true!' she said angrily.
'You think that because she has…everything and I
nothing. As if I cared for a few baubles and furs.
Truly you and she make a good pair!'

Since this was his ambition for the future, it was
hard for him to decide why this last statement
seemed such an insult. 'I don't understand,' he said
abruptly, 'why you are always so angry with me.
Have I earned such enmity?'

She blinked. He had the habit of making these
surprisingly direct remarks, which sat so ill with his
usually casually polished conversation. She was
startled into forgetting that he had offended her
twice with his comments on her character and ad-
mitting, 'No. It is just that, when I am with you, I
feel as if I want to fight with you.'

'Because you think I betrayed your confidence to
my mother?' He gave her the straight, blue Latimar
look.

'No…for if you tell me you did not, then I believe you.'

A slow smile spread across his fair face. 'I am glad of that, for I am a good person to share secrets with. And, actually, I do not have your secret over this, for you told me only meagre details.'

She sighed. 'I should not have said even what I did. And how your mother knew…I cannot see how.'

'Why don't you tell me all about it, Rachel?' Hal folded his arms and looked attentive. Most of his interest was for his parents' part in the story, certainly, for their past was part of the history of the world he occupied. But some was reserved for Rachel, so nervously engaging. He could not help noticing that the colour coming and going in her face, the light changing in her expressive eyes, improved her looks, already arresting. Also, whatever Rachel Monterey was, she was extraordinarily easy to talk to.

Rachel took a breath, conscious that her cursed tendency to blush was upon her now. She looked down at her clasped hands, then up into Hal's face. 'It was this way…' she began, stopped and began again. 'My grandmother, Madrilene, came to the English court when she was but seventeen—the age I am now… She was half-Spanish, half-French and a ward of the old King, Henry. Almost at once she fell in love with your father, who was a good friend of the King. She was—even when I knew her in her old age—a passionate impulsive creature, and must have been more so at that age… Anyway, she saw your father and wanted him, pursued him, I suppose…but he was married to your mother and would not be led astray.' Rachel paused again. This story, told in the house of two of the characters in her tale, was difficult to tell without her grandmother being seen as the villain.

Hal signalled for more wine to be dispensed for himself and Rachel. When it was, he leaned more comfortably against the broad cushions. 'Yes? And then what happened?' Rachel was embarrassed, but he was not. He was a sophisticated courtier of the most glamorous court in the world. He had heard it all before—apart from it being more personal on this occasion.

'What happened then,' Rachel said bleakly, 'was that my grandmother lost the battle between herself and your father and was dispatched forthwith back to France and from there to Spain, where she found some sort of solace with my grandfather, and her daughter—my mother. That is all,' she ended lamely.

'All? I don't think so,' Hal said softly. 'Otherwise, why should my mother—usually a sensible person—resent you so?'

'Well…' Rachel looked away, then back at him. 'Of course that was not…all. For my grandmother never got over him—not having him poisoned her life. And that would not have happened if she had not felt the force of her love was returned in however small a way.'

'That is what my mother felt,' Hal said thoughtfully. 'And the resentment she felt for your grandmother is now transferred to you.' He sipped his wine, adding, 'I am sorry.'

Rachel smiled wryly. He was sorry. Well, who was not—for her? Poor Rachel Monterey, so wellborn, but un-dowered. Poor Rachel, whose father had been a gallant officer of the throne of England, whose mother—so lovely—had chosen badly. Poor Rachel, born into Spain in privileged circumstances, but reduced by her grandmother's gambling to penury. Poor Rachel, whose only contact, a simple Spanish priest, had said, Dear child—to ensure your future, your personal goods must be sold and you can then go to England, the home of your relatives. You will be a poor girl, but you will be with your family…

'And apart from being a keen horsewoman,' Hal asked, after a moment of watching the varying emotions darken her eyes, 'what was your grandmother—Madrilene—like?'

It gave Rachel a strange feeling to hear the name on his lips. In spite of their differing colouring, she thought Hal very like his father. No wonder her grandmother had become so obsessed with a similar attractive creature. 'Oh…' She became aware of his enquiring expression. 'She was beautiful; even old, when I knew her, the way she walked, the way she used her hands and her vivid presence drew all glances. She was also,' she added wryly, 'not to be trusted with a peso when there was any game of chance in prospect. She was rich when she met and married my grandfather, still rich when my mother was alive but…towards the end of her life she had lost it all in one way or another. One way or another usually involving cards or dice, or horse races… well, whatever can be gambled upon.'

Hal laughed. 'Well, I can understand that.'

'Are you a gambler?'

Hal didn't answer. Did he gamble? Yes, he did, it was the ruling passion in his life, or had been until he had set eyes on Katherine Monterey. As this thought struck him, he glanced to the floor where there was now a general move towards the party breaking up. It was well into the early evening and the children needed their rest, they were becoming tearful and cross. George and Judith decided they would stay another night; their children chose to take their little ones home to their own cots. The female adults fluttered about finding outdoor clothing and fitting it on to tired and wailing tots.

Bess and Harry bade a fond farewell to those leaving and Hal was delegated to escort duty. The rest of the family retired to the parlour.

'I think it went very well,' Bess said, relaxing into her chair by the hearth.

'Indeed it did,' Harry agreed, taking his own place near her. Judith dropped a kiss on the top of his head in passing, and put a full glass in his hand. He sipped appreciatively.

'It was lovely,' declared Judith. 'Was it not, George?' George agreed, and busied himself finding seats for everyone. He hastened to the door to welcome two latecomers. Katherine had flown up the stairs to her chamber to repair her toilette, and Rachel had been helping to clear the table in the hall. They took their chairs, spread their skirts and raised their glasses to their lips.

Katherine set hers down and spoke. 'My dear Lady Bess, you should be very proud of your efforts today. So many guests, such fine food—so much of it prepared by your own hands! It is all very praiseworthy.'

Bess smiled wryly. She wanted no praise for what was a pleasure, and resented the patronising tone the girl used. She had seen how her younger son had reacted to the exquisite Katherine but hoped it was just another case of beauty making its usual impact on Hal's susceptibility in this area. He had always been so; even as a child he seemed to love the more physically attractive among his small circle, however kind and worthy the others. It was a fault, Bess had always conceded indulgently, but then children were like that. Now Hal was no longer a child, it worried her more, for beauty did not last nearly as long as other qualities and those qualities did not have room to emerge when a woman traded only on her looks, as the lovely Monterey demoiselle did. Bess's sharp eyes had noticed that Katherine had annoyed most of the ladies tonight by

flirting with their men, and—even though it was all
in the family today—it was unacceptable behaviour.

Most of Hal's women, so far, had been like that,
Bess mused, her blue eyes wandering over Katherine, who could have come from the same mould.
Involuntarily her eyes moved to the girl sitting beside her, then quickly away. Better that known and
familiar devil, than the one incalculable in the shape
of Rachel. Last night Bess had liked Rachel Monterey, today she saw nothing but her likeness to a
distressing phantom from the past.

'What are you thinking of so carefully?' Harry
asked her, leaning forward. She smiled to see him
so well today. Those attacks of his came and went,
and she felt strongly one must make the most of
each day of good health.

'That Hal is very taken with Katherine Monterey.'

'Hal is always taken with any female of passing
good favour.'

'I think this may be different. After all, she is the
granddaughter of an old friend of yours and I feel
he would not have made it so plain if he were not
serious.'

Harry laughed. 'I believe you are right. Our son
is not a fool, and John Monterey, despite his disability, is a hard man.' He stretched out his legs,
blissfully free of pain today. 'What about the other
little girl? I rather like her, but understand she is
some kind of poor relation to the Montereys, with
no means at all.'

'No.'

'But very taking looks, you must admit. Since she came here I have had the strangest feeling—as if I have known her before, although I cannot think where. I'm getting old, I suppose.'

'Or have known too many girls to remember just the one,' Bess said tartly. Harry looked surprised. His Bess rarely spoke in such harsh tones, and especially not to him. At least, not for years. It was obviously a night for ghosts because, looking across the space which divided them, he saw again the challenging look she had worn nearly four decades ago. In that moment his memory clicked. He looked again at Rachel. 'I have it now! She is the spit of Madrilene de Santos.'

'So she should be, for she is her granddaughter!' Elderly husband and wife, lovers for three generations, stared apprehensively at each other. Then Harry smiled delightedly.

'Dear Bess, you are not still holding that against me, are you?'

'I might be.' Bess rose and made her dignified way to the cupboard which held her stock of wax candles. The room had darkened suddenly beyond the dusk of encroaching night; there would be a summer storm. She replaced the candle stubs in the parlour, then moved into the hall, carrying the remainder of the stout white candles. Rachel rose and followed her.

'May I help you, my lady?' she asked hesitantly. Without speaking, Bess put some of the candles in her hands and together they went about their task. The clouds carrying rain were spread haphazardly across the sky now, leaving stretches of clear lilac where the swiftly sinking sun shone bravely. Rachel was chosen by one of these broad strips entering through the high windows as she attended to one of the many-branched silver candelabras on the oak table. Bess paused in her own work to stare at her.

The red rays played over Rachel, discovering the blue tints in her black hair, the brown and gold lights in her eyes and the unblemished perfection of her skin. With these attributes and her proud carriage, Bess thought reluctantly, the girl was a significant beauty. It was a very unwelcome perception because she could so clearly see Madrilene de Santos in her granddaughter and remembered that the Spanish girl, in spite of being spoiled and ruthless, had also been young and vulnerable.

Bess sighed and went away into the kitchens to see how her servants were faring with the task of returning their immaculate facilities to order after two days of entertaining.

Rachel wandered disconsolately back into the parlour where she found a projected card game under discussion.

# Chapter Five

'Oh, Father-in-law!' Judith was saying laughingly. 'Not cards.'

'Why not, my dear?' Harry turned in his chair to smile up at her. 'Katherine and Piers suggested it. As for myself, well, as you know, I can never resist a challenge. Hal, you'll support me, won't you?' He gave his younger son an affectionate glance as he came into the room smoothing his wind-ruffled hair. 'And Rachel, of course.' He included the diffident girl hovering by the hearth in his warm invitation.

Rachel had played games of chance many times. Her grandmother had been addicted to such activity, and Rachel had absorbed the basic rules of any game with the warm Spanish sunshine. Since coming to England, however, even if there had been a rare youthful party visiting Abbey Hall, Katherine had made it clear it was not her cousin's place to join the entertainment.

Now she looked about the company with bright

anticipatory eyes. What fun to be part of such a lively pursuit! Although tonight's game was not one she recognised, she quickly assimilated the rules. Hal, on her right, gave her a congratulatory glance.

'You have played before, lady. We must all take care you do not remove the very shirts from our backs.'

She glowed under the compliment, and he looked again, surprised to see such beauty flowering.

It was a lighthearted exercise, with much gaiety and laughing exclamation. Rachel, who had been a solitary child and an even more bereft adolescent, found herself in a warm and different world. Perhaps it was only a little of the Latimar magic, but she truly felt valued for herself this evening. Lady Bess did not look her way, but her husband—on Rachel's left—helped her make her play and congratulated her on her success. George and his lady smiled and nodded across the table.

Only Katherine appeared resentful of the move to include her and several times remarked that she looked tired enough to retire. Hal, after his initial comment, contented himself with giving her the odd speculative glance. When the play was concluded, with the honours divided between Harry and Hal, the assembly removed to the hall for last drinks and plates of little spiced cakes.

Harry Latimar patted the seat beside him and invited Rachel to join him. 'Come, sit here and tell me about yourself, my dear,' he smiled.

'There is little to tell, my lord Earl. I was born

in Spain where I lived until quite recently—then I
came to England. To Abbey Hall.'

'And your grandmother was once my friend,'
Harry said casually. 'Did she ever speak of me?'

Ever speak of you? Rachel thought wryly. She
spoke of little else, and probably thought of you
constantly! 'She remembered you kindly,' she compromised gravely.

'I doubt that,' Harry returned with a glint in his
eyes. 'But she had a way with all living creatures.
Particularly horses, and I understand you have inherited that talent.'

'I dearly love them.'

Harry nodded. 'Very well. You took a lively
mare from the stables today, I have heard. How did
you find her?'

'Oh wonderful! She is a beauty, so well trained,
yet still has retained her own spirit and personality.'

Why, it could be Madrilene speaking, Harry
thought. The passionate Spanish girl had forfeited
their friendship by her relentless pursuit of him as
a man when all that side of him belonged to his
wife, but he had retained the greatest respect for her
as a prideful human being. What had happened to
this little girl, so like her relative in looks, but so
beaten and timid in her manner? He said, 'Yes, any
female must submit to circumstances—and training—but manage to remember their own selves during the exercise.'

There was a double meaning in his words, Rachel
decided. She looked at him carefully. Latimar was

old now, yes, and suffering from a recurrent illness.
But about him clung the aura of extraordinary
events—his younger son had inherited that indefinable glamour which came from brushing shoulders
with the great men, and women, of his time, and
resisting the submerging of his own character. As
Harry continued to talk, she warmed to him. She
found him fascinating and it showed on her face.
He, in turn, responded to her interest.

The evening progressed very pleasantly for both
of them and at length Harry said to Katherine, 'You
are shortly going to Greenwich, Katherine—I do
wish you would leave this charming girl with us for
a while. I don't know when I have enjoyed someone's company more.'

Katherine, who had been watching them jeal-
ously for some time, gave a little laugh. 'That
would be quite impossible, dear Earl Harry. Rachel
is my body servant, I would be quite lost without
her.'

'Your servant?' Harry raised his eyebrows. 'I
thought she was your cousin.'

Katherine coloured. 'Well, of course…but she at-
tends to my needs. My hair and clothes…'

'Indeed?' Harry looked down his shapely nose.
'Well, should you be so lacking in maids at Abbey
Hall, I am sure my wife could find you someone
suitable to take with you.'

Katherine flushed even more brilliantly. She was
adept at making the comment designed to reduce
another, but Harry had spent half a century per-

fecting the skill. She turned to Judith and began to speak with her in halting tones.

'You are naughty, Father-in-law,' Judith said later in a reproving undertone.

'I don't like ladies who behave like a Queen without the crown,' Harry said haughtily.

'You don't like her? I thought she was favoured by you and Lady Bess.'

'She was a nice little girl,' Harry said, 'and we were indeed fond of her, but now she has grown to be exactly like her father. You knew him?'

'Ah, yes, Ralph Monterey,' Judith said reminiscently. 'Yes, I knew him when he was affianced to Anne. A very...proud young man, as I recall.'

'Mmm, and he was not kind and nor, I fear, is his daughter. However, I must not criticise her, she is young yet.'

Embarrassed by this exchange, Rachel got up, murmuring that she would replenish the glasses. Judith took her place and slipped her arm through Harry's. 'That is so, of course. I think Hal has taken a great fancy to her. Do you think a match between them would be suitable?'

Harry's eyebrows shot up again. 'Hal? Certainly not! What a terrible idea, Judith. Hal needs an entirely different sort of woman, and Katherine another sort of man. One like young Roxburgh.'

'Piers? But earlier I heard you speaking of Rachel's lack of estate. Piers has even less, you know.'

'Tcha! Why is it women are always reminding one of what one has said earlier?' Harry asked testily. 'It is most annoying… I was not suggesting they wed—Katherine and Piers—merely remarking they would be good for each other.'

Judith laughed. She could remember that when George had announced he wanted to marry her—at that time she had been Hal's nursemaid—Harry had been very opposed and they had argued most bitterly. But how successful the marriage had been! She wondered if Harry ever thought of that these days…

'So,' she said, 'Piers would do for Katherine. Who would be suitable for Hal, then?'

'The Spanish girl,' Harry said firmly.

'Rachel?' Judith said doubtfully. 'I don't think she is Spanish, you know.'

'She has her share of the blood, though. Her grandmother was a delightful mixture of France and Spain. I knew her very well once,' he added.

Now Judith looked surprised. 'Did you? I had no idea.'

'It only came out tonight, and…' Harry chuckled sardonically '…your mother-in-law is fit to be tied to be thus reminded. Her name was Madrilene and she caused me a deal of trouble once.'

Judith squeezed his arm. She smiled mischievously. 'Your wicked youth! Tell me all about it.'

Harry looked into the fire without answering, wondering why faces and situations from the past appeared more real to him these days than what was actually happening now. He passionately loved his wife, he adored his family and was interested in all their works, yet—all this evening a ghost had stalked his imagination. Two ghosts, in fact, for Rachel and Hal could have been himself and Madrilene again.

The way Rachel turned her head, gestured with her pretty hands, was all Madrilene. The way Hal threw back his head to laugh, laid a card on the table with that take-it-or-leave-it air, that could have been himself forty-odd years ago. Strange. Strange and somehow very exciting was the way blood—significant blood—will out. He and Madrilene de Santos had shared that peculiar and exotic mix—his family had been English aristocratic adventurers from Saxon times, hers, in different countries, the same.

In Harry's children the strain had been diluted by Bess's sensible combination of Norman knight and yeoman farmer, except for Hal, who was the wild card in their pack. Harry felt as one does when opening an ancient trunk of clothes, lifting the contents and inhaling scents from the past. He closed his eyes and Bess came swiftly to his side.

'Now, dearest, you are tired. It is time you were abed, and myself also.' She gave him her hand and he rose immediately, slightly confused by the wine and the memories. None of these memories detracted at all from his allegiance to Bess, he thought. That time when Madrilene had been a part of their lives had been merely a reaffirmation of that allegiance. He and Bess went slowly around the hall, bidding all good night. When he bent over

Rachel's hand with the courtesy so much a part of him, she found her eyes filling with tears. As he straightened up, he lifted her chin with one finger and smiled down into her eyes, before taking Bess's hand and moving away.

'What is wrong?' Hal asked, removing her empty glass and substituting it for a full one.

'Why, nothing.' She swallowed. 'Except that he is so very charming, your father.'

'The word he used to describe you,' Hal remarked. 'He has a way with women, my father, even at his advanced age.'

He did not mean the comment to be derogatory in any way, but she took it so. It was not Hal's fault; he was disturbed and unsettled by the atmosphere in Maiden Court tonight; the affinity between Rachel and his father had affected him in a way he could not understand. They were like two fascinating strangers. Rachel, he had conveniently slotted into place as the not-very-interesting appendage to the girl he had fallen in love with yet, tonight, it was Rachel, not Katherine, who had showed to advantage.

Rachel thought, He must reduce it to that! A man and a woman flirting. She kept her eyes on the couple climbing the stairs and did not reply. Much later, the party broke up and, yawning, followed their host and hostess up the same stairs.

Afterwards Rachel came to be glad Harry Latimar had had this last happy evening with so many of his family present and Maiden Court extending the hospitality it was famed for. For, during the balmy early summer's night after a nourishing and sweetening fall of rain, the Earl passed peacefully away in his sleep.

Bess, who still shared a bed with her husband, was awoken by the rain drumming on the roof and turned to him and so heard his last word, spoken without waking. It was, of course, her name. No tears came to her then; she simply took him in her arms and stayed thus until the dawn crept into the room.

Then she rose and knelt by the bed to say the prayers learned in her youth and which were no longer used, but somehow seemed more appropriate in their doleful splendour than those more modern. Her lips moved caressingly over the traditional plea: Go forth, Christian soul, into the light...

At last she stood a moment, looking down on the man who had fulfilled her life for so many years, then bent to kiss the cold lips, but paused no longer, for she had seen his graceful soul leave his body hours since and what was left was no more than a beloved shell to be buried with honour and due respect.

The man she loved had gone away now to a place she could not follow yet, and so she dressed quietly and went slowly down the stairs, pulled open the door of the hall and stood gulping the pure rain-washed air. Hal found her a half-hour later.

'Mother? You are about early.'

She stretched up to kiss him. 'As are you.'

'My room overlooks the stables, as you know. There was some disturbance and I went down to investigate. It was all a commotion about Rachel Monterey's horse—apparently the poor creature had the staggers this morning— Why, what is wrong?' His mother's eyes were fixed on his face, but he could swear she did not see him, or hear any word he spoke. She gave a start and laid a hand on his sleeve.

'Hal…I have sad news for you…your father is dead.' He looked at her, unbelieving for a moment, then something in her face told him this was no aberration on her part. He turned ashen, and she put her arms about him. 'My dear son, it was so peaceful, had we all the choosing we would wish to be so well treated by the good Lord.'

In spite of her comforting arms around him, Hal suffered such a deadly blow he gasped. Struggling for control, he said, 'I will fetch George…or perhaps you have already roused him?'

'No, I have not. It is early yet, and I think I just want you for the moment. My son.' Bess looked up into his haggard face. 'I thought, as I was coming down the stairs, that I would like to walk to the Queen's Rest. Your father and I went there so often when he could no longer ride.'

Hal concentrated all his efforts. Women, he thought, were so brave. Without taking sword in hand and charging into any battle, they had more stomach than any man living. He reached up and took a cloak from those hanging just inside the hall. Placing it carefully around her shoulders, he took her arm and they walked through the rose gardens and up towards the little building.

Rachel saw them go from her bedroom window. She had spent a restless night and was up early, wondering whether to repeat her ride of the previous morning. She was curious as she watched Hal's bright head disappear into the garden and reappear outside the Queen's Rest. She was dressed, so decided she would satisfy her curiosity.

Within view of the Queen's Rest, she paused, pretending to examine one of the flowering rosebushes, decorated with rain drops. Hal was in the doorway, staring out at nothing. Rachel realized she must have taken unconscious note of all his facial expressions because now he wore one unrecognized. It aroused an emotion she could not identify. Letting go of the flower spray, she hastened along the cobbled path.

'Hal? Is anything wrong?' She looked past his broad shoulder to where his mother sat, with the same expression on her smooth face. Rachel touched his arm and he started.

'Rachel…I…we…have sad news this day. My father…is dead.' He looked almost impersonally down into her face.

She paled, then moved past him into the little house and said falteringly to Bess, 'My lady, please accept my most sincere condolences for your great loss.'

Bess looked up blankly. 'I'm sorry, lady, did you speak?'

Rachel looked helplessly at Hal, who said nothing. Alarmed, Rachel took his arm.

'Hal! Speak to me!' At the urgency in her voice he took hold.

'Yes, Rachel?'

She breathed a sigh of relief. 'Do the rest of your family know yet? Your brother, his children?'

'No...only we three know as yet.'

'Then I think you should take your mother into the manor and advise them. Then—' here inspiration came to her '—you must ride out to tell those on the Maiden Court estate. They should be told, you know, he was greatly loved. You owe it to them...and to him.'

Hal braced himself. 'You are right. I will take Mother to the house, then ride out. Please, if you will, ask for my horse to be saddled, and your own. You will accompany me.' Without awaiting her reply, Hal turned into the little house, gently took his mother's arm and steered her carefully down the path.

Rachel and Hal said nothing to each other as they rode their horses out towards the first village. When the village was in sight, Hal drew rein and both horses slowed.

'Was it bad?' Rachel enquired. 'With your family?'

'Oh, no.' Hal half smiled. 'My family are staunch in the face of adversity. In fact, are famous for it.'

'I meant—was it bad for you?' Rachel asked. Hal turned his reins in his bare hands; he had come from the house bareheaded and without suitable protection in the way of gloves. He glanced sideways at his companion, also shabbily clad, but not for want of care. Rachel simply did not have the necessary clothing. She gave him a shamefaced look in return, then said, 'I am sorry, of course I may not trespass on your family's privacy.'

Hal said slowly, 'Since you ask, I will tell you what happened. My brother George took the news with both dignity and self-control. He laid a hand on my shoulder and said, "Gently now, Hal, remember what Father always declared about dying."'

'And what was that?'

'He… Father always said when one of his dear friends was gone, "Remember, my boy, a death is no more than a star falling from the skies. There are many more such stars and babies are born each minute and the flowers will still bloom in the spring."' Hal smiled. 'That was his philosophy, I think.'

'I am sure of it,' Rachel said gravely. 'For, when I ventured to tell of his death in your yard, one of your boys—Wat, I think he is called—said, "Thankee for telling me, ma'am, now I must feed the pigs." What he meant was the same, and that was—life goes on.'

Hal stared at her. 'You will forgive me if I don't find comfort in that sentiment at this moment,' he said stiffly. He prepared to ride on. Rachel sighed. She had said the wrong thing as usual, but what could one say? There were no words of comfort for the newly bereaved. Perhaps he would find solace in comforting others. She urged her own mount on.

Hal followed, resentful eyes on her straight back. Primrose had been deemed unfit to be taken out and Rachel was on Belle, and he had to admit they made a beautiful pair. He thought, This girl has lost all her near family. Her mother and father before she could know them, her grandmother just before leaving for a strange country. Who had comforted her? And, curiously, her funny little anecdote about Wat had diverted his mind—mainly because it so aptly fitted Harry Latimar's attitude to life: Deal with the immediate first, then take time to think about the rest. Even pigs needed attention when the world was falling apart, and—perhaps—there lay the ability of the human race to carry on in the face of overwhelming misery.

If Hal, and Rachel, had thought they would be carrying fresh news to the estate that morning, they had underestimated the power of the country grapevine. Carters had been about since dawnlight, milkmaids, too, and most of the surrounding countryside knew that their liege lord was dead. Harry had been a popular figure, his youngest son was regarded as a chip off the old block and everyone was glad to receive him on this sad day. It was a difficult, emotional enterprise, but Hal showed himself equal to it.

Some of the older tenants remembered the Earl in his wild youth; they equated it with theirs, half-forgotten now, but not entirely. With them Hal assumed a jocular, sometimes half-bawdy tone, recalling tales he had heard in his childhood. Others, younger, remembered only the responsible practical man Latimar had become—this man had dandled their children from his knees, danced at harvest horkeys, always been there with a sympathetic ear to the trials of country living. Both had been parts of the whole, Rachel guessed, the complete package was embodied in his younger son: Hal Latimar was a mixture of sophisticated courtier and child of the English soil.

It was late afternoon when they turned their horses for Maiden Court. On arrival Hal lifted Rachel down and turned both animals over to the stable boy. They entered the manor and went straight to their respective rooms. Hal found peace there and sank on to his bed to sleep. Rachel found Katherine, pettish from imagined neglect.

'Really, Rachel! I would have thought that today of all days you could have been on hand to assist me. I have been pushed and pulled around by servants since dawn!' In fact, Katherine had been wakened in the late morning by a tearful maid, sobbing with her news, but ready to do her duty with hot water and hair dressing, and assistance into 'my lady's chosen gown'.

'I will be happy to help you now, Katherine,' Rachel murmured.

'I am happy to hear it! Firstly, I understand the funeral is to be in three days' time. To allow for Madam's daughter and her family to attend from their home in the North, and other exalted persons to make ready. Secondly, there will be time for my new white silk gown to be hung in the air and pressed. Of course, I had planned to take it to court for some more joyous occasion, but must employ it into another service now. Still,' she said complacently, 'a number of very important people will see me in it...' Katherine sat with a sigh before her glass. All day she had been listening with her sharp ears to the conversation around her. The Queen was to be informed of the Earl's death, along with other luminaries of the court. Messengers had been dispatched to all parts of England to similarly spread the news. There had even been talk of advising nobles across the seas.

Rachel, on her knees before the brass-bound trunk containing her cousin's clothes, gave her own sigh as she took out the white silk dress and stood up with the gleaming folds over her arm. She wondered if Katherine Monterey had any human feelings at all: the Earl had been a part of her life since she was a baby. Surely she should feel something! 'And I think the pearls would look well with the gown.' Katherine was pursuing her own selfish thoughts. 'Take them from my box so they might take the air a little—they can be dull if deprived of light.'

Rachel laid the gown over a chair and found the jewellery box. She extracted the pearls and, running the translucent spheres through her fingers, had a pang of regret. She, too, had had just as finely matched a string once. Her grandmother had presented them to her on her twelfth birthday, saying only a woman with truly perfect skin should wear them. They had been sold, along with her other jewels, to finance her trip to England.

Mid-morning three days later Rachel reviewed her own meagre wardrobe for suitable mourning wear and eventually put on a dress she actively disliked. It was a dull colour between plum and purple, another cast-off worn once by Katherine for a masque two years ago at Abbey Hall, and discarded. And no wonder, Rachel thought, surveying her reflection, for it had been unflattering even for her cousin's dazzling fairness. On her it was a positive insult! She told herself she wore it as a mark of respect, and that was all that mattered, but it was hard just the same to appear in a colour which turned her skin ashen and made her hair the colour of one of Wat's prized Clydesdale mare's hooves. Rachel wandered disconsolately down the stairs to the hall. It was empty.

The table was laid as usual for the midday meal. Along its polished length were baskets of fresh bread and jugs of spring water, and ale and wine. From the parlour at the end of the hall Rachel could hear the murmur of voices—in there was the family discussing their loss. No place for her there. As usual, the feeling of belonging nowhere swept over her and she took a chair by the open door, folded her hands on her lap and closed her eyes.

She must have sat there for some time, for the sunlight which first illuminated the floor at her feet gradually crept up her dull skirts and on to her white hands. She started and opened her eyes as a tall man ducked his head to enter. She rose and dropped her respectful curtsey.

'I am Jack Hamilton, lady,' he introduced himself. This, then, was Hal's brother-in-law; Rachel had heard the arrival earlier.

'Rachel Monterey,' she returned. 'Is anything wrong, my lord? I mean...more wrong?' Jack removed his cap and turned it in his hands.

'My horse—Valiant. He is very old and the journey here too much for him. I need a hot mash for him, and also some physic, but am at a loss. Lady Bess has naturally decreed no work here for to-day—' Rachel straightened her shoulders. Here was something she could do. She had been treating her mount, Primrose, for four days now.

'I will make the mash, my lord Earl. Physic for the horses is kept in a white-painted cupboard as you enter the stable. I will join you there.' She gave him her hesitant smile before hurrying towards the kitchens. Jack paused in the doorway a moment looking after her. He had no idea who she could be. The name Monterey rang a bell with him, but he could not make the connection, he could only think to himself that in their short exchange the girl had inspired a confidence he rarely granted.

There were five women seated around the scrubbed kitchen table when Rachel entered. They had all been weeping and raised tearstained faces to the intruder. Rachel smoothed her skirts nervously. 'Please forgive my intrusion.' She addressed the cook, Margery. 'If I may take charge of one of your pans, mistress, a little oatmeal and various other things, I will be gone in a moment.' Margery raised a plump hand.

'Becky, get the lady what she needs.' Rachel, conscious of the staring eyes, did what was necessary, laid a clean cloth over the resultant mixture in the bowl and, carrying it carefully, left with all speed. The five other women settled in their chairs again. Margery sipped her ale thoughtfully.

'I like that lady,' she said at length. The other women nodded. Sweet and kind, they agreed. Gentle, one said, but with dignity.

Wat, the only male present, said from his place at the hearth, 'And a rare one with the horses. That was a mash for that old devil the family from the North brought wi' them, or I miss my guess.' Valiant, Jack Hamilton's destrier—warhorse—who had for years borne his soldier master into many a battle, was old now and bad-tempered. Jack tolerated his foibles because of their history together.

# Chapter Six

Rachel found Jack in Valiant's stall. She held the bowl of mash firmly while he dug in with both hands and offered it to the great grey horse. At first it seemed Valiant would eat with a good will, but soon he shook his massive head and retreated shivering to the back of the stall.

Rachel cast a compassionate glance at both horse and owner. 'It is,' she said gently, 'something I have seen many times before. The only answer is the humane *coup de grâce* from a loving comrade.' Jack gave her a stormy look. He had lost one irreplaceable friend recently, must he lose another?

'It is too soon to speak of that.' Hal had entered the stall unnoticed by the other two. In his hand he held a bottle of liniment, his father's sovereign remedy for any equine problem. Removing his doublet, he rolled up his linen shirt sleeves and, tipping some of the brown liquid in his palms, advanced on Valiant and began to rub the trembling legs. Jack joined him. Rachel put down the bowl and did the same.

After a half-hour Hal straightened up. 'That is enough for the present. We will leave all now in the hands of God. We are wanted in the house, I think, Jack.'

Jack nodded and threw a blanket over his destrier. 'Yes, indeed, I am derelict in my duty today.'

'No such thing. We all must grieve in our own way,' Hal replied, smiling. 'And my father would be the first to agree that.' Without speaking, the three walked towards the manor.

Harry Latimar, an Earl of England, a friend all his long life to its ruling family, but—in his heart— only squire of a minor estate in Kew, and beloved husband of that estate's beloved mistress, was laid to rest that afternoon. The grand and the great of the land attended. Elizabeth Tudor, her ambitious and embittered paramour, Robert Dudley, Earl of Leicester, and others from the English court came to pay tribute. The aforementioned sat in the little chapel, awaiting the funeral cortège which wound its slow and respectful way along the country lanes from Maiden Court.

The coffin was borne by his two sons, George and Hal, and Jack Hamilton and his son, Dudley. Following behind walked a very motley crew: Bess and her daughter, Anne Hamilton, local gentry, estate farmers and villagers, household servants and at the back little Wat, shoulder to shoulder with

Rachel Monterey who had insisted on so doing. Katherine Monterey, taking her seat behind the Queen and spreading her white silk dress, had been extremely aggravated not to be able to order her maidservant to the contrary.

'I will do it,' Rachel had said stubbornly, 'and if you don't like it, you must put up with it.' She tramped the dusty mile and a half, shook her skirts and entered the chapel. Inside the old building was packed to its oak rafters. In the privileged front pews sat the Queen and her intimate friends. Behind the Latimar family was George's wife Judith and their two redheaded daughters with their children, Katherine Monterey and Anne Hamilton. In the main body of the congregation the mourners sat on a first-come, first-served basis. An odd arrangement, some might think, but very much in keeping with Harry Latimar's curious attitude to such matters.

Outside among the broken tombstones of the graveyard and beyond for a clear hundred yards around stood many others who had come to show their respect. Farmers who had left their fertile acres for a snatched hour, farmwives who had abandoned their kitchens and dairies—everyone, anyone whose lives had been touched and enriched by the man they came to honour. The radiant sky darkened as they stood there and a light rain began to fall.

Rachel, on entering the chapel, stood uncertainly at the back until Anne, glancing over her shoulder, gestured for her to come forward, making space on the hard pew between herself and Katherine. Rachel hastened up the narrow aisle; Katherine gave her a scornful look as she sat breathlessly down. The pastor, slightly intimidated by the company today, cleared his throat, fixed his eyes on the coffin laid gently before him by its grave bearers and delivered the few words allowed by his religion. Rachel acknowledged them with bent head and clasped hands, but in her heart spoke the old, grand words of the old order. Then the coffin was raised once more and carried out to its final resting place.

Katherine was to the forefront of the final ceremony, with demure eyes and suitably modest demeanour, but her sharp blue eyes noticed all. Why—there was great Elizabeth Tudor actually weeping! At one point she even swayed and was supported by Robert Dudley's glittering tissue-clad arm! And Jack Hamilton, veteran of a thousand fierce encounters with England's enemies, so laid aside his dignity to allow the painful tears of maturity to course down his cheeks!

All around her was, in the Lady Katherine's opinion, a quite disgraceful display of emotion. And the place of interment did not please her either. With her own eyes she had seen the magnificent marble tomb erected on Latimar land, but the man who had commissioned and watched its building, had ordered that he would not be laid therein. That was for future Latimar generations—the English earth was good enough for him. No, nothing was in order today, Katherine thought.

At the moment when the family came forward with flowers to fling down into the yawning grave, Hal had faltered, the rosebud clenched in his fingers. A sigh had risen from the watching crowd as he appeared unable to pay this last tribute, then Rachel Monterey had stepped out from the throng and taken the bloom from him and let it drift down from her own white hand. She had then taken Hal's arm and guided him back to his brother. Such needless drama offended Katherine and her face was haughty as she made her way back to the manor.

All had been invited to Maiden Court to sup after the funeral, but only those with the leisure to do so came. Those who could not approached Lady Bess and received her sweet smile and thanks for attending thus far. She knew her estate, she knew country folk for she had sprung from them and knew the personal effort all these men and women had made to come this day. She appreciated it and knew how much her husband would have.

Despite diminished numbers, Maiden Court was still filled to capacity for the feast to crown Harry Latimar's funeral. The servants scurried here and there, trying to satisfy the flow of guests. The food and the wine were more than adequate, the house was as efficient in tragedy as it had been in joy. Rachel, looking around the crowded hall at the assembly, thought a chance traveller knocking on the door and expecting hospitality would have been forgiven for thinking he had chanced upon some kind of celebration. For there was so much laughter here, and merriment of the kind which had existed in the old King's reign. They would have liked this, Rachel thought, Harry and Old King Hal. She knew their history together—

Katherine was at her elbow, frowning. 'Do you think you could help a little, Rachel? Lady Bess really has too much to do this day.' Bess had been hurrying about since returning to the house.

'It is her way of getting through her grief,' Rachel replied without thinking.

Katherine said sharply, 'It is not your place to decide your betters' feelings!'

Rachel turned away.

'Harsh words,' Piers Roxburgh murmured, offering Katherine wine. 'And no one born with that look in their eyes should be reminded of their place.'

'Whatever do you mean?'

'You have obviously never been in Spain and had words with a Spanish grandee.' He laughed.

'Are you trying to annoy me?' Katherine enquired icily.

Hal caught Rachel's arm as she prepared to lift some empty dishes from the table. 'What are you doing?' he demanded. He had little memory of the recent ceremony, except for standing at the graveside, suddenly unable to remember where he was or what he was supposed to be doing. Unaccountably, Rachel had come to help him.

'I have been reminded that I must earn my keep,' she answered crossly.

'Put down the crocks. We have guests and, as a friend of the family, you are not required to do the servants' work.' She looked at him, the warm colour coming and going in her pale face. A friend of the family?

'Hal.' George joined them with Robert Dudley. 'The Queen has expressed a wish to walk down to the Queen's Rest. Robert and I will accompany her.' Robert was looking Rachel over with interest obviously awaiting an introduction.

Hal smoothly supplied it. 'My lord Earl, may I present the Lady Rachel Monterey? She is a distant cousin of your old friend Ralph, and a friend to the Latimar family.'

Dudley bent over Rachel's hand. 'A great pleasure, demoiselle. Shall we, George…?' The two men moved away and she gave him another look.

'What?' Hal murmured. 'You are both those things, although…' a smile tugged at his mouth '…I stretched a point declaring Ralph Monterey a friend of the great Earl's. Both favourites of the Queen and vying for position, I believe they cordially hated each other.'

She had hardly noticed the first part of his introduction, but the last— A friend to the Latimars! To her it sounded like the grandest title in the world. 'Thank you,' she said quietly.

'Don't thank me,' he said brusquely. 'Just stop juggling with the dirty pots.'

Later that day Katherine finally achieved her ambition and managed to be close enough to Elizabeth to be introduced to her. The Queen had decided to stay the night and had dismissed all but one lady-in-waiting and two gentlemen who would be accommodated with Leicester at the lodge. As darkness fell Bess ordered the fire lit in the parlour and saw her royal mistress comfortably seated beside it while she bade farewell to those of the rest of the company who had lingered at Maiden Court. George had taken his family home and the Hamiltons had retired. Katherine hovered in the hall, waiting for Hal to appear to take her into the parlour.

Dudley rose as they entered, Elizabeth looked inquisitively at the fair young woman before her. This was Ralph Monterey's girl, she thought. Ah, Ralph, she mused sentimentally, dead in his brilliant youth...how handsome and amusing he had been. Months since Ralph's father had written asking her to consider taking his granddaughter into her service, Harry Latimar had also requested she do so. Two such loyal gentlemen—now both dead—must be accommodated. Elizabeth considered Katherine as Hal led her forward for her deep curtsy. Mmm, quite beautiful, she observed. She made one of her lovely eloquent gestures to indicate Katherine might seat herself. Hal stood behind the upright chair, laying his hands on its back in a proprietory manner. Dudley resumed his seat, saying, 'I had the pleasure of meeting your charming cousin earlier, my lady.'

Not a propitious start, Hal thought, seeing Katherine stiffen.

'A very distant cousin,' Katherine said dismissively. 'A connection from Spain, in fact.'

Elizabeth stiffened in her turn. Spain? Not a heritage any decent Englishman, or woman, would want to claim these days.

Rachel, entering with refreshments at that moment, received the battery of her hostile eyes. She paused and Hal came and took the wine jug from her nervous fingers and set it on a table.

'My Lady Rachel Monterey, Your Majesty,' he said formally.

'Of Spanish descent, I believe,' Elizabeth said, noticing that Rachel's curtsy was more graceful, and her manner more regal, than that of her cousin. 'Who were your parents?'

Rachel blushed her cursed fiery colour and gave their names in a muted whisper. Nothing Spanish there, Elizabeth thought. 'And my grandmother was the Lady Madrilene de Santos,' Rachel continued, lifting her square chin, 'and her father Don Santino de Santos, whose fourth cousin was Catherine of Aragon, once Queen of England.'

Silence fell in the pleasant room, the fire crackled orange and red and Hal lifted his eyes to Bess's well-plastered ceiling. What in Heaven's name induced her to bring that into it? he questioned silently. Yet a part of him applauded Rachel's refusal to deny family.

Elizabeth looked thoughtfully into the fire. Madrilene de Santos. A name from the past, but familiar. Yes—an image rose before her of a black-haired, vital lady she had met on the few occasions her father, Henry, had remembered his obligation and invited his younger daughter to court. Horses…Elizabeth fumbled in her memory…and something else. Oh, yes, some scandal connected with the Spanish girl and Harry Latimar.

Robert Dudley, also looking into the flames, chuckled to himself. He knew the whole story, and very amusing it was. Robert liked to think of Latimar, so much a friend of the old Tudor King, so beloved by his children, Edward, Mary and Elizabeth, as being very human. And human he had been during his episode with Madrilene de Santos! He slanted a mischievous look at Hal. Hal acknowledged it with the straight, blue Latimar look.

He did not care for the way this evening was progressing. He was prepared to support Katherine because he loved her. He was also more than prepared to support Rachel because she was now his friend. But how very uncomfortable all this was! He was relieved when his brother, George, entered the room. George had ridden back to the lodge, but remembered suddenly that he must assume a responsibility upon his father's death. That of Katherine Monterey. He bowed before Elizabeth, who invited him to sit down with them.

Dudley said, 'A sad day, George, but not melancholy.'

'Indeed.' George turned to Elizabeth. 'Madam,

this might not be the time, but I was privy to my father's concerns before his death and one of them was to ensure that his friend's daughter's future was settled. I speak of Katherine Monterey.'

From anyone else such direct speech would have annoyed the Queen very much, but she was used to George's bluntness. And such candour deserved a similar response. She said, 'I have not given the matter my full attention as yet, but think I can ask the Lady Katherine to join my court for Yuletide.'

Rachel, looking at Katherine, thought, Well, that has pleased her. A definite time, not merely the promise of consideration in the future which Bess had warned her might be the case.

Hal thought, She will be there with me for all the magic of the Christmas season.

Katherine offered her thanks with a becoming blush and much fluttering of her white hands and Elizabeth rose to say goodnight. Bess met her in the hall and accompanied her to her room. The five left in the parlour looked at each other.

'How wonderful!' Katherine said, turning her flower-like face up to Hal. 'You must tell me all about Greenwich. It will be Greenwich, will it not?'

'At first, then Hampton. Her Majesty likes to keep Christmas at Hampton if possible.'

'How excited I am!' Katherine sent Robert Dudley a coquettish glance. 'To be at court with all those glamorous and important people.' He responded with his own charming smile and, looking up, met Hal's stare. He returned his eyes to the fire, thinking how pleasant it must be to have the feeling Hal obviously had now. But I am no rival for you, my boy, he assured Hal silently. I am long past that.

For so many years Leicester had loved and danced attendance on Elizabeth Tudor in the hope that she would one day grant him the supreme honour of becoming her consort. Throughout the long years of being pushed aside, made little of by her noble friends, being positively reviled and persecuted by her chief advisor, Lord Cecil, that hope had died a bitter death. Several years ago Robert had decided he could no longer wait for the ultimate prize—or a legitimate heir. His was a proud name—his father and one of his brothers had been executed by Mary Tudor in the wake of their attempt to put Lady Jane Grey upon the English throne.

Robert was now the last of his line and wanted what was every man's right: the perpetuation of his blood. He had married a lady of the court and Elizabeth had thrown him into the Tower as a result. He had been eventually released, and he had his beautiful son... That was enough, Robert considered, for any man approaching his half-century. He recalled now that all three Latimar males had spoken eloquently for that release.

Katherine was saying, 'We have much to do before I leave, Rachel. I must have new gowns, and my furs and jewellery will need attention. I suppose you, too, must examine your own wardrobe.'

'I am to go with you?' Rachel asked in consternation. 'But surely not.'

'Of course you will go,' Katherine said impatiently. 'I am sure all the worthy ladies in Her Majesty's court have a suitable...relative to care for
them.'

Rachel could have cried, and would have done if
she had been that sort of woman. Earlier she had
been taken to the heights to know that Hal considered her to be a friend of his family. Now she was
cast down once more to know that she was after all
just a glorified servant of that family. She would
have dearly loved to go to the royal court, to see
what happened there, to be amongst the people she
had heard so much of from her grandmother, Madrilene. But not as a servant! Everything that was
proud in her nature cried out in protest.

Robert Dudley rose. 'I see the remainder of the
evening is to be spent in the age-old discussion of
ladies' fashion. I will take my leave now for the
lodge.'

Hal followed him out to the stables to make sure
he was safely mounted—he had noted that Leicester
had taken a great deal of wine that day. He then
turned back into the manor. Katherine was at the
foot of the stairs in the hall. She smiled and held
out her hand.

'What a day, Hal! How delightful this sad occasion has turned out for me.' He took her hand
and raised it to his lips. Her words jarred slightly

on the sensitive part of him, but the intoxication of the touch of her hand and her smile obscured this.

'Katherine…as you say, this is a sad day for all of us, but I feel I cannot let this moment pass without saying something to you.'

'Yes?' she murmured. What was coming now to add to the other extraordinary events of the day?

'I love you, Katherine,' he said gravely, abruptly discarding his polished guise of courtier. 'And would ask your leave to apply to your grandfather for your hand.'

Katherine considered. She had seen today how favoured was this young man's family, how well regarded by the First Lady of England. Of course, he was a second son and might never be particularly well-to-do, but she could do worse… In any event, she could always change her mind, could she not? It took only a few seconds to assimilate these thoughts, then she smiled again.

'Dear Hal, I hardly know what to say. You scarcely know me…' She lowered her eyes modestly.

'It was love at first sight, sweetheart,' Hal declared.

Love at first sight? Katherine thought. How romantic! And a fitting tribute to her… She allowed him to take her hand again. 'Even so,' she said carefully, 'I am anxious not to tie you to any promise you might be making because you are rather upset at this time.'

It was a shrewd remark, for Hal would admit to

himself he barely knew what he was doing or saying since his father's death. More evidence, he reasoned, that his beloved was sensitive and caring.

'I love you for saying that, darling,' he acknowledged, 'but would repeat—I fell in love in the first moment of meeting you.'

Rachel, coming out of the parlour at that moment, saw them by the stairs and immediately put the correct interpretation on the scene. It had been an emotional day for her, now she could have shouted aloud: Oh, it was all wrong! Katherine was all wrong for Hal. She stood transfixed in the doorway for a moment, knowing she could not change anything that was happening, then turned back into the parlour.

George Latimar was almost asleep beside the fire. His face, guarded when fully awake, was vulnerable at this moment. All his conscious life he had been aware of others' private feelings, and consequently suffered for it. Now he was acutely aware of the distress Rachel was experiencing. He said, 'I am getting old, Rachel. A full day exhausts me in these times.' She laid another log on the fire without speaking. 'Do you want to go to Greenwich with Katherine?' he asked casually.

She shrugged. 'Does it matter if I want to go or not? Katherine will have her way whatever I say. And does it matter what I want anyway?'

'Oh, my dear girl, one does not get what one wants in this life with that defeatist attitude.'

Rachel moved away from the fire and sat on one

of the hard wooden arms of his chair. 'There speaks one of the favoured species: a Latimar, whose lightest word is of account in this land.'

George thought about it, then agreed. 'Yes, we are indeed well regarded, but consider this: a Spanish friend oft used to quote an old proverb from his homeland. Roughly translated, it went, Beware when you are getting all you want for corn-fed cows are not in luck just before the Yuletide season.'

Rachel smiled ruefully. 'I know the saying well—but then the Spanish have a saying for every eventuality.'

'Also,' George continued, 'money, position, a secure place in the world do not measure a man's worth. Or so I think.'

'All three,' she declared, 'are useful commodities. I have neither one, so I should know. Especially money. Had I a degree of that, I would now be sitting in a Spanish castillo considering my marriage options. Instead I am forced to play nurse- and chambermaid to my lady Katherine. And if you are now thinking I can refuse to go to Greenwich to attend her, I can assure you that, were I to do so, I would be dismissed forthwith.'

George said quietly, 'I am sorry.'

'George—may I have a word with you?' Hal was in the parlour now. The two at the fire started. Rachel rose and made for the door. As she came to Hal she looked up into his face. What she read there was just what she expected—he now wished to dis-

cuss the matter with his brother. He bowed and
stood aside to allow her to pass. When she did not
move he looked at her enquiringly.

'I wish to speak to my brother in private,' he said
at length. What was the matter with the girl? She
looked quite distressed. For the first time he noticed
that around the brown of her pupils was drawn a
fine, darker line; it was strange and beautiful. 'Rachel?' At last she moved and he closed the door
behind her and advanced to the fire. 'May I get you
a glass of wine, George?'

'Thank you, no. But you have one, of course.
What can I do for you, Hal?'

Hal found a glass and filled it. He dropped into
the chair opposite—his father's chair. He gained
comfort and confidence from touching the wooden
arms, made smooth from much handling. He hesitated, then said, 'It may not seem quite the time to
speak of this, but I have to leave Maiden Court
soon.'

'You need advice?'

'Indeed. On my own personal business. It is this
way: Katherine Monterey and I find we...love each
other. I intend approaching her grandfather at Abbey Hall on my way to court, and wondered what
you might think to this. You know me, you know
her. So, what do you think?'

George reflected. He did indeed know his little
brother, born when he was a grown man. He had
watched young Hal grow up—a very likely boy,
strong and intelligent, sensitive and with all the best

virtues of the Latimars. The most, in fact, like the man who was just now assigned to his grave. Yes, Hal had all the attributes of the family, but also the weaknesses.

At Petrie Castle, where he had served his page-ship and later at Ravensglass, where he had gained his silver spurs, the report had been the same: young Latimar has everything required for a great soldier, or a clever and wily politician. He is charming and intelligent and has every necessary social grace. But he is too soft! He is forever putting himself in the shoes of the opposition, be they on the battlefield, or in the clouded and dirty council chamber of politics. George thought of this now.

He said: 'It is a tradition in our family to choose our own mates. My grandfather did so—choosing a Devon farmgirl; our mother did the same, choosing a star of the Tudor court. I followed that example with Judith—your nursemaid, if you will remember—and Anne, our sister, chose Jack Hamilton, a most unlikely candidate for her very desirable hand.'

Hal knew what his brother was saying. They—the Latimars—were an unconventional breed. 'All those marriages,' he said, 'were supremely happy. I have now made my choice. Please encourage me, George.'

George sighed. 'Father did not...like her,' he said quietly. 'And I know of no man whose opinion I value more.'

'I wanted you to approve,' Hal said. 'Both of

you, of course, but...Father had special criteria...
Mother... But you and I are men of the world. Can
you not give me your blessing at least?'

George sighed again. 'I will, in part,' he said
carefully, 'but would also say this: Look around
you, Hal. At those around you. It could be your
destiny lies with someone you have not considered
yet.' He dared not say more; Hal had always had a
peculiar dislike of George's gift of the 'sight', inherited from his mother who had received it from
her paternal grandmother. On the rare occasions
they had discussed it, he had dismissed it as 'somehow Calvanistic—that joyless creed!' The Calvanist
sect believed they were judged at birth, and nothing
they did in their lives changed that judgement.
George suspected Hal drew a comparison with his
own privileged birth.

Hal tossed off his wine. 'Then I must be content
with that, I suppose.'

'Have you mentioned it to Mother?'

'No, I would not intrude on her thoughts today,
but I am sure she will approve. She and Father have
been friends to Katherine's family for years—you,
in fact, were one of her uncle Tom's best friends,
and knew her father, too. What was he like?'

'Ralph?' George looked thoughtfully into the fire
for a few moments, then said, 'He was very like
Katherine—especially in looks. Very handsome,
very fair, and very self-assured.'

Hal refilled his glass. 'That tells me little of his
character.'

'Ah, his character…well, I would say that was also like his daughter: very articulate and amusing in company, very skilled in courtiership—Elizabeth loved him greatly, I believe.'

'Hmm.' Hal was pleased with the description. 'And he died in a duel of honour, I have heard. I must have been a child then, but you will remember it?'

'I do indeed,' George agreed. 'It was, you could say, a classic case of the old adage—if you live by the sword, you die by it. Or, in this instance, the duelling pistol. It is said that Ralph Monterey fought fifty times before he met a man who was not so easily persuaded to give up this tiresome life.'

Hal frowned. 'Well, from your tone I gather you felt as Father felt about Katherine. So there is no more to be said between us. But as you know, George…' he paced about the room '…life at the court is different from here in rural Kew. Tempers run high, there is always someone trying to cut you down… I imagine if the Queen loved Ralph Monterey greatly he must have had an uneasy time of it.'

'As you do,' George suggested.

'No, no,' Hal said, 'for I am not one of those who seek her patronage in that way—'

'Long may that be true,' George remarked.

Hal gave his brother a black look. 'That is not to say,' he continued repressively, 'that those gentlemen who do are less in my eyes. Your best friend, Leicester, is among them, after all…'

George acknowledged the thrust, but qualified it. 'I know that, none better…but I also know that he loves her and has done for most of her life. That, I think, cancels out any charge you might make.'

There was a silence in the parlour now. George broke it. 'We must get to our beds now. It has been a long and distressing day.' He rose with all the grace characteristic of his family and put a hand on his brother's shoulder. Both tall men, they looked into each other's eyes.

'Say you wish me well over my affair with Katherine,' Hal said after a moment.

'Of course I wish you well in all you do,' George said.

Left alone in the room flickering with firelight, Hal was disappointed. He would have liked it settled there and then. He would have liked George—head of the family now—to say, Let us send for the Maiden Court pastor and have him witness an official betrothal betwixt you and Katherine. I will, myself, approach John Monterey and all will go ahead! Then perhaps she would have no reservations. However, the two would shortly be at Greenwich together and, without conceit, Hal knew this was his world and he showed to advantage in it. He banked the fire, pinched out the candles and made his own way to bed.

# Chapter Seven

The following morning Robert Irwin, the Latimar lawyer, attended upon the family at Maiden Court to read Harry Latimar's Will. The bequests were numerous in this document, but only the immediate family were present in the parlour. The Hamiltons, Jack and Anne and Dudley, were dressed for riding and would leave after the midday meal. Bess, of course, and George and Judith, and Hal. Hal had asked Katherine to join them, feeling she would so soon be a member of the family and she sat with Dudley and George's children. Bess was in her late husband's chair by the hearth.

It was a very intimate family group, Robert thought, clearing his throat in his chair by the window. He unrolled the stiff parchment he held and began to speak.

Hal, his eyes on Katherine's lovely profile, hardly heard the words spoken. Yes, yes, everyone at Maiden Court and in the outlying estate who had

touched his father's life had been remembered. He
scarcely took in what was being said.

'And now,' Robert Irwin intoned gravely, 'as to
my personal effects: I bequeath, with great love and
affection, my deck of playing cards, and my diamond ring, to my younger son, Hal.' An affectionate ripple ran around the room. All those present
knew the cards referred to, and the ring. The cards
had once belonged to Harry's greatest friend,
George Boleyn, the Lord Rochford and brother to
Anne Boleyn. The ring—a great table diamond
etched with the royal arms—had been presented to
its owner by Henry Tudor.

Katherine had sat through the earlier reading in
disbelief. True, Hal was mentioned to receive the
revenue from various profitable sources, and naturally it was the older son's right to inherit the Latimar manor and the estate. But, it was well known
that Harry Latimar had been possessed of a vast
personal fortune when he died. Careful manage-
ment and fortunate investment over the last two decades—with practical Bess's encouragement—had
turned the acorn of profit from the estate into a great
oak of money. Surely, Katherine reasoned, some of
it should have come to Hal? But he was actually
smiling: they all were, as if the document just read
was a pleasant entertainment. And the Earl's jewellery! That alone must represent a king's ransom,
for Latimar had always been a dandy. But all those
marvellous jewels, with the exception of the diamond, had been left divided equally between his

heir and his daughter, to keep, to wear, to dispose of as they wished. Ever since she was a child and Harry a frequent visitor at Abbey Hall, Katherine had admired his glittering gems and, latterly, had hoped some might come her way...

Robert Irwin refolded his parchment, tucked it into his belt and rose, bowing. He refused an invitation to stay for the meal and took his leave. Jack Hamilton got up, murmuring he would go out to the stables for a moment. At the door he beckoned to Rachel and she followed him out. The others poured more wine and George opened the window to let out some of the heat of the fire. It was a radiant day, with all summer's glory in it, the sky a crystal dome in which a round butter-coloured sun was suspended. The open window let in the scents of the season, rich earth, the fragrant smell of flowers and newly scythed grass.

Judith said, 'What a happy will!'

Happy indeed, thought Katherine sourly, when one's husband inherited an Earldom, a thousand acres of land and many sacks of gold at the sweep of a pen.

'You don't mind, Mother, George and me getting all the jewellery?' Anne asked.

'Of course not. I have the only things that mean anything to me,' Bess replied, touching the ruby heart on her breast and turning her left hand to look tenderly at the betrothal ring on her finger. 'I am well content with everything Harry did.'

'But surely—!' They all turned to look at Katherine, who had spoken quite loudly. 'I mean—I am a little concerned for you, dear Lady Bess, for there was no proviso in the will for you to continue making your home at Maiden Court.' Anne and Judith looked shocked, and Bess hid a smile. This lovely Monterey girl had a lot to learn about the Latimar family...

George said gently, 'There was no need for there to be, my dear. My father knew that.'

'But what when you are gone? I mean...your heir might feel differently, or his wife might, and Lady Bess...women are more long-lived than men.'

'My heir will be my brother, Hal,' George returned equably, 'and after him the next male in the clan—my grandson, little Robert.'

'Katherine,' Hal said uneasily, 'perhaps now is not the moment to discuss this.'

Walter appeared in the doorway to summon them to lunch. When Hal and Katherine were alone, she tossed her hair and said defiantly, 'Well, dearest, such matters must be considered, you know.'

Hal looked at her doubtfully. 'But perhaps not today. Come and eat now.'

She said angrily, 'You don't seem to mind getting absolutely nothing! Fobbed off with a little gold, a ring and an old deck of cards. And I know Maiden Court is not entailed—George has a fine house of his own, he does not need it. It could have been yours.'

'But George loves Maiden Court,' Hal said patiently, 'and I don't want it—at least not until it is

my turn. He has already asked me to stay and keep
it in trust for him. And I have plenty for you and I
to be very comfortable on. As I will explain to your
grandfather in due course.'

'But it is scarcely riches, is it?' she said pee-
vishly.

'No, not riches,' he agreed. He disliked this conversation intensely. He knew women must be practical—all his life he had been conscious of his
mother being so in her marriage. But Katherine's
strident tone earlier, her expression of discontent
now, grated on him. She even looked different, her
golden softness hardened.

'Anyway, I suppose we must eat…' Katherine
said. 'Where has Rachel run off to? My hair—' He
took her arm none-too-gently to escort her to the
hall.

'Ah, Hal and Katherine,' Bess said as they came
to the table. 'Now we are only missing Jack and
Rachel.'

'They are in the stables, my lady,' offered Walter.

'Jack is taking leave of Valiant.' Anne sighed.
'And no doubt leaving minute instructions with Rachel about his welfare.'

'Why should he do that?' Katherine demanded.
'If necessary, I am sure Hal could look out for the
creature.'

'But he loves Rachel,' Piers murmured, 'and an
ounce of love is worth a pound of medicine, as we
all know.'

'Poor Jack,' Anne said, 'he does so hate to leave his dear friend behind. But, of course, the old fellow could never make his way back to Ravensglass now.' There was general sympathy around the table, except from Katherine who was wondering why the animal had been brought if he was not up to it. A moment later Jack and Rachel came in; Jack went to his mother-in-law and apologized for being late to the board, and Rachel took her place between Piers and Katherine.

'Whatever have you been doing?' Katherine asked crossly. 'It never seems to occur to you that I might need you.'

'I think my lord Hamilton needed me more,' Rachel returned.

'What nonsense! You are getting very self-important suddenly, Rachel.'

'He asked me out to see Valiant and to ask me to care for him when he left. I could not refuse.' She was buoyed up with confidence. As Katherine had said, Hal Latimar was more than capable of doing all that was necessary, and Jack had conceded this, but…

'I know no man is better with a four-footed animal than Hal, my dear, but you…you seem to understand Valiant very well.'

'I do,' she had replied, eyes shining. 'I suppose it is because I was trained and encouraged by a master, well, mistress really. My grandmother Madrilene always said that a brave horse was like a brave man. Difficult and temperamental and dangerous. But she also said a loving word and a gentle hand could work wonders with both species.' Jack had looked at her thoughtfully. He wondered why the slim dark girl before him reminded him so strongly of his mother-in-law, his wife, his sister-in-law—in fact, all the Latimar women. She was not at all their like in looks or manner.

'When the time comes,' he had continued, 'I can rely on you to do what is right?' Rachel had agreed he could. Now Katherine's remarks reduced her, as they always did.

At the head of the table this day was Elizabeth Tudor. She would be leaving as soon as Robert Dudley came from the lodge to collect her and take her on to the palace. Meanwhile, she was relishing her last moments at Maiden Court—always a favourite among her nobles' homes. Of course, now that Harry Latimar was dead the link would be weaker, but not altogether severed. Harry's older son was always willing and able to apply his fine mind to whatever his monarch required. But, 'twas always a temporary thing with him, Elizabeth had to admit, understood between them that his real life was not within her court but in the rural Kew.

His sister Anne had taken herself off twenty years ago to the fastness of the Northern border. The Queen had no real quarrel with that either: Jack Hamilton was a valuable asset to a sovereign determined to keep the borders of England safe. Hal, the younger son, was still within her immediate sphere but he had, like his kin, proved somewhat intransigent and hard to handle. Undoubtedly gifted in all the necessary skills of her gentlemen, Hal would not be forced into the silken slippers of the courtier any more than his father or brother had been.

She caught his eye now and smiled. He was, in spite of his shortcomings, the most attractive male, she thought. In love, or so he believed and her sharp eyes had noted, with that fair-haired Monterey girl. That would not last, the Queen mused idly. Hal was privileged and spoiled, but this lady was both these without another essential ingredient enjoyed by the really noble—kindness. Katherine Monterey was not kind, or even thoughtful about her contemporaries or subordinates.

In due time Hal would find this out and the love affair would be off, Elizabeth thought. Quite in order, too, for she had always preferred her male satellites to be unencumbered: indeed, it was positively ruinous to their careers to fall from grace in this way, if not downright dangerous as it had so nearly been for Robert Dudley.

By the mid-afternoon the bustle of the royal departure was over. Immediately after, the Hamiltons left for the North. Bess embraced Anne fondly. 'Do write when you get a moment, love,' she said.

Dudley, the handsome and assured Hamilton heir, paused with one foot in the stirrup to acknowledge Hal's farewell. They had been, with Piers Roxburgh, pages at Petrie. 'Take good care of yourself, my friend,' he said swinging up into the saddle. 'And I do mean good care—there is word about that you are courting Monterey's daughter.'

Hal, the wind lifting his blond hair, looked up. 'I hope you approve, Dudley.' The young men regarded each other gravely, then Dudley laughed.

'Approve? Dear Hal, I never know whether this penchant you have for approval is the result of a desire for security, or a gambler's wish to hedge his bets. If 'tis the former I would say—and even in the remote area of the border a young man reviews the feminine characters available to him—don't count on it with Monterey's daughter.'

Hal stepped back. He said, 'If you were not one of my oldest and dearest friends, I would pull you off that horse and knock you down for that comment!'

Dudley laughed again and bent to grasp Hal's hand. 'You never change! Always the bold move. But remember, boldness can be a useful tool only in the hand of a careful man.' He followed the others out of the yard.

One morning in the third week of November a peremptory message arrived from the Queen, ordering Hal to Greenwich and asking, almost as an afterthought, that he bring Monterey's daughter, the Lady Katherine, with him. As it was a full fortnight earlier than expected, it threw Maiden Court into a flurry.

Katherine, elated by the summons must, *must*

have at least one new gown. Her furs must be dis-
interred from her trunks and hung for two days at
least in the privies that they might be rendered immune to the destructive moths. Her underlinen must
be washed and aired and mended, her jewels taken
out and washed and polished that they might out-
shine any others possessed by ladies with whom she
would share quarters. Her slippers, her riding boots,
her cloaks must all be attended to.

She herself must be made ready for the grand
entrance into the world she knew she belonged in.
Rosewater for her hair, milk baths for her skin—
Rachel thought she would go mad tending the
shrine called Katherine Monterey.

She was to go with her to Greenwich, as handmaiden, keeper of these clothes and jewels, yet had
no moment of her own to see for her own needs.
Not that she had many gowns to look to, or any
jewellery to pick over. As for furs—it was a problem to know what to wear for the journey ahead,
the weather being cold, and she being singularly
lacking in anything except a thin woollen cloak.

Very suitable, Katherine said when Bess drew
her attention to her cousin's lack. Much as Bess
disliked Rachel, this comment sat ill with her ideas
of propriety. Whatever Rachel was, she was a Monterey, after all, and a lady by heritage of some distinction. Bess consequently sorted through her own
luxurious cloaks for the solution. But she was a
very small woman, and extremely slender. Rachel
was taller and more amply proportioned.

'Why has the girl no decent clothes?' demanded Hal, who had returned home to escort the party to Court and come upon his mother sorting through the trunks.

'Well, my dear, she has no money of her own and is dependent on charity,' Bess said vaguely.

'Then Katherine should have seen to it—she is the girl's nearest relative, however many places removed.'

Bess sighed and let drop a trunk lid. 'Knowing that does not solve the present dilemma.'

'Something must be ordered then.'

'There is no time. You leave for Greenwich in two days.'

Hal considered. 'I have the velvet and sable cloak—never worn—presented to me by Father on my last birthday. It could be made to fit very easily.' Men no longer wore full-length cloaks, and this item, which fashionably fell to Hal's mid-calves, would suit a woman's height very well. The extra material used to accommodate his broad shoulders could be contrived in some way to fit Rachel by any competent dressmaker. Bess sat back on her heels. 'But, darling, that is a very valuable thing! Your father was waiting almost a year for the ship bringing the fur...'

'Do you think Father would mind, then?' Despite his grief and reluctant acceptance of Harry's death, Hal was the only one at Maiden Court who could speak naturally of him.

Bess took her son's hand in order to rise. 'I suppose not. Actually, he seemed to like Rachel very much.'

Hal looked at her averted face. 'Indeed. But not for any memory of a past association. Father always judged anyone new on present merit—and Rachel is good company, you know.'

Bess withdrew her hand and turned away. 'Is she?'

Hal presented the cloak to Rachel the evening before the departure. He had made no great production of the affair—simply sought out the dressmaker working on Katherine's new gown and told her what was needed. Now he came into the parlour where the family was gathered with it over his arm and went to where Rachel sat on the window seat. 'I understand,' he said casually, 'you have no suitable cloak for travelling. I hope you will accept this.'

Startled, Rachel rose and he threw the cloak over her shoulders. Instinctively she raised her hands and smoothed the luxuriant soft fur against her neck and face—how rich it made her feel. She turned to examine her blurred reflection in the dark panes of the parlour window and received an image of muted grace. 'I love it!' she declared. 'Thank you, thank you, Hal!' She raised herself on tiptoe to kiss his cheek.

Hal was conscious of warmth and sweetness in that split second. Then he removed a strand of her long black hair which had strayed on to his gleaming arm, gripped her velvet-clad elbows and leaned down to kiss her mouth. It was the briefest exchange, but it was observed by all in the room. Bess, at the hearth, remembered Madrilene's vital and sudden movements which were so attractive, and so annoying to her; George and Judith shared a simultaneous memory—a sparkling snowy day when they were beginning to acknowledge their love. Katherine's blue eyes flashed acquisitively; she recalled Lady Bess's plea with dismay. If she had known that the result of her casual dismissal would be this, she would have allowed her cousin one of her many rabbit-fur wraps. Now she would have to arrive at one of the greatest palaces on earth in the company of a servant dressed in finest Russian sable. How mortifying!

Then the moment passed and Hal said briskly, 'Well, I am glad you like it,' and stepped back. Later, when Rachel found out that the cloak had been one of Hal's cherished possessions, she was even more pleased with it.

## Chapter Eight

The morn of departure came after a night of hard frost. The roads were as unyielding as iron and Bess was for putting off the journey. Hal was reluctant to do so—he knew his Queen; when she summoned one it was wise to come running or suffer her displeasure. That might mean little to him, but he was eager that Katherine begin her association with Elizabeth on a tranquil note. 'We will be well mounted and clad,' he said consideringly, 'Jonas and Paul—' the Maiden Court grooms appointed to accompany them '—are confident enough of the conditions. Also, five of our party are excellent in the saddle.'

Bess knew he spoke of Piers, himself and Rachel and the grooms. Not Katherine, who even she could see was spectacularly undistinguished on a horse.

She said, 'Very well, my dear. I imagine you know your own business best, and Elizabeth must have her way. I suppose it is you she really wants at Greenwich and not Katherine?'

Hal half smiled. He had not given his mother the exact terms of Her Majesty's summons, and hoped that while his love was resident at Greenwich she might attain the recognition she deserved from the Queen.

He and Bess were breaking their fast early before Katherine and Rachel came down to the hall because he had wished a private word. He was worried about leaving Maiden Court so soon after his father's death. He knew he had been Harry Latimar's favourite and therefore felt responsible. Bess, he thought, had changed in some indefinable way since losing her mate. She looked smaller somehow, and her bright silver hair dimmed. But her eyes, raised now to his face, were as clear a blue as his own and still held the unquenchable light so familiar to him. Katherine's eyes were a similar blue, but did not have quite that expression, as if nothing and no one could deny her right to hope… Unaccountably he found himself thinking of a pair of darker eyes.

'What are you thinking about?' Bess asked, refilling his ale mug. 'I hope you are not worrying about leaving me at this time.'

Hal turned his beaker on the polished table without answering. He had scarcely touched the full plate of food Bess had pressed on him. He was suddenly filled with foreboding. Bess waited, allowing him time to choose his words, thinking how like Harry he looked when struggling to break away

from the habitual armour of the advantaged courtier
to grapple with real and personal life.

'I am worried,' Hal said eventually. 'For life has
changed here, has it not? Not just losing Father, but
in other ways… I have changed, I do believe.'

'Of course you have,' Bess smiled. 'For there
is…Katherine now.'

Hal had not meant that exactly; he had changed,
he felt, in a very fundamental and significant way.
Never before, in his fortunate life, had he considered the future; now he did. His regard for Katherine had—like throwing a pebble in a pond—radiated all kinds of other thoughts on women in
general. He said abruptly, 'You don't like her, do
you?'

Under his straight blue look Bess flushed. 'I have
known her since her birth—she is almost family,'
she said, flustered.

'No, she is not,' Hal countered gently. 'She is no
relative at all and therefore not subject to your
strong feelings about family. You may say what
you truly think.'

'Well, then…' Bess seized the nettle '…no, I do
not like her, but that is not important. You like her.
Parents should have no say in whom their children
choose, for 'tis entirely irrelevant. Youth must find
its own way.' As she spoke these words she remembered with regret how her parents had adored
Harry, how in their turn she and Harry had come
to love Judith and Jack Hamilton.

Hal had his own thoughts: for the second time

that day Rachel's vivid face flashed before him, and a part of his mind tucked away his mother's words to think about on another occasion.

Soon after, the party left Maiden Court for Greenwich. Bess saw them off with misgivings. She wondered what would happen to Hal and Katherine Monterey at court. How soon would it be before the girl provoked a situation where her son would have to make some kind of stand which would threaten his career, his well-being, or even his life? It would come, Bess felt, as sure as death, for Katherine was that kind of girl and Hal that kind of young man. She hugged her fur wrap around her and shivered as she watched the dwindling figures fading into the November fog, then turned back into her warm house.

Katherine settled into her new place with complacency. This was the most glamorous time of year in any court and in England especially so. The days, the nights passed in a delightful blur of revelry. Afternoon indoor games, evening masques and banquets, a seemingly endless procession of entertainers in the great hall: mummers, acrobats, tumblers, merchants with fabulous wares to sell—anyone with something to offer the jaundiced courtiers was welcome at Greenwich in this season. The court danced and played all day and far into the night, slept until noon, then rose to begin again. This suited Katherine very well, for she had the necessary clothes and jewels and ambition to take part thoroughly. And she learned swiftly to value her greatest asset—that of the jealous attention of one of the most attractive and eligible men in the assembly, Hal Latimar. Yes, Katherine was very happy and did not spare a thought for the girl she had brought with her.

When Rachel had arrived at the palace she knew immediately that here was yet another place where she would have no standing. The journey was uneventful; Hal was surprisingly efficient on the road and in their brief visit for refreshment at two inns along the way. He had the happy knack of authority combined with the common touch so endearing to all. Katherine had complained all the way: she was cold, her mount was skittish, her complexion was suffering from the bitter blowing wind, her food— the best the inns could offer—was inferior, she should have had a closed carriage to transport her even such a short distance. Rachel bore the brunt of her cousin's displeasure, but eventually was able to leave her side and trot up to join Piers Roxburgh. Hal, dropping back, received a rueful smile from Katherine.

'Dear Rachel, I fear she is not apt to rise to the occasion.'

'Perhaps she is nervous as to what awaits her,' Hal said thoughtfully, his eyes on the two figures in front. His critical gaze noted that both had an easy and accomplished seat on their horses, made restive by the poor conditions underfoot and the thunderous sky above. Raising his eyes to the sky, he knew why the animals were so nervous—there would be a storm before long. 'Not something you need to consider, darling. You will be adored the moment you set foot in Greenwich.' Katherine regained some of her diminished sense of importance hearing this loving comment.

And it seemed Hal was right, for she made an immediate impact. Rachel, on the other hand, found herself firmly in place as her cousin's handmaid. Katherine, introducing her to the other ladies in her dorter, omitted to mention their relationship. Rachel was not even granted a sleeping place in the same room, but was lodged down a cold stone corridor with girls she saw at a glance were ladies' maids, rather than…ladies. Never mind, she thought, drearily. I expected nothing else. One of the girls, friendly enough, pointed to one of the enormous beds and told her space would be made for her there. Rachel knew sharing a bed was common in any royal palace but as the room filled up with chattering women she realized here it must be at least ten to a mattress. 'And,' the friendly girl came back to say, 'I expect you'll want to return that cloak to your mistress. We don't have room for anything that grand in here.'

'It is my own,' Rachel replied stiffly, and then flushed as the girl gave her an interested speculative look which plainly showed she thought this rather different newcomer had a protector—and a rich one by the looks of the fabulous garment. Rachel turned

away, biting her lip. The room had a window and
she went to look out with blurred eyes. There was
little to see for it overlooked a narrow dusty court-
yard and faced the blank wall of the apartments
opposite. She stood there, fighting back tears for a
long time, aware that the room behind her was now
lighted and its inhabitants were changing their
clothes. A touch on her arm.

'We eat now, didn't you hear the bells? I'll show
you where if you like.'

Rachel removed the cloak and dropped it on to
the window seat. 'You're very kind,' she said with
a catch in her voice.

'Not at all,' the girl said cheerfully, reassured by
the drab ugly gown the cloak had concealed. 'I am
Amy Price, and you are—?' Rachel gave her name
and followed her companion down to the great hall
full of smoke and glitter and hundreds of voices all
raised at once. Amy led her to a table—well below
the salt, Rachel noticed—so littered and shining
with grease she was reluctant to accept food from
it. She sat down. The little, overworked pages came
seldom to this table and the food when they did
bring it almost cold. Rachel pushed it around her
plate, looking about her at the silk-clad walls; at
intervals were hung enormous circles of beaten silver which reflected the dancing candlelight and the
shimmering, spangled clothes and rich jewels worn
by the assembly. She was suddenly desperately and
desolately lonely—even a glimpse of Katherine
would be welcome, but her cousin, too, was appar-

ently lost in the mêlée. She did see Hal Latimar, however, what seemed like a half a mile distant sitting with a group of gentlemen at the foot of the royal dais, empty tonight as the Queen was entertaining guests privately in her apartments. Moodily, Rachel kept her eye on the glittering blue-and-silver figure as it ate and drank and laughed with its similarly gorgeous fellows.

When she returned to her dismal room her cloak was gone and a weary servant mending the fire told her, 'A fair lady come to get it; said as how she would find more use for it than you.'

In mid-December there was an early fall of snow. Rachel woke to a heavy silence and from her crowded bed she saw the white flakes swirling beyond the window in the wind tunnel created by the close stone buildings. She eased herself cautiously away from the girl gently snoring beside her. During the night the covers had been pulled off her in her position on one extreme edge of the bed and that no doubt explained the painful ache in her bones. She sat up and as quickly lay back, dizzy and sick. She was freezing cold and yet sweat was beading on her forehead and trickling between her breasts under her demure linen nightgown.

I am ill! she thought hazily. Ill in this alien place with no one to care for me. Although she had tried to be pleasant and accommodating with the other girls in her weeks at Greenwich, she had not made friends with them. Even Amy shunned her now, thinking her stand-offish and 'different'. She performed her duties for Katherine, but when the other ladies in her cousin's dorter showed signs of interest in her, attracted by her unusual looks and lovely voice, Katherine made sure those duties were kept to a minimum. There was nothing to do for most of the day except gossip and she had nothing in common with the others in her circle; they fell silent at her approach and talked behind their hands when she sat apart. Before the weather became too poor to walk in the grounds she found some pleasure in exploring the gardens, but her mind cried out for some stimulation and there was none that she could find here. A tentative query as to where the libraries were—she had always found solace in books—had brought forth blank stares and cries of 'You can't go in there!'

I have managed badly as usual, Rachel thought, trying to swallow through a throat suddenly lined with sharp knives, and now I am sick with no one to help because I don't fit in anywhere. Neither flesh, nor fowl nor good red herring—the silly country phrase kept repeating itself in her fevered brain.

By the time the others stirred Rachel was in a near coma, alternately burning hot or shivering cold and staring glassy-eyed. Amy Price, who had not fulfilled her early promise of being a friend, nevertheless looked at her in consternation. The other girls, dressing quickly in the freezing room with the swirling curtain of white beyond the window, looked askance at the figure on the bed. 'You'd best inform her mistress, Amy,' one said. 'She ought to be put in one of the sick rooms straight away. It may be the sweating sickness.' The words struck terror into the hearts of those listening, for any disease could sweep through such close quarters like fire in a hay loft. Amy lifted Rachel into the middle of the bed and tucked the coverlet over her. Then she dressed herself and made her way to Katherine's apartments and tapped on the door. Receiving no answer, she went in and identified Katherine's gleaming blonde head amongst the other yawning ladies.

'Please, my lady—'

Katherine stretched in the feather bed. She had come to bed very late and had no wish to be awakened. 'I shall lie in this morning, Rachel,' she mumbled.

'It is not Rachel, my lady. I share her room and have come to tell you she is sick. Sore sick.'

Katherine's eyes snapped open. 'Sick? How so?'

'Fevered, and out of her mind with it.' Amy deliberately avoided the diagnosis pronounced earlier, for fear there would be no help for Rachel who, after all, was this lady's responsibility. Amy had been a personal maid to successive ladies of the Greenwich court for five years and had found them a particularly uncaring breed, especially where contagious sickness was concerned. In fact, in this age of limited medical knowledge, it was better to avoid falling sick than to hope for a cure if you did so.

Katherine frowned, but sat up and reached for her robe.

'I will come,' she said, mainly because she thought this irritating girl would not retreat unless she did. She stood at the door of the maids' room and peered in. The other girls had gone and Rachel was alone. 'Hmm.' She approached the bed and, standing well back, examined her cousin. 'She does indeed look poorly. Now, what are the arrangements here for a situation such as this?'

Not a word of sympathy, thought Amy grimly. 'The arrangements?'

'Yes. People must fall ill from time to time at Greenwich—what happens to them?'

Amy sighed. There would obviously be no compassionate care from this quarter. She felt guilty about Rachel herself, knowing that it was not her fault she was shunned, it was the penalty of being different. Amy resolved there and then to do her best for the patient, but she must have help. 'She can be removed to one of the sick rooms, a physician asked to attend, a nurse engaged.'

'Ah, well then,' Katherine said, relieved. 'Please see to it all, will you?' She made for the open door but Amy was there before her.

'Physician and nurse must be paid,' she said bluntly.

'Oh, money… If you come with me now I will give you sufficient for the purpose.' As easy as that, thought Amy, accepting the heavy purse. 'Do your best for her, won't you?' Katherine dismissed her with a dazzling smile which failed to dazzle at all.

Amy would have done her best if she had not that night fallen prey to the sickness herself. Before that she had seen Rachel comfortably installed in the room designated, stood by while a physician shook his head dolefully, applied leeches and prescribed nostrums to be administered by the nurse whom Amy also commissioned. Amy paid the doctor and promised to pay the nurse the following day, by which time she was ill herself. Unlike many at Greenwich she had family nearby who, on hearing of her plight, came to carry her off and care for her themselves. Despite their loving attention Amy died within twenty-four hours and, although they mourned sincerely, her relatives were pleasantly surprised by the amount of gold she had about her person. It would pay for a handsome funeral and there would be ample left for the kind of headstone not usually provided for a girl of her class.

On the third day Katherine descended the stairs to the great hall to attend a masque. She wore shining blue and silver and her costume was matched by that of her escort who also wore diamonds in his ears and on the buckles of his silk slippers.

'Dear Hal,' she said, slipping her arm through his. 'Is this not all the greatest fun? Truly I believe I did not begin to live until I came to court.'

'I am glad you are enjoying yourself,' Hal replied, both appreciating and resenting the glances his companion was receiving as they went on to the dance floor. They parted for a while in the pattern of the dance and when they came together again Katherine said,

'How far away Abbey Hall and Maiden Court seem, do they not? I have not heard from my grandfather—have you heard aught of your family?'

'Indeed. My mother is a good correspondent and tells me all goes well there. She asked for you, and the Lady Rachel.' He spun Katherine in a shimmer of sky blue and silver and set her down, looking hungrily down into her face. 'When I next write I can tell her you are more beautiful and successful than ever.' He released her to skim up the line and in time be returned to him. 'And as to the Lady Rachel? I have not seen her about. Is she well?'

Katherine allowed a slight frown to pass over her fair face. 'I cannot in all truth say that, Hal. Some days ago she fell ill and I was constrained to engage a physician and also a nurse. I felt it my duty, you understand.'

'Of course. But she is well now?'

'I cannot say…' The figure was concluded and the dancers were dispersing to seek refreshment. Hal helped Katherine to wine and they stood about with friends drinking.

During a pause in conversation Hal asked, 'You cannot say? But you have assured yourself she is recovered?'

'Not personally, for she was removed to a place to be nursed and I am not sure where. But I am not concerned for I have done all I can.' Katherine finished her wine and accepted an invitation to view the play now being performed in one of the anterooms. Hal stood tapping one fingernail against his empty glass. Katherine could not be expected to know that persons of no estate were very vulnerable should they fall ill in a place like Greenwich. The great and powerful received the best of care; those in the lower orders were similarly attended by their fellows. Into which category did Rachel Monterey fall? he wondered. He would like to find out, but hesitated to involve himself. But if he did not, who would? He had not been courtier for so long he had forgotten the way he had been raised: it was the Latimar creed that Latimar friends were cared for. Putting down his glass, he left the hall and ran lightly up the staircase.

Dame Mary Rashleigh was in charge of the sick at Greenwich. In her still room she mixed and concocted the remedies to alleviate most of the minor ills which beset the community. More serious conditions—deep wounds and amputations—were dealt with by the barber surgeons. The court physicians were called in to give their advice and theories on anything which did not fall within these boundaries. All medical factions were usually at a loss to know what to do with the frequent outbreaks of various plagues. The so-called sweating sickness was one of these unaccountable areas. No one could explain why the disease chose such diverse victims—rich and poor alike, strong and weak—with such impunity. The symptoms were always the same: aching bones and muscles, high fever, shivering and chills and extreme loss of bodily fluids. Hence its name. Unpredictable, too, was its outcome—whatever their station in life, or former health, some survived and some did not. Dame Rashleigh had correctly ascertained Rachel Monterey had contracted this malaise and dealt with her within the confines of her experience. Restrict the sufferer to a room without air, for the bouts of violent ague must be denied any current of fresh fuel, administer no liquid for what the body did not take in could not be sweated out, keep a cool room to combat the raging hot fever. There was little more to be done and the Dame felt she had performed her duty. As far as she could see this patient had no friends, no one had enquired for her—after the first day no doctor or nurse had attended. Dame Rashleigh was therefore greatly surprised when Hal Latimar came knocking on the door of her modest apartments.

Hal refused a drink but did accept her invitation to sit down. It was pleasant, she thought, to receive a visit from so charming a young man with charming parents, too. She remembered his mother, the Lady Bess, very kindly and told him so. She then commiserated with him about the untimely loss of his father, also kindly remembered. Five minutes were spent recalling the old days, then Hal said, 'I understand the Lady Rachel Monterey is being cared for by you.'

'Yes,' Dame Mary said after a moment when she could not quite remember the name. 'A sad case. The girl has been sick several days and no prospect of recovery.'

'Why so?' Hal enquired gently. 'She is—was—a strong person.'

'She is known to you...? A friend?' the Dame enquired delicately.

'She is distant cousin to a family who are great friends to the Latimars,' Hal said blandly. 'She came to court in the service of the Lady Katherine Monterey. You will recall that lady's father? A favourite of our Queen? And her grandfather, the Earl of Monterey?'

Dame Mary suffered a slight constriction of breath. The girl lying so apparently friendless had powerful relatives, it seemed. 'No one told me of this,' she said defensively.

'Ah, no.' Hal smiled placatingly. 'She came to Greenwich, as I said, in the company of the Earl's granddaughter, who made certain arrangements on her cousin falling ill, but failed to realize that these arrangements must be reviewed.'

Dame Mary bridled. 'Reviewed or not, sir, I have done my duty regarding the young woman.'

'I am sure, I am sure. Now if I might just see her for a moment—just, you understand, to set the Earl's granddaughter's mind at rest.' It is like a French exercise, Hal thought—the pen of my aunt... He felt ridiculous, yet would not give up the enterprise until he had satisfied himself. The Dame rose majestically.

'Certainly you may.' She went to the door and called out. To the servant who appeared she said, 'Show this gentleman to Lady Rachel's room.' When the woman looked blankly at her, she enlarged, 'The girl in the turret room.' She then sat down again and reflected how times had changed. In the past the well connected were also well known.

Hal followed the servant down the corridors. At the end of one she opened a door and gestured within, before retreating to continue her work which she was sure was more than one body could be expected to do. Hal advanced into the room.

It was tiny. At one end a three-paned jutting window gave it its name, the glass grimy, the catches corroded from disuse. There was a single bed in the centre, a small hearth with a sulky fire issuing grey smoke. Beside the bed was a table on which stood a glass of water filmed with dust. Rachel lay on the bed, her black hair spread over the dingy pillow; her small face, turned up to the low ceiling, was as pale as wax. She was so still that Hal approached the bed with trepidation, but as he did so she opened her eyes and stared up at him.

'Hal—' Her voice was no more than a breath. Beneath the coverlet the outline of her body was sharply defined, her white arms and hands were transparently pale lying above the faded embroidery. Hal took one of her hands.

'I am here, Rachel,' he said, pressing it. Immediately her lashes fluttered and her eyelids fell, cutting off the dark stare, but her hand turned in his and held. The well-contained but always present Latimar anger ignited. Rachel was one of the clan and was now abused. Hal extracted his warm hand gently from her cold one and went to the window. He struggled with the warped fastenings, but succeeded in opening only one. Cold air flowed into the stagnant room with drifting snowflakes. He strode to the door, wrenched it open, shouting. To the servant who came eventually he said, 'Mend the fire in this room, woman! A bright blaze, if you please. And bring warm milk and water in quantity, and be quick about it!' He returned to the bed and looked down on Rachel. Her shift was limp and wet with sweat. It must be changed. When the servant returned, carrying a basket of logs, he stood over her as she knelt by the fire, saying, 'I need clean linen for this lady immediately. And where is the milk and water I requested?' The woman looked up.

'I have asked, sir. But the Dame has given no instructions—it is difficult, sir.'

'I am instructing you now,' Hal said, in the grip of a cold rage. 'Finish with the fire and get the milk. I will see for the linen.' Before the girl's startled eyes he left the room and walked swiftly down the stone passage. He pushed open each door as he went, finding nothing to help him until the last. On the bed there he found a pile of night shifts. Lifting them, he went back.

The girl on her knees before the hearth had gone, presumably to find the nourishment he had asked for. Certainly Rachel needed it. How was it possible that she had become so bone thin in the course of a few days? A timid movement at the door announced the return of the servant, carrying a jug from which spiralled steam. He said peremptorily, 'Set it down on that table— Come here and help my lady into a fresh night shift.' The girl gave him a dubious look. 'Get on with it!' He went to the window and pulled it shut, remaining with his back to the room, arms folded.

# Chapter Nine

He remained standing thus for a time he could not calculate. Behind him came sounds which made him heartsick. He had never had the sweating sickness—in fact, he had had a life remarkably free from any disease. But friends had been struck and all said the worst of the symptoms had been the agonizing pain in bones and muscles, especially when any movement was made. Hearing Rachel's cries now tormented him. At length it ended and Hal turned back.

'Shall I give her the milk now, sir?' the servant asked.

'I will do that,' he answered brusquely. 'You will leave now, but hear this—you will return often this night to remake the fire, to see my lady is covered warm and as comfortable as possible. I will report to the Dame shortly and return in the morning to ensure all is as I have ordered. If it is not, you will be dismissed, without reference.'

With a last frightened look the girl left and Hal

returned to the bed. He had not raised his voice in the last minutes but Rachel stirred restlessly on the bed. He looked somewhat helplessly at the jug. His mother had always ignored current medical advice on almost every occasion. Her sovereign remedy for fevers, for example, was to offer constant liquid— common sense, she maintained, for what was lost in sweating must be put back. Fresh air formed the staple of her curious strategy, as did cleanliness in the sickroom and appropriate herbs carefully combined and administered. Once over the crisis, the invalid would be tempted with delicious food in small amounts. Others looked askance at this turning on its head of learned opinion, but those lucky enough to be nursed by Lady Bess usually recovered.

Now Hal struggled to remember what he must surely have absorbed over the years. Milk he had and water in a beaker. Rachel stirred and moaned and he lifted her awkwardly and held the mixture to her lips. She turned her head away and struggled weakly.

'No, no, it is better you take it,' he said. In spite of his amorous history Hal had never been in such an intimate situation with a woman before. Women came to him painted and perfumed for love; if the ladies in his circle were sick or hurt they were cared for by other ladies and did not appear in male company. At home, his mother had kept her ills to herself and his brother's daughters the same. But, Hal thought, coaxing Rachel to drink and smoothing the damp hair from her forehead, there was an odd satisfaction in knowing another side of a girl. At last he was content she had taken enough nourishment to sustain her through the night and laid her back on the pillows. He even fancied she looked a little better; some of the waxen colour in her face had been replaced by a more natural pallor. He set down the beaker and lifted one of her hands and held it between his two. She turned her head and fixed her dark eyes on his face.

'Hal? You are still here?' She had no memory in her fevered state of the last half-hour.

'Of course.'

'Will you…could you…stay until I sleep? Lately—lately I have had the most frightening dreams.' He returned her hand under the covers.

'Induced by fever, sweetheart. There is no call for fear—I will stay until you sleep, and be here when you wake.' Her eyes, made enormous by the loss of flesh from her face, reflected the candlelight and were the colour of the brandywine he had drunk earlier in the great hall; they focussed with difficulty.

'You will do that for me? Why?'

'Why?' He could hardly answer that himself. He said lightly, 'Because you are a cousin of a family closely bonded to mine, and I have been derelict in my duty towards you since we came to Greenwich.' She was too weak to attempt to understand this, but managed a painful smile before drifting back into sleep.

Before leaving, Hal checked the fire, kicking into place a log which had not yet been caught by the flames, opened the window the merest crack and covered the jug of milk and water. On his way down to the great hall he stopped off at Dame Rashleigh's apartments.

'I trust you found the lady well cared for?' the Dame said.

Hal sat down and crossed one long leg over the other. He accepted the wine offered. 'Well, not entirely, my lady. You mentioned earlier your memories of my mother and she, you will recall, had definite ideas as to the nursing of the sick. In fact...' he gave his inherited and charming smile '...I believe she once nursed a future king back to health.' Bess Latimar had indeed done this: Henry Tudor's prized son, Edward, owed his early life to Bess. 'Of course,' Hal went on, 'I am but an amateur in this field, but feel—' He then gave the most detailed and minute instructions for Rachel's care during the night and rose. 'I shall be back tomorrow,' he added, 'to visit.' Dame Rashleigh blinked and escorted him to the door, marvelling that times had indeed changed since she was young. In those days young gentlemen like Hal Latimar concerned themselves with the important things in life—their horseflesh, their clothes, the jousting lists...

Hal returned to the hall with a wry smile on his lips. He had never yet considered any tomorrows in his life, or taken up any cause which did not directly concern himself. Now he had and wondered

at himself. Entering the hall, he looked around immediately for Katherine. She was seated in one of
the alcoves with Piers Roxburgh. Piers rose on his
approach and looked warily at his friend. He knew
the other man so well he was instantly aware of the
difference in him, but not why. 'Well met, Hal,' he
said extending his hand.

'Indeed.' Hal ignored the outstretched hand,
looking at Katherine. She smiled. Having viewed
the play, she had come back to the hall in search
of her cavalier. When he had not appeared she had
enquired for him and been told he was visiting a
sick relative. Putting two and two together, Katherine had correctly assumed he was with that annoying thorn in her flesh, Rachel Monterey. Wishing to teach him a lesson, she had pondered on
some way of doing so and concluded that Piers
Roxburgh might be useful. She had sent a message
to Piers and hence the tête-à-tête Hal had come
upon. She looked mischievously at the two young
men to see what might occur.

'You have eaten tonight, Hal?' Piers asked tentatively. He was quite aware of Katherine's tactics
and—as much in thrall to her as Hal—could not
resent them but, a veteran of a dozen confrontations
with other courtiers, he had developed a sixth sense
about who to tangle with. Even laying aside their
long friendship, this experience told him only a fool
would bring Latimar to the point: easygoing and
idle Hal might be, but when it came to a real fight
Piers would rather not be opposing him.

'No, I had no heart for it on hearing that Katherine's cousin was severely indisposed.'

'Her cousin?' Piers looked nonplussed.

'The Lady Rachel Monterey,' Hal said grimly.

'Ah...Rachel? I am sorry to hear that. What ails her?'

'The sweating sickness,' Hal replied baldly.

'Oh, no!' Piers had attended the funerals of various of his friends who had succumbed to this plague. 'Is there aught I can do? Anything—?'

'Not more than I have already done, I think. Truly, Piers, you would be amazed by what I have been about in the last hour!'

Piers grinned. 'I am sure you were more than equal to it, my friend.'

Katherine looked disapprovingly at them both. This scene was not at all what she had planned. She rose gracefully. 'I feel,' she said, addressing Hal, 'a little faint. 'Tis this talk of sickness...'

He responded instantly. 'I beg your pardon, sweetheart. Of course, you must be as concerned as I about your cousin.'

'My distant cousin,' Katherine said firmly.

'Well...yes...but you know it has occurred to me that we have not included her as we might since coming to court. I suggest when she is fully recovered we remedy that.'

Katherine slipped her arm in his. 'That could hardly be, Hal. She is, after all, a very poor and distant relation.'

Over her blonde head Piers threw Hal an enigmatic glance. He could have advised his friend not to pursue this particular tack. But Hal, of course, was not to be advised.

'But, darling, she is family, after all.'

'Hardly mine,' Katherine said coldly. 'And not at all yours. Shall we continue on to the dancing?' She put pressure on the arm she held.

Piers, following behind, laughed inwardly. It was not, he knew, in Hal's understanding to fail to stand up for a friend, and when it came to family...

'You do understand what I am saying, don't you, Hal?' Katherine asked as they joined the dancing. He bowed.

'I understand everything you have said,' he returned gravely. Piers, still listening, chuckled. But that does not mean he will act upon it, he thought.

Life at Greenwich whirled on towards the season of gaiety. The year coming swiftly to an end had been eventful in many ways. England was extending her boundaries all the time—Walter Raleigh had left for the Americas to establish a colony and been duly knighted for his success; another plot to overthrow Elizabeth and substitute her Catholic cousin, Mary Stuart, had been discovered and its instigator, Francis Throckmorton, was now a handful of half-forgotten bones. In parliamentary circles there was discussion of forming a group of noblemen 'to pursue to the death anyone plotting against the Queen' and it was rumoured that even the disgraced Scottish Queen had signed this paper. En-

gland had supported the Dutch in their war against
Spain and one heard a great deal these days that
another fine sailor—Francis Drake—had distinguished himself by his determination in attacking
Spanish ships and that the Spaniards had retaliated
by confiscating English ships at anchor in Spanish
ports. All these events, and more, were reviewed at
length among the elite at Greenwich court, as well
as a more domestic, but equally interesting, matter.

Hal had, as promised, returned the morning after
he had stormed Dame Rashleigh's preserves in the
sick rooms. He had been pleased to find all he had
ordered had been done and a more hopeful atmosphere was present in the turret room. Rachel, although still desperately ill, had been well enough
to smile a greeting.

There had followed a fortnight of these morning
visits undetected by the rest of the court. It was no
hardship to Hal to rise early; he abhorred the habit
of his friends of lying abed until noon and Greenwich was practically snowbound at present, pre-
venting him from riding abroad. And he found he
enjoyed his new activity. At first he and Rachel just
talked a little of this and that, then, as she grew
stronger, played cards, or he would read to her. After the first time Hal never made the mistake of
being alone with her—he had no wish to compro-
mise her or to be compromised himself. Application
to the Dame—busier now that true winter was with
the court—had produced Martha Pipe, rather dour

but thoroughly respectable and trustworthy. Martha was at her post when Hal broached the subject of Rachel's return to court life.

'I know I have to,' she sighed, looking over his bright head at the window where snow fell in brief flurries. 'But am reluctant to take up my duties again.'

'What exactly are your duties?'

'Oh, well…I rise and dress, then go along to Katherine's apartments where I help her dress, arrange her hair. Then she goes down to break her fast and that is all for me until she requires a change of costume.'

'Is that all you do? Nothing for…yourself? You go to eat in the hall…'

'Eat, yes, but I am not part of anything there. How could I be?'

Hal frowned. 'Surely your cousin invites you? If not to eat with her, I know how strict the rules are…but to the plays, the entertainments?' He could, of course, have asked Katherine this question in the weeks before Rachel's illness, but it had not occurred to him to do so. He was not always with her, and had assumed she had looked after her cousin when he was not there to observe it.

'No, why should she? Also, if she did, how could I go? I have not the suitable clothes.'

'Ah, clothes…' Hal smiled. This was familiar ground for him—no female of his acquaintance would ever admit to having a suitable gown for any occasion. Rachel did not return his smile. At this very moment she was wearing a borrowed night shift!

'They are important, Hal,' she said gravely. 'In this place particularly. Certainly at first I tried to become…part of things. But 'twas impossible. One glance at my poor dress, my lack of jewels, my general air of being disadvantaged…' Her voice trailed off before the expression on his face. Of course he did not understand, she realised. Hal Latimar took his fellows as he found them; no outward gilding mattered to him. But it did to the majority. She was ashamed to have been poor-mouthed before him. 'It doesn't matter,' she said.

'But it obviously does,' he countered. He was ashamed, too—a Latimar connection being too shamefully clad to appear before her peers! 'And can easily be remedied. Mistress Pipe!' He turned and addressed the woman toasting her feet before the blazing fire. 'We require a dressmaker immediately. I would suggest Mistress Jourdan, she is French and I have heard her spoken well of.'

The startled woman jumped up and scuttled from the room. She did not know what the fine gentleman was about, but Dame Rashleigh would. She duly consulted with her and the next hours were filled for Rachel with a delightful confusion.

The dressmaker arrived with two handmaidens equipped with tape measures, in their wake a trail of merchants carrying materials.

Rachel was confused but her companion was not. Hal, one leg crossed over the other, pronounced on

the silks and satins and patterns and ideas presented
by Marie Jourdan. When the door finally closed behind them all, he said to Rachel, 'Are you pleased?
Do you think everything will be to your liking?'

'I am sure it will,' Rachel answered breathlessly.
She climbed back into the haven of her bed and lay
back.

'But—as to jewels? You mentioned them earlier.
I have about me a few.' All gentlemen of the court,
on rising, donned some jewellery. Hal stripped off
his pendants and bracelets and rings and dropped
them on to the table by the bed. 'Choose what you
will of these.' Rachel looked at the pile of glittering
gems and her eyes filled with tears. The hard stones
brought back hard reality.

'Now what is wrong?' Hal asked. 'Have we tired
you? Are you feeling ill again?'

She shook her head. 'I feel well enough, but this
is all madness. I was carried away with the excitement.'

'It certainly suits you,' he said, smiling. 'Two
weeks ago you looked ready for the winding sheet,
now you look…much better.' He had been about
to pay her the compliment of saying she was beautiful, a compliment which belonged only to Katherine. He turned the subject. 'If you cannot accept
the baubles, very well.'

'I can accept none of it,' she said. 'Does a lady
allow a gentlemen to buy her clothing?'

A smile tugged at his lips. 'Frequently.'

She gave him a look inherited from one of her Spanish ancestors. 'I said a lady, Hal.'

He straightened his face. 'I take your point, Rachel. But as your nearest male relative, my good friend the Earl is unable to perform this duty, I will stand proxy for him. As such I must insist you do not appear in company again in those—' He waved an arm at her few poor gowns laid over a trunk.

'I seldom appear at all in the company you are speaking of,' she returned tartly.

'But will in the future. Pray allow me to know best in this area, Rachel. Now…' he got to his feet '…I must go. You rest now and I think I will visit no more but simply let Nature take her course. I will come here in three days to escort you to the Eve celebrations.'

Rachel took a breath. The Eve of Christmas celebrations were the beginning of the grandest of the Yuletide festivities. It was a time which mixed the classes; the Queen accepted homage from any of her subjects who presented themselves at Greenwich—grand nobleman or humble workman from the stews which surrounded the London palace alike. Hospitality was offered to all, and to the needy a basket of food to take home to their families to begin the new year aright. Men travelled from all over England to take advantage of this largesse—many beginning their journey weeks before to combat the likely bad weather—and every entertainer who could walk came to perform. It was a time of fascinating excess and Rachel, who had heard tell of it, would very much like to be a part of it.

But I couldn't, she thought, as the door closed behind Hal. I would not dare! Hard on this thought came another: How angry her grandmother Madrilene would be to know her granddaughter felt unequal to this challenge. Rachel pulled up the covers under her chin and looked towards the window. The snow had at last stopped falling but it was colder and fantastic patterns of flowers and stars had formed on the panes.

How Madrilene de Santos had hated the cold! 'Cold, cold,' she had often declared. 'All England is suspended in icy cold. The rain, the sleet, the snow, and *always* the wind blowing! Trying to freeze the very blood in your veins. And the people, pinched and bloodless. Except for my Harry—one could warm one's hands on the fire he radiated when near.' The child Rachel had pondered this. How could a human being be like a fire?

Older, at Abbey Hall, she had understood part of her grandmother's reminiscence, for the house was as grey as her stories, and the people there, although sometimes merry and cheerful, frequently had the look described. Now Rachel thought she understood the rest: Hal Latimar radiated the kind of warmth one associated with a welcome fire burning in a home's hearth on a cold day each time he was near. And he wanted to take her to the Eve celebrations! But he will not come, Rachel cautioned the persistent ghost of her past.

*     *     *

But he did and found Rachel dressed and ready in one of the flattering gowns for which he had chosen the design and the rose pink material. He took her down the great staircase, holding her cold hand in his warm one and introduced her to all as his good friend. Rachel was well and truly launched.

Katherine was furious. She, too, had looked forward to the Christmas revels and they were all spoiled for her as her despised kinswoman took her place on the stage. 'You would think all here had never seen a woman before!' she said angrily to Piers as they left the antechamber on the second day of January, having witnessed Elizabeth receiving her new year's gifts. It had been a very regal occasion; Her Majesty had graciously accepted valuable and rustic offerings with equal thanks. From all over England men had braved the discouraging snowy conditions to present their tokens of allegiance. Only the expressly invited of the courtiers had been allowed to witness this ceremony and one of them had been Katherine Monterey. She had not appreciated the honour. She had been quite casual about it, even to the extent of asking Piers Roxburgh to escort her, a breach of etiquette which had not been missed by Elizabeth Tudor's sharp eyes. But Katherine could think of nothing but Rachel.

'Why do you hate her so?' Piers asked as they descended the main stairs.

'I don't. But I question her right to the place she appears to occupy now.' Since Hal had introduced Rachel to the assembly on the Eve of Christmas, she had been truly taken to the heart of Greenwich. A new face was always welcome, and what a pretty face this was! Gentle and dignified, too, with an unexpectedly amusing turn of speech. The men admired her femininity and looks, the women her kindness and interest in their dress and coiffure. As quickly as Katherine had acquired a reputation for being a cruel flirt, Rachel was accounted a sweet addition to the proceedings.

'What place?' Piers enquired. 'She is a beautiful girl, but so are hundreds of others here. Why should that disturb you?'

'Because she has no right to any place,' Katherine said stubbornly.

'She has the right of looking the part, anyway. No one can pretend to the kind of look she has in her eyes, or that instinctive carriage of head. You have to be born with that.'

'If you are trying to annoy me, you are succeeding,' Katherine said angrily. By then they had reached the dancing chamber and the first person they saw was Hal with Rachel on his arm. Katherine would have swept past them without a word, but Hal stepped in front of her and bowed.

'I have not seen you all day, Katherine.'

'I had an invitation from the Queen to observe her receiving her Yuletide gifts.'

Hal smiled delightedly; he knew it was an invitation to be coveted. 'A singular honour! I am so happy for you, sweetheart.'

Rachel, who had seen immediately that her cousin was in a temper, attempted to pacify her. 'Do tell what Her Majesty received. I have heard some of the gifts are wondrous.'

'I scarcely noticed,' Katherine said petulantly.

'I did,' Piers said cheerfully. 'If you will take some refreshment with me, Rachel, I can satisfy your curiosity.'

'Not at all!' Katherine cut in, taking his arm possessively. 'Hal has made it clear he cannot bear to be parted from Rachel lately. I would not dream of letting you take her away.' There was an awkward pause; Rachel flushed and Piers looked discomforted.

Why must she say that, and with such an expression on her face? thought Hal. It had not been easy, he knew, for Rachel to take her place in the society he had persuaded her into. But she had done splendidly and he was proud of her. Her beautiful new wardrobe was only half the story—she had been sought after and accepted for herself, for her intelligent conversation and bright-eyed interest in the new people she met. Some of the men had tried to take this interest further, and these overtures she had met with a charming dignity, cloaked in obvious innocence. Hal, who had seen many a pretty head turned by such attention, had admired her for this particularly. His father had once said to him that the ability to turn away an advance without offence was a talent which could not be learned. All in all, Hal liked Rachel very much; she had carried her flag with honour in the last fortnight, been the centre of attention and achieved a hard won confidence. The last thing she needed was Katherine chipping away at this confidence. He took her arm in a none-too-gentle grip.

'We will all take refreshment, I think,' he said, steering her through the crowds. Piers offered his own arm to Rachel and the two couples arrived at the tables together. On coming through the crush Rachel had been saluted by many courtiers and one of them approached her now. Ned Oxford was one of the gallants who had been so taken with her and rebuffed, but he was not daunted. He was a young bachelor who, in spite of being wealthy, had managed to gain his majority without being netted, or even betrothed. He could afford to marry the woman he chose and he thought that woman might possibly be Rachel Monterey. She was well connected; her kin, the Montereys, were a family revered in royal circles, her sponsor—apparently—in this assembly a member of another illustrious family, the Latimars. He bowed low and said, 'Lady Rachel, you promised you would join me for cards this evening.'

'I did, yes.' Rachel would be glad to leave this difficult situation. She made a move towards him.

'It is not yet full dark, Oxford,' Hal said genially. 'And the lady has not eaten—'

'I have sufficient viands in my apartments,' Ned

returned. 'I am expecting you also, Hal, and...' he bowed courteously to Katherine and Piers '...any friends you might choose to invite.'

'Would you like to go?' Hal asked Katherine.

'I am not sure. My grandfather always said that gambling is a fool's pursuit.' All three young men looked at her, outraged. 'However, I suppose it will pass the hours.'

'You're a brave woman to say that to two of the most dedicated gamblers in this assembly,' Piers said to her in an undertone as they mounted the stairs to the gentlemen's private quarters.

She tossed her hair. 'Oh, well, if you are talking about Hal, I shall change all that once we are wed.'

'Then I foresee stormy seas ahead for you,' he murmured. He left her at the door of Oxford's rooms, pleading he was tired and needed sleep. Hal suspected it was a lack of funds which prevented Piers joining the party, but did not comment.

After that rather awkward beginning, Ned's soirée was surprisingly successful. Hal could always be relied upon to add lustre to any group and Rachel showed a special talent in charming some of the older, and very sophisticated, members. Lords Rizborough and Saunders, sated with so much revelry in the last days, had drifted up to Ned's room intent on finding a comfortable place to sleep, but were kept enthusiastically awake by a lovely dark-eyed lady. A lady who also displayed an uncanny facility for the game of cards in hand.

By chance they played the game Hal had taught her during her convalescence. She had quickly learned the rules and was soon able to give him a challenge. In this more experienced company she still found it possible to hold her own. In the snow-hushed turret room Hal had given her no quarter, but had been as stern as any tutor she had had when a child, refusing to concede any lapse on her part. Tonight a more indulgent spirit prevailed, particularly from Will Saunders and John Rizborough, who both admired a pretty face.

Even so, when they broke for refreshment, Will said wryly, 'You are no beginner, lady.'

'Oh, but I am,' she protested. 'Although I dearly love to chance a coin. My grandmother...' She paused.

'Yes, your grandmother? Who was she?'

'Her name was Madrilene de Santos,' Rachel said hesitantly.

Saunders exclaimed delightedly, 'Now I understand! My father was a squire at court aeons since. He spoke often of a beautiful Spanish lady who had taken the English court by storm and was a rare hand with a horse or a hand of cards! He described her as being shiningly lovely; looking at you, I can well imagine he spoke true.' He tapped Rizborough on the shoulder. 'John, you have many years on me; d'you recall Madrilene de Santos?'

Lord Rizborough, an old roué of the kind which was a little out of style these days, clasped a hand over his heart. 'Madrilene de Santos? My dear fellow, she broke my heart three decades ago! Why do you remind me of such sadness now?'

'Because this is her descendant—my lady Rachel is her granddaughter.'

'Madrilene's granddaughter...' Rizborough said sentimentally. 'How strange and wonderful.' Those around the room caught the mood. The ladies present were inclined to think the situation very romantic. They liked Rachel as much as their grandmothers had hated Madrilene. Once again Rachel had sparked memories and a response over which she had no control.

## Chapter Ten

'Why did you mention your grandmother?' Hal asked Rachel later when they stood before the open window looking out at the frozen view. The snow had ceased falling at last and the sky, in which a bright moon surrounded by stars hung in pearly splendour, was clearly visible.

'I'm not sure, except that I felt her ghost tonight. She told me of so many evenings like this in her past—and how much she relished them.'

'As you did tonight.'

'Oh, indeed, and am ashamed of myself.'

'Why so? I staked you five gold pieces and you have trebled them. Should you ever need to do so you could make a fine living at the tables.'

She put out one finger and touched the silver tracery of stars on the glass. It was freezing cold and she was suddenly burning hot. She said, 'I am many leagues behind you in that skill, Hal. I watched your play—doesn't it disturb you to know you have so much knowledge of what is in another's mind?'

'At the card tables? No, for real life is much harder, you know.' The shadow she had learned to look for crossed his face. Instinctively she knew he was thinking of the demons he had half expressed at Maiden Court when Katherine had arranged the flowers she had gathered. She sought for something normal and friendly to say, but could only think of: 'But you always know what is in my mind, too. You knew I was sick so you came and made me well, you knew I was unhappy at court so you remedied that, too. Now you have re-made me, Hal.'

It was another strangely intimate moment between them and he did feel exactly that. He felt like the god who made a statue of a woman and then was so charmed by his creation he brought her to life.

Around them everyone was taking their leave. Will Saunders bent over Katherine's hand. 'I understand you are the Lady Rachel's cousin? My compliments for bringing her into our circle. Lady Madrilene must have been your relation, too—tell me, have you knowledge of what became of her?'

All evening Katherine had had to endure her cousin being made much of, complimented on her gown, her hair and her skill at the game. She herself had been virtually ignored—it was insulting! 'I have,' she answered Saunders. 'She died in penury—her gambling debts, you know—and her granddaughter was forced to beg a place at my grandfather's board.' The spiteful little sentence resounded in the air and Saunders drew back, dropping the hand he held. Katherine turned to Hal. 'I hope you are ready to escort me back to the hall now.'

'Indeed I will,' he said. He turned courteously to Rachel. 'Won't you come with us, Rachel?'

'Thank you,' she murmured, much embarrassed, 'but I believe I will just say my farewells and retire to bed now.'

'A rather elderly party, was it not?' Katherine said with a yawn as she and Hal walked down the passageway.

'I was interested in the elderly members,' he replied coolly.

She looked up at him in the flickering light of the wall sconces. It was not the first time lately he had used that tone and it occurred to her he was no longer speaking constantly of their future together. However much she was enjoying herself at Greenwich, Hal was by far the most attractive and possibly the most eligible of her suitors—she did not want to lose him. Hers was not a subtle personality, but occasionally she noticed that although she attracted men readily enough they were easily distracted. She laid a hand on his arm.

'Dear Hal, perhaps I was just not in the mood. Perhaps I would have liked to be alone with you this night—as much as is possible in this place where everyone seems to be looking.'

His face lightened. 'I am sorry if I spoke coldly

just then, sweetheart, it is just that…well, you are often a little distant with Rachel, who you must know looks to you for support.'

Katherine kept her eyes lowered on the stone flags they were walking over; she had no wish to put herself in the wrong again. 'Mmm…' she said thoughtfully. 'Of course I appreciate that but…you know, Hal, there has been a certain amount of talk about Rachel. And, in fact, you.' She sighed.

'Talk?' he asked arrogantly. 'Who dares to talk about me?' He stopped walking.

'The ladies in my apartments—Rachel being installed there at your persuasion, with all those fine new clothes.'

'Oh, the ladies in your apartments…' Hal said, amused. 'Ah, yes, I see.'

'It is not funny, Hal. I have a certain standing with those ladies and it is now undermined.'

'By Rachel? Don't be ridiculous, Katherine.'

'Oh, Hal…' The passage was draughty, the teasing air lifted and played with her fair hair. She sank back against one cold wall as if exhausted. Immediately he was all concern.

'What is wrong? You are surely not troubled about a little gossip? Why, at Greenwich or any of the royal houses gossip breeds like rats in the store cellars. If I were to take any of it seriously I would be forever defending myself.'

She raised her head and her blue tearful eyes met his. 'That is the point, can't you see? You understand these things and can manage accordingly. I, on the other hand, have been protected all my life from such scandal.' She plucked a minute lace-edged handkerchief from her sleeve and dabbed her eyes. 'Why, my grandfather would die of shame to know I had been subjected to any such humiliation.'

A totally irrelevant and disloyal thought crossed Hal's mind: Katherine had never known her father, by all accounts a man who regularly promoted the kind of scandal she spoke of now and who had compromised many a good lady in his life. Her grandfather, however, was in a different and more chivalrous mould.

'Well,' he said slowly, 'no doubt 'tis all a storm in a cup. The weather is poor here at present, the entertainments have lost some of their appeal—small wonder the gossipmongers will fix on something diverting to chew over. My advice to you is to ignore it all. And tell Rachel to do the same.'

'Rachel—' Katherine was aggravated that he should bring her cousin's name in. 'I am not concerned about Rachel! She is the cause of my dilemma.'

'Should you wish to send her away then?'

'Back to Abbey Hall?'

'Why, no…back to Maiden Court.' His mother would not welcome this, he knew, but he was reluctant that Rachel be dispatched home as if she had done something wrong.

'Oh, I see! She creates a stew here and then is rewarded by being taken in by your family.' Even Katherine's shallow mind had been able to grasp that Hal's family, the Latimars, were something quite unique in England.

'Katherine,' Hal said softly, 'surely we are not arguing, you and I?'

'I think we are. Really, Hal, I wonder if you know how strangely proprietory your attitude to Rachel is now. I—and others—cannot account for it.'

'Then they must mind their own damned business, must they not?' exploded Hal.

They were both now furious and each took a breath and looked down the passageway. As they did so, the root of their quarrel came gracefully towards them accompanied by Piers Roxburgh. Piers had found himself unable to sleep and had decided to join Oxford's party after all. When he got there the party was over and he had offered to take Rachel to the hall. The newcomers observed the faces of the others in the uneven light. Piers thought, Lord! it is an age since I saw Hal so angry—or so painfully alive. Rachel, her eyes on Katherine, thought, What can have offended her now?

Piers took the initiative and grinned at his friend. 'Rather a chilly place for a love tryst, Hal.' The wind outside had now reached howling proportions, it rattled the windows and tried to steal the flames from the candles protected by the horn shields. Hal inclined his head in acknowledgement but did not speak. His companion did.

'Ah, Piers, we did not see you in Oxford's apartments tonight.'

'I fear I had no silver to risk tonight, my lady.

Or indeed on any other.' Hal felt a spasm of irritation. He thought of the many occasions he had lent Piers money, paid off his debts, listened to his constant song of poverty. Katherine gave her musical laugh.

'I am sorry to hear that. May I console you by offering you my arm to take me down to the hall?' Playing with fire, Piers allowed her to suit her words to action and the two walked away.

Looking after them, Rachel frowned. She turned to Hal, murmuring, 'I'm sorry.'

'For what?' Hal ran a hand over his hair, disarranged by the draughts.

'For—?' She laughed suddenly. 'I hardly know exactly, except that I always seem to be present when Katherine is angry with you. I feel somewhat responsible for you both.'

'Why? You now have a life in your own right, and need take no account of others. Especially me.'

'I will always take account of you, Hal.' The words were out and she wished she could recall them. He looked so embarrassed. 'You are my cousin Katherine's intended, after all,' she continued lightly, and saw him relax. It must be the success of the evening which has made me so unguarded in my talk, she thought, but I must be careful in the future not to lose his friendship by speaking so intimately. We both know he could not cast me even a casual glance when he has Katherine.

If she could have read Hal's mind, she would

have been surprised by how wrong she was. His embarrassment was caused by the instant leap of pleasure his senses made at her words. In that moment he had been reminded of the strange premonition he had experienced all year of something wonderful coming to him. But that was explained by meeting and falling in love with Katherine, was it not? Confused by the way he felt and the way he knew he ought to feel, Hal took Rachel's hand and hurried her along the corridor. 'That is so, naturally, and in that capacity I should be allowed to ask you: How feel you for Oxford? He appears very taken with you...'

The hard weather continued for several weeks, then abruptly gave way to warm winds and rain. The sudden thaw made the roads a churning sea of mud and the traditional remove to Hampton was delayed for a week, then put off indefinitely as the Queen was laid low with a severe cold which spread, despite the efforts of her physicians, to her throat and thence to her lungs. Those of her subjects who had made the journey to fête her in the near year departed in some anxiety for their homes, the rest of the court carried on with their lives cautiously, for when the Queen bee was out of sorts the drones must tread cautiously.

'But really,' Katherine said in the ladies' apartments one bleak February day, 'I cannot see how it benefits her to have the rest of us deprived of any pleasure.' This when the news came that the eve-

ning's entertainments had been cancelled yet again.
For near a month now Greenwich had been hushed
and as silent as a palace could be, its gentlemen
speaking in whispers over the odd game of cards,
its ladies taking up their embroidery to pass the
hours.

'Her Majesty is ill,' Rachel said from her seat by
the window. She was working on a fine piece of
cloth, bright with silks, but almost invisible in the
poor grey light. 'That being so, we would not wish
to make merry, would we?'

Katherine sent her a venomous glance. Rachel,
so adaptable in any circumstances, positively
glowed in the gloomy room. She was not reliant on
gaiety to thrive and had spent a pleasant few weeks
exploring the libraries, no longer forbidden to her,
and had made a friend there. Walter Corlin, one of
the elderly librarians, was working there, catalogu-
ing the many valuable books collected over the
years of the Tudor princes. He and the pretty dark
lady had fallen into conversation and—hearing of
his task—she had offered to help. She wrote a good
clear hand and was interested in the volumes, many
of which were in French, practically a third language to her. She and Master Corlin had occupied
the hours very contentedly and the square of fine
linen she was labouring over now was to replace
the binding of a rare old book collected by Henry
Tudor during one of his visits to his cousin Francis,
King of France.

'Some of us are happy to leave Her Majesty's

affairs in the hands of the good Lord, Rachel,'
Katherine remarked. 'But naturally we have a different view to you and your backward-looking
friend.' There was a tense pause. The other girls
looked sideways at Rachel, who looked puzzled.

'I don't understand you, cousin,' she said.

'I am sure you do. The library with Master Corlin, the chapel with Master Corlin—need I say
more?'

'You have said quite enough,' Cecily Rampton
said hastily. She and Rachel had begun a tentative
friendship recently. 'Such things are best not spoken of at all.'

'Oh, well,' Katherine said, rising and shaking out
her skirts, 'if I am not allowed to say a word of
warning, then I must stay silent. And now I have
to attend Master Reeve for my Latin instruction, as
must you, Jane, and you, Isobel.' Before her illness
Elizabeth Tudor had been shocked to find that many
of her ladies were lamentably ignorant of the kind
of education she had had. She had therefore arranged that a tutor be available to remedy this and
kept a sharp eye upon who took advantage of the
facility. Katherine had been a poor student at Abbey
Hall, she was a poor student now, but she knew her
duty. The girls left the room and Cecily and Rachel
were alone. Rachel folded her embroidery with
careful hands, then looked up.

'I didn't understand what Katherine was saying,
can you explain?'

Cecily joined her at the window. 'I can, and 'tis

this: you know well how Her Majesty feels for the old religion…the Catholic religion?' Rachel nodded. 'Well, then; most times she is happy to let the thing alone but occasionally her notice is brought to it. As it was with the Throckmorton affair. And then she gets anxious about those of her subjects who might feel that Mary Stuart is some kind of rallying point for them in England and she fears revolution. 'Tis so at this time.'

'But England is Protestant,' Rachel protested. 'No one may practise any other faith.'

'Indeed. But they do. They do. You have heard of a lady in Kent who was pressed to death for her adherence to her beliefs?' Rachel shuddered, she had heard of it.

'But what has all this to do with me?'

'Master Corlin is Catholic and makes no pretence otherwise. It is rumoured he is one of other such thinkers who will shortly be arrested on suspicion of conspiring against the Queen. Katherine has… has…mentioned to various sources that you were raised in Popish ways and, what with your association with him—well, you can see how it is.'

Rachel turned her head to look out of the window. The rain was unrelenting, it fell dagger sharp on to the cobbles below. A chill which did not come from outside entered her bones. She said falteringly, 'I cannot speak for Master Corlin—we have never discussed the subject—but for myself I can. Such charges could have no possible substance for I have done nothing. Nothing. I don't understand why my cousin would raise the matter.'

'Nor do I, but she has and in the right quarters.' Cecily was afraid for her new friend. These affairs were incalculable—they lay dormant for years, then sprang up full of malignant life, touched off by an event such as the brave Kentish lady. Mary Fortescue had been mistress of a small rural estate, completely loyal to the English throne. Some of her outlying farmers had been found guilty of not attending chapel regularly. Lady Mary had spoken for them before the justices, pleading that the man and his three sons had been busy with planting, with hoeing, with harvest... Malicious rumour about her had sprung from nowhere and she had been in her turn questioned, arrested and brought before the tribunal, who had professed itself unsatisfied with her answers and sentenced her to death. Unaccountably, whilst dying in agony, she had suddenly re-embraced the faith of her youth, thereby confirming her tormentors' suspicions and raising a storm throughout all England. Her tragic story had been discussed at Greenwich at great length, following so soon after the Throckmorton business, and whispers of similar rebels crackled around the palace like a bracken fire. But Rachel had had no notion she was involved.

'What should I do?' she asked Cecily, who shrugged.

'What can you do, except stay quiet and wait for it all to blow over? Soon we will leave for Hampton—no doubt leaving all the bad humours and spite behind.' She sounded unconvinced even to her own ears, so added more cheerfully, 'It has been a long winter, dear Rachel, and so close confined some tend to exaggerate every little piece of gossip.'

But why gossip about me? Rachel wondered. She had truly believed she had made a place for herself here; now it appeared she was still as outcast as ever and in a more serious way than the endurance of a few slights. She put a brave face on it when the other girls came back, but her heart was heavy. The worst of it was knowing Katherine had deliberately set out to harm her. Why? She had longed so much for loving kin to cherish but had only met rebuffs from the closest, and now positive malice.

Another day she would have sought solace in the library or in the chapel—common sense told her both were forbidden to her now. Who could she turn to, talk to? Hal Latimar, of course! Her heart lifted at the thought and she changed her dress and went down to the hall with a light step. But he was nowhere to be seen and did not appear in his usual place at the supper table. As she was leaving the hall, she heard his name spoken and shamelessly listened. Her spirits sank again, for Hal had been dispatched to Hampton in the last hour. Her Majesty was on the mend and had sent him ahead of the royal party to ensure all would be ready. So there was no comfort there and Rachel went to her bed that night, feeling totally alone. As usual.

* * *

Hal had been at Hampton Palace for three weeks before the Queen and her entourage arrived. He had been happy, for spring had shown her timid green colours in the last few days and one of the owners of the palace had laid his gardens out to take full advantage of this season. Thomas Wolsey, Henry Tudor's chancellor and mentor, had devoted his life to his royal master, making only the mistake of trusting him. And loving him. The present Queen's father, ruthless man, had taken first his friend's grand house—called a court in those times by malicious enemies—then his reputation and finally his life, for Wolsey had died not so much from the illness which had officially killed him but of a broken heart that his King had forsaken him.

Hal thought of none of this as he roamed the luxuriant acres, admiring the wealth of new colour in the formal gardens, wandering under the bud-laden trees in the orchards, visiting his family home in nearby Kew. He was waiting, along with other nobles, to greet the royal barge as it approached the palace, swept up the broad waters of the Thames. Behind him the ancient bricks of Hampton were tinted rose red by the sun, on the ground at his feet an ocean of bluebells defied the March sky. Hal settled his short fur-trimmed coat about his shoulders, adjusted the wheel of his dazzling ruff and proceeded to the stone jetty.

Elizabeth was helped to land with ceremony. As she came to Hal he bowed very low and she stopped and held out a pale hand to be saluted.

'Good day, Latimar. I trust all is prepared for me?' So desperately insecure in her young years, when each time her father permitted her to visit a royal residence she had been accustomed to indifferent service, Elizabeth in her powerful years exercised a curious delight in delegating well-bred courtiers to ensure her welcome.

'Indeed it is, madam,' Hal said, 'and I am happy to see you so much recovered.' The weak sun struck living gold in his hair as he straightened and swept off his hat. She smiled again and proceeded. Hal raised a gleaming arm and shaded his eyes to look out over the water. There she was!

Katherine was in the fourth barge, very beautiful in blue velvet with a creamy lace ruff, the sunlight enhancing her blonde fairness. She lifted a hand when she saw him and then she was being assisted up the slippery steps. As she and Hal followed the others she laid the same white hand on his arm. 'I am so glad to see you, Hal!' Dazzled as usual by her smile, he forgot he was about to ask her where her cousin was and they parted in the great hall, the most impressive Katherine had ever seen. It was over one hundred feet in length with a carved and hammerbeam roof. The walls were hung with glowing Flemish tapestries which told the old Bible story of Abraham's trials; vivid silks depicted this ancient tale. At the east end of the hall a fan-vaulted window shed light on the dais where royalty feasted during meals which often lasted five hours and more. Katherine was impressed—Greenwich had been well enough, but here was grandeur on a large scale! 'I feel,' she said happily, 'that I am going to enjoy myself very much here. And now I must go and make myself beautiful for the evening meal.'

That first evening was very merry. Elizabeth was grateful for her return to health. She loved Hampton Palace for many reasons—it was far enough from the smoke and mists of the capital and the plagues which dwelt there. It offered a variety of sporting pursuits impossible at Greenwich—riding in the clean air of the park, tennis, tournaments of strength, archery in the green open spaces, and tranquil dallying on the wide river, with occasional pauses to eat and drink picnic fashion in the meadows adjoining. Add to all this the masques and playacting she delighted in and it was not surprising she was content and contentment bred a contagious joy among a society which took its cue from its first lady. Manners were also informal here and Hal knew he would be able to spend more time with Katherine, without censure. That night he sat with her for the evening meal and led her in to the dancing later. As they lined up for the first measure he asked after Rachel.

'Rachel? Er…you have not heard, then?'

'I have heard nothing—' He had to let go of her hand as she danced away with the gentleman who bowed before her. It was some time until they were face to face again and he could ask her what she meant. She sighed.

'Must we discuss this now? On the first evening we are together?'

'Just tell me.' The music was insistent, the lady on Katherine's right frowned as she was jostled.

'Lady, sir, please may we continue?'

Hal gripped Katherine's wrists and the man next to him said, half-laughing: 'Latimar, pray move along or continue your conversation out of the line.' Hal gave him a chilling glance and innocent Tom Loxley wondered if he was about to see the legendary, if seldom witnessed, Latimar temper. But Hal merely put a firm arm about Katherine and removed her to one of the stone alcoves surrounding the room. She looked up at him with ice in her hazel eyes.

'Really, Hal, I was enjoying the dance.'

'I asked you a question, sweetheart,' he said softly. 'What is there to hear about Rachel?'

Katherine sighed again. 'She was arrested—along with Master Corlin and others—a week ago.'

'Good God! And no one thought to inform me?'

'You? Why should they inform you? Naturally a messenger was dispatched to advise my grandfather.'

'What was she arrested for?'

'Oh…treason, or whatever name is attached to Catholic sympathisers plotting to overthrow the Queen.'

Hal could have laughed out loud if he had not been so furious—and astonished. 'But, Katherine—

I have seen no evidence of Rachel being sympathetic to the Catholic cause.'

Katherine took an enraged breath. 'I have been dragged away from my friends—must I now endure a philosophical discussion? I cannot tell you any details, Hal, for I don't have them. All I know is that Rachel was arrested, taken to the Tower and that my grandfather has been informed.'

'The Tower!' Hal glanced behind to see if the little glazed window behind him was open—he was suddenly so cold. Arrested and confined to her apartments while further enquiries were made was what he had imagined. 'Katherine,' he said patiently, 'your grandfather may well have been sent a message, but he is a sick man, as you know, and probably not able to act. Meanwhile, Rachel is in the Tower and—have you enquired as to her welfare?'

'I have not! How would it look for me to enquire for a…traitor?'

'I wonder how it looks that you have not enquired after your kinswoman!'

'Distant kinswoman! Well, thank you for that, Hal. Now, if you will not take me back to the dancing, I must go alone.' She turned and left him.

Hal started after the jewel-clad figure, then stopped. He had fallen out with Katherine over Rachel yet again… He must make it right with her as soon as possible; now, however, there was more pressing business. But how to go about it? As he pondered, Ned Oxford passed in front of him and Hal put a detaining hand on his arm.

'Oxford, may I speak with you?' He drew the other man into the alcove. 'Can you tell me aught of Rachel Monterey's case?'

Ned's ruddy colour heightened. 'Only what I heard at Greenwich. That she was arrested on a charge of treason and taken to the Tower. Really, I had no idea... As you know, I have been showing an interest in her...I was never more mortified to know—'

'Did anyone do...*anything*?' Hal cut into the blustering speech.

'My dear fellow, what? A charge like that is not made lightly.'

'Did the Queen sign the warrant of arrest, do you know?'

'I believe she did; such a serious matter, you know.' Ned gave Hal a half-shamefaced look, then added awkwardly, 'I advise you not to involve yourself, Latimar. I know she was your protégé—'

'She was not my protégé,' Hal said coldly. 'She is my friend.'

'Yes, well...'

Hal turned on his heel and left Oxford mumbling. He scanned the dancing chamber and saw that the Queen was not there. He asked a page and was told Her Majesty was watching a play in one of the antechambers. From the doorway Hal saw her, seated with the Earl of Leicester, closely flanked by a half dozen other nobles. He had no idea how to go about any of this. He was a very junior member of her court, probably the Queen would not even listen to him. Ned Oxford's advice to keep out of the matter was good advice—it was a brave man or woman who meddled with Elizabeth Tudor's obsession with stamping out the religion so closely associated with her Scottish cousin.

The play was ended now, the Queen was laughing and clapping her hands and preparing to rise. Without forming any plan in his mind, Hal stepped out in front of her as she came to the door.

## Chapter Eleven

He bowed. 'Madam, may I speak with you?' Elizabeth looked surprised by such an unorthodox approach, but she had had a very pleasant evening and was disposed to be accommodating.

'We have seen a splendid performance and now will refresh ourselves. Join us if you wish, Latimar.'

'In private, if I may,' Hal said quietly.

'Well, really…' Elizabeth turned to Leicester. 'The young men of our court grow impertinent, Robert!' Leicester, his eyes on Hal, did not reply.

Hal's eyes narrowed before the rebuke but he stood his ground. 'It is a family matter, madam, with which I would value your help.'

'Oh?' The Queen's interest was caught. 'Then let us go into the writing room…' Once there she sat down and indicated that Hal should sit, too. Robert Dudley went to look out at the spring rain falling gently outside.

Elizabeth moved in her chair. 'This damp

weather torments my bones… Tell me this family matter which weighs on your mind.'

'I have heard this night that a cousin of one of my family's closest friends has been arrested and removed to the Tower.'

The Queen frowned. 'The cousin of—?'

'The Lady Rachel Monterey, madam.'

'Oh, the Spanish girl.' Elizabeth's face hardened beneath the enamelled mask of paint. 'I know little of that affair.'

'You signed the arrest warrant,' Hal said. 'And the lady is English, not Spanish.'

'You are very free with your insolent contradictions, sir,' the Queen said. 'I am still awaiting discussion of the family matter you mentioned.'

'Lady Rachel is John Monterey's granddaughter's cousin. The Montereys have been friends of my family for generations.' There was that ridiculous French exercise statement again…

The Queen attempted to rise. 'Interesting though this scrambling about in the family trees of Latimar and Monterey might be, Latimar, I fear we wish to hear no more of it. Robert—if you please.'

Leicester turned from the window but made no move, prevented by a straight look from Hal.

Hal took a breath. 'Madam, I said this was a family matter and it is. I beg you in the name of my family who have all given you unswerving loyalty for so long to help me in this.' Elizabeth stared at him with unblinking eyes. 'I pray you to let Rachel Monterey out of the Tower.'

'Why should I do that?'

'Because I believe—and my family all have be-lieved—that you are against imprisoning the inno-cent.' Leicester smothered a sardonic chuckle. He had spent many of his young years so imprisoned. Elizabeth herself had suffered her share of similar treatment.

The Queen directed a chilly glance over one vel-vet shoulder, then said, 'Since you are so vehement in your pleas, Latimar, I will permit you to speak for her at her trial.' Again she prepared to rise, ham-pered by her aching bones and full skirts.

'That will not do, madam.' Hal was now treading where few angels would dare. 'The Lady Rachel has recently survived a serious illness. The weeks, months, in prison might kill her.'

'Do you imagine her incarcerated in some dank, rat-infested cell?' Elizabeth asked sarcastically.

It was, Hal realised suddenly, what he was imag-ining—it was what drove him to confront this dan-gerous woman in this stuffy room with the soft rain falling into the winter-starved earth outside. 'I don't know,' he replied. 'Do you?'

There was a long pause. Now he has gone too far, the foolish young cub, Leicester thought rue-fully. Elizabeth Tudor liked to control emotions and events in any interview she was conducting and this one was fast slipping from her grasp. Also, she prided herself on knowing what went on in every square inch of her kingdom. She had her own de-mons in this area—her own mother, Anne Boleyn, had been summarily arrested in the dark of night, as had Rachel Monterey, before being transported to the Tower to await her grisly end. This young man's father, Harry, had begged for her life, probably in the same impassioned way Hal was doing now. Elizabeth thought of this and it softened her. It showed in her eyes.

'If your gracious Majesty will sign her release into my custody,' Hal pressed on, 'I will swear on my life to bring her before any court you name in the future.'

Another silence, then the Queen said quietly, 'Robert, bring me writing materials, please.' Leicester raised his eyebrows, but produced parchment and pen and ink. Hal laid a writing block gently on her lap.

Elizabeth chewed the end of the quill—a habit retained from a scholarly childhood—then scratched a few lines, waved the paper to and fro to dry it and folded it decisively. She reached into her purse and extracted her seal. She gave paper and seal to Hal. 'You may finish the job, Latimar.' Hal carried both to a table and, under Leicester's ironic eyes, tilted one of the candles so the wax ran, then pressed the seal carefully into place.

'Perhaps I may now be helped up,' Elizabeth said. Hal bowed very low as the other two left the room and he heard the door thud behind them. He passed a hand over his hair. He had no idea how he had done it, but he had! Now he intended to make all haste to the next step.

\* \* \*

Rachel was afraid. She had been housed in the
Tower for eight days and eight nights now, and
could see no glimmer of hope. The room she had
been escorted to along dismal stone passages, after
a bitterly cold and windy river journey, was not
unduly bleak—its floors were covered, and its tiny
window and the narrow bed no worse than she was
used to. It contained adequate lighting in the form
of inferior candles and she had been allowed to
snatch various items of clothing before leaving
Greenwich. It was the atmosphere of the place
which destroyed her and the fact that she had been
forbidden to speak to anyone either at Greenwich
or upon arriving at the prison. Also, she had no
distraction—a book or a piece of sewing. A court
official had battered on the door of the ladies' apartments, requested her attention, shown her the warrant of arrest, then handed her over to two palace
guards. The ladies in her room, roused from sleep,
had fluttered about her hysterically. Only Cecily
had had the presence of mind to thrust a few es-
sentials into a trunk and help her to dress. 'Be
brave,' she had said, her face pinched and frightened in the hastily lighted lamplight. 'I will ensure
a message is taken to your grandfather Monterey.'

When Rachel was alone in the little room in the
Tower she had considered this remark and had it
been appropriate in her present circumstances might
have laughed. Rachel felt she knew her cousin's
grandfather well enough to know the words 'high
treason to the throne of England' would over-

shadow any inclination he might have to give her assistance—even supposing he was well enough to do so. She wished in those first few hours of her confinement that she had listened more carefully to the charges rattled out by the pale young man standing between the stalwart guards. She could only recall that one phrase, but there must have been others...

The next week had passed for her in a dreamlike haze. She remembered asking for books or needlework to pass the time and not receiving either. She remembered asking if the window could not be opened to let in the pale sunshine and a surly guard showing her the stout iron nails which prevented this. As if anyone could escape from this room, she had thought wryly, looking down a hundred feet or more at the cobblestones below.

Now it was the ninth night and she was sitting on the hard pallet of her bed, thinking that her meagre allowance of candles had run out and presumably she would be in darkness from now on. There was the sound of tramping footsteps outside, but this was usual. Some other poor soul being brought to share my fate, she thought bleakly. Sometimes in the dead of night, from another part of this terrible place, she had heard agonised screams and her blood had trembled. So far she had not been molested in any way, but perhaps tonight was her turn... She was therefore astonished to hear a key rattling in her door, then it was flung open and Hal

Latimar stood in the doorway. He ducked his head and came in, looking disparagingly about him.

'A poor place, Rachel,' he said.

'The only one on offer,' she replied faintly. Was this a vision? she wondered. She had heard that refusing to eat—as she had consistently turned away the horrible meals after a disgusting mouthful or two—produced such hallucinations. But…no! Hal Latimar was all too real, prowling around the narrow perimeters and scowling, removing his feathered cap to reveal his golden hair, casting malevolent looks at the armed guard looming in the doorway. 'Oh, Hal! Take me away from here!' She got up from the bed and flung her arms about him. And, yes, he was very warm flesh and blood.

When she had kissed him at Maiden Court in thanks for the cloak he had been surprised; this time it all seemed very natural to return her embrace and stroke her hair, which was hanging loose about her shoulders. He noted with displeasure that the weight she had gained since recovering from her sickness was lost again. He said, 'Collect your belongings, Rachel, and we will leave.'

'Where are we going?' she asked, throwing her things wildly into the little trunk. She never thought to ask him how he had obtained her release; it seemed so entirely natural that she was in trouble again and Hal had come to rescue her.

'To Maiden Court. The Queen has released you into my care, and what safer place than my home?'

'But…your mother has agreed to this?'

'She doesn't know yet,' he replied cheerfully, picking up the trunk and taking her hand.

'Has Her Majesty dropped the charges against me, Hal?' Rachel asked when they were in the barge, which was consuming the river miles to Kew. Dawn had just broken and the sun was rising over what would be another mild, if damp, day. Hal had indeed made all haste to extract Rachel from the Tower, but first his horse had thrown a shoe a few miles from Tower Hill, then the prison governor, long abed, had been intransigent about receiving his visitor and, finally roused, had taken what seemed an eternity to peruse the document he produced. Trying to hold his temper, Hal had eventually gained his consent to remove the prisoner. By then it was almost morning and he had been surprised to find Rachel sitting fully dressed on her bed. It took him some time to realise the extent of her disorientation, but at last he had by keeping fast hold of her hand while he engaged a barge and riverman, then persuaded her on to the boat.

'What exactly are the charges?' he asked, watching her huddled in his cloak in the bows, the wind whipping a bright colour into her pale cheeks.

'I have no idea,' she said sadly. 'I was so frightened I could not take in what was said when I was arrested, and as far as I know I have done nothing wrong.'

'How did it happen, then? Someone must have

spoken against you—even the fanatical tribunal must have some evidence, however contrived.'

'Oh, Katherine, I suppose…' she said vaguely.

'Katherine?'

Rachel realised what she had said and hastened to retrieve her damning words. 'Just rumour, Hal—and Katherine is so staunch a Protestant. I know I have frequently angered her in certain ways over the months.'

'What ways?' He had given Rachel his cloak and the wind was brisk and chill—he was chilled to the marrow.

Her hand moved in an instinctive gesture to her breast where her golden cross lay—the only jewellery left to her in the Tower. 'Well,' she said judicially, 'I was brought up in the old religion and its solace for me dies hard…but I swear to you I have not practised it since arriving in England…only sometimes I say the old prayers in my head and touch my cross for comfort.'

'And for this you are accused of treason? And by your own cousin?' It was a rhetorical question, for he knew well that such trivia was all that was needed to make a case against someone on political grounds and innocent comments were frequently used to condemn. It must have been just such a series of events for Katherine and Rachel, or so he told himself.

'Oh, don't ask me, Hal,' Rachel cried, pressing one hand to her aching head and shivering. The sun was bright but had no warmth and Hal's cloak was the typical courtier's wear—short and made of thin silk trimmed in wolverine fur.

'Where is the cloak I gave you for your trip to Greenwich?' he asked suddenly. 'Why did you not include it in the clothes you took to the Tower?'

'It was not available to be included,' she said in the same brisk tone he used, 'for Katherine took it away from me the very night I arrived.'

'I see.' Sooner or later Hal knew he would have to consider Katherine's part in all this, but he shied away from it. 'You can always find an excuse for those you love,' Piers Roxburgh had once remarked wryly, and Hal knew this was true. He wanted to find excuses for everything Katherine did or said, for he loved her. From the moment he had set eyes on her he had loved her. She was his dream and he must not lose sight of that dream.

'Sir, we are near to Kew,' the bargeman said. 'Where do you wish me to find land?'

Hal looked at the riverbank. Maiden Court was not a manor overlooking the Thames, but it did have access to its water along narrow streams. 'I will take the tiller,' he said, getting up and making his way to the stern of the barge. 'I know the way.'

Rachel remained in the bows, dipping her head beneath the willows which trailed their progress, feeling very tired and unreal, but still able to notice the striking blue of the iris, the delicate cups of the rose-tinted water lilies.

Bess Latimar had not yet risen when her visitors arrived. Her maid came gently to wake her—as all at Maiden Court were, she was anxious for her mistress these days. Bess made no wild display of grieving, she appeared to eat well and fill her days as always with the housewifely duties she loved, but she was simply fading away. She came to life when she came down this morning to find Hal in the hall. They embraced.

'Mmm…my tall son,' she said, standing back to look up at him. It was a moment before she noticed Rachel standing by. 'Good day, Rachel.' Rachel dropped her graceful curtsy, murmuring a greeting. Bess waited for refreshment to be brought, then looked enquiring.

'I have brought Rachel to stay for a little while, Mother,' Hal said.

'Oh?' Bess waited to hear more.

'There has been a little trouble for her at court,' Hal put it mildly.

'Trouble? What trouble?'

'I was arrested for high treason and put into the Tower,' Rachel said flatly.

There was a silence in which Hal could hear Margery's voice raised in the kitchen as she chided one of her maids and, through the open hall door, little Wat laughing with one of the other stable lads. The familiar sounds of home, he thought. I have missed them.

Bess sat down in her chair by the hearth. 'Were you involved, Hal?'

'Only in so far as I went to Her Majesty and

asked her to reconsider her actions as regards Rachel.'

'And how did she react to that?'

'She saw reason and signed another warrant for Rachel's release.'

'Are the charges dropped?'

'No, but I believe with Her Majesty more kindly disposed they will come to nothing.'

Maybe, thought Bess, but from experience she knew anyone who had taken part in such an affair would not be favoured in the future.

Rachel, who had not taken a seat, shivered and felt she would prefer the grim Tower to this difficult scene. She said, 'Hal, could I possibly…?' He was immediately at her side.

'Of course, you are tired and cold. Mother, may I ask someone to show Rachel to a room? She has been sorely treated in the last days and then subjected to a hasty river journey during which the wind was sharp to say the least.' He gave the order, removed Rachel's cloak and watched her taken up the stairs with anxious eyes.

Madrilene's granddaughter, thought Bess wryly, an honoured and cherished guest in the home her grandmother tried so hard to set asunder! The whole thing would have been laughable if it had not been so ironical.

'Why did you do it, Hal?' she asked when they were eating the breakfast hastily produced by Margery and he had told her the tale.

'It was a matter of family, Mother,' Hal said,

chasing the last of a delicious meal around his plate with a fresh-baked crust.

'Whose family? Not yours?'

'Rachel is a Monterey cousin,' he said, setting aside his plate and raising his beaker of ale.

'She is a distant relative of the Montereys,' Bess said bleakly. 'No blood of yours—and my rival's granddaughter. Can you imagine how I feel having her in my home, at your invitation? What is she to us? To the Latimars?'

Hal put down his beaker. 'She is more than… Madrilene's granddaughter, as I am more than Latimar's son, George's brother, and so on. She is a person in her own right.'

'Why do you care so much?'

Asked such a direct question, Hal searched his mind for an answer without finding one. Bess sighed.

'How long do you wish her to stay?'

Hal got up and put an arm around her thin shoulders. 'Thank you, Mother. I have to go back to Hampton and I will see how the land lies over Rachel and let you know.'

She put one hand over his. 'Be careful, Hal. Elizabeth—Her Majesty does not like interference, and in this area she is obsessive. It may have suited her to give you your way over Rachel for a time, but her policy over such…people is written in stone.'

'Rachel is not one of those "people", Mother, so has nothing to fear from any policy. Now I must go. Will you see me away?'

'Have I ever not?'

When he was mounted, she asked, 'What of Katherine? Does all go well with you both?'

He grinned. 'That is what I must hasten back to Hampton to find out.' He leaned down and touched her face, then her faded hair, chirruped to his horse and was gone. Looking after him, Bess was obscurely comforted that he had not sought out Rachel to bid her farewell.

Hal could not see Katherine the day he returned to Hampton Palace. She was in conference with her dressmaker, he was told. In the late evening he again impatiently sent a message to her apartments, but received the curt reply that she would see him on the morrow. Well, he thought, she is angry with me and who can blame her? However, he was not too disappointed, for what he really needed now was sleep. The last forty-eight hours had drained him of energy and he wanted to be fresh and confident to explain away his words to her, and his actions. Although the gentlemen's quarters were crowded and lacking in privacy, he was one of those fortunate people who could sleep in any situation and, rolled in a blanket, did so peacefully throughout the entire noisy night.

Rising with the sun the following day, he washed and dressed and made his way down to the kitchens. The overworked servants there found time to give him a reasonable meal, after which he strolled

out into the grounds. At length he found himself on
the archery lawns and sat down to watch the squires
trying their skill. Seeing him, they invited him to
join them and, so engrossed was he in the game, he
did not hear the breakfast bells. Regretfully, he realised that now he would have to wait some more
hours before speaking with Katherine. But during
the mid-morning, the squires looked towards the
palace entrance as a collection of courtiers came
towards them. One of the ladies was Katherine.

Hal smiled and raised a hand, gestured her to the
seat he had recently had. She ignored him, turning
to her companion with an animated expression.
Very well, he thought, still angry... He took the
seat himself to watch events and saw that his love
was as poor at this sport as at all others. During a
break he again got her attention and she came
across the grass to stand before him. He sprang up.

'Katherine! I must speak with you. Please sit
with me.'

'I might as well,' she said sulkily. 'It looks very
simple, this game, but I have not fared well.'

'There is a secret to it,' he offered. 'One must
consider the wind blowing, the damp which may
affect the bowstring—'

'Well,' she said, arranging her skirts on the
bench, 'whatever the secret, I cannot do it.' She fell
silent and raised a hand to touch her hair. Hal
turned sideways on the bench to look at her—she
seemed very ill at ease, an unusual state for the
confident Katherine. Turning her rings one by one,

she said slowly, 'You said you wished to talk to me?'

'I do. To apologise for my manner and tone the other evening, I know 'twas unforgivable, but I ask you to forgive me. I was in such haste to do something for Rachel—I secured her release, after some difficulty.'

'Oh, Rachel…yes, we all heard of the daring rescue. It was quite the topic of conversation yesterday, until something else took its place.'

Her voice was so neutral, yet there was an undercurrent of something else.

'So you do forgive me?'

'Forgive you? Oh, yes, but…I was wanting to tell you something, Hal.' Again she nervously patted her already immaculate hair. 'The other startling news was about Piers.'

'Piers? I have not seen him since I left Greenwich.' Hal felt slightly deflated. He had dreaded and longed for this meeting with Katherine; longed to see her and dreaded that he might with his hasty words have ruined his chances. Now she scarcely listened to his apology, but prattled about Piers. 'What has he to do with what we are speaking of? With us?'

'Oh, everything! But I hardly know how to start—'

'At the beginning is always a good place,' he said, distracted for the moment as another gentleman joined the archers. It was Piers. 'And if Piers has everything to do with the proceedings, there he is. Shall I invite him to join us?' He half rose.

'No!'

Hal sat back down, arrested by her exclamation.

She recovered herself, smoothed her skirts again and began to speak. 'It is this way, Hal. Since coming to court, I have been aware of great differences between us, you and I.'

'Naturally. I have spent most of my life in the company of those you are just beginning to know. I am used to the manners at Greenwich and Hampton—the way in which those here conduct their lives. It is all strange to you and of course you have made mistakes.'

She gave him an aggravated look; she did not like to hear she had made mistakes. 'I am not speaking of that!' she said crossly.

'Then what?'

'I am trying to tell you about Piers. While you were gone his father sent for him. You will know about his father?'

'I know he has never acknowledged him,' Hal said, trying to see where all this was leading.

'Well…anyway, he sent for Piers when he was dying. Piers was too late, but when he got there he found he had inherited all. Can you imagine?'

'I can indeed.' Hal was thoughtful for a moment. As an illegitimate son Piers could inherit no title, but 'all' constituted considerable wealth and estate. 'But I still don't understand what this has to do with us.'

Again the nervous fiddling with her hair. 'You know, you have probably seen that Piers and I are...good friends, but it is only recently that I have seen how well suited we are.' She looked to see the effect of her words and saw that it was dire. Hal jumped up. 'Now, calm yourself—'

'Calm myself!'

Piers chose this unlucky moment to finish his bout. He handed his bow to another and came across the cropped grass towards them. 'Hal, I wanted to ask you—'

'I have questions for you, too, Roxburgh,' Hal cut in.

Piers, perplexed by his tone, said, 'I wanted to enquire for the Lady Rachel.'

'The Lady Rachel is well enough, but your enquiries are a little late.' Piers looked at Katherine, who suddenly found something very interesting in the trees opposite her.

'I was not at Greenwich at that time,' Piers said patiently, 'but on my way to Kent—'

'Ah, yes, to visit the father who had to be confronted by death before he could bear to receive you.'

Piers went white. 'What is the matter with you, man? I wish to assure you that I would have tried to help Rachel if I had been there. When I returned, you had already reclaimed her from the Tower.'

'And you made good use of my absence to betray our friendship!'

'God in glory, Hal! What are you talking about?'

'I believe you know, and the sight of you fills me with such disgust I shall remove myself before I forget I am a gentleman and my father's son.' Hal moved towards the path to the palace. Piers stepped out before him and Hal put out an arm and pushed him forcefully aside.

Piers staggered and all but fell. Recovering his balance, he looked at Hal aghast. 'I don't understand any of this, but I know an insult when directed at me. I will ask two friends to attend upon you, Latimar!'

Hal strode on. Over his shoulder he said, 'You have no friends save me, Roxburgh. But no doubt your newfound wealth might buy you a few.' He continued on.

Piers stared after him. The archery group, having been interested observers of the incident, left their game and hurried to him with curious questions. In the flurry Katherine made good her escape back to the palace.

## Chapter Twelve

Two gentlemen sought Hal out later that day and asked him to name a time and date when he would meet Roxburgh. Hal put them off, not because he was shy of the inevitable outcome of his clash with Piers, but because he wanted to do something first. He knew Piers's reputation and, whilst not ignoring his own considerable skill in any kind of combat, he knew the difference between a talented and well-trained warrior and a veteran. That evening, he requested an audience with the Queen and was granted it. He then asked for leave to go to Maiden Court.

'Is it that you wish to go home to visit the Spanish girl?' Elizabeth asked, proving that she did indeed know most of what went on in her kingdom, for Hal had told no one Rachel was with his mother.

'She is not Spanish,' he said wearily, 'but English. And, no, that is not the reason I ask permission to go.'

The Queen had granted this interview at the end

of the evening when she had retired from the hall and was ready for her bed. She wore an imposing royal purple chamber gown, a cap much beribboned and embellished with exquisite lace and her most forbidding expression.

Hal, invited to sit, had chosen a chair to the left of her writing table. Scholarly himself, in spite of other gifts, he noticed she had been reading in Latin and making intelligent notes of the volume. The scent from a great silver vase of lilac filled his nostrils. He said thoughtfully, 'Some hold 'tis unlucky to bring lilac into a dwelling place, madam.'

Elizabeth rose from her chair and came to the desk. She riffled some papers with a long finger, straightened her quills. 'Is it so? I had not heard that, but then luck—or good fortune, I prefer to call it—is very much in the hands of each of us. We make our own, I think.' Hal, who had risen when she did, smiled uncertainly. He had never been in the royal apartments before and was not quite sure how to act. A great black hound, its coat shining ebony in the candlelight, was stretched before the door—Bess Latimar never allowed any of the dogs up the stairs at Maiden Court, and certainly not in the bedchambers.

'Have I then your sanction, Your Majesty?' he asked.

'Mmm?' Elizabeth was studying her carefully written notes. 'Look you here, Latimar, you are accounted proficient in this language. See if you can tell me where I have gone wrong.'

Hal leaned over her shoulder. On one long fore-finger she wore a ruby, the size and colour of which he had never seen before; it absorbed much of the flickering light in the room into its ruby depths. He picked up the book and compared it with her writing. After a moment he said, 'The reference is Biblical, I think, madam.'

'Angels at the supper table?' She frowned up at him.

'No, the phrase "entertaining angels unaware" is a way of expressing that sometimes one is blessed with love without knowing it. It is nothing...' he smiled again, down into her eyes '...to do with inviting angels to the board to sample good roast beef.'

The Queen laughed and moved away. 'You have a way with you, Hal. So I cannot find it in my heart to refuse your leave. Go you to Maiden Court and—as you did for me when I was leaving Greenwich—ensure all is ready when next I visit.' She dismissed him.

Rachel had been dismayed when she discovered Hal had left without bidding her goodbye. She did not even know when he intended coming back. She came down from resting to find him gone and herself an unwelcome visitor. Lady Bess was not so cruel as to say this, but merely made it clear by not taking her meals with her guest. 'My lady is resting, my lady has been called away,' the servants told Rachel at the dinner and supper hour. Rachel was relieved, therefore, when Hal rode into the stable yard at noon two days later. She was coaxing Valiant to take his daily walk at the time and, sleeves rolled up to the elbow, skirts tied up away from the paddock mire, felt she was looking less than her best.

Hal dismounted lightly. 'Well, Rachel, how are you this fine day?'

'Well, thank you,' she said, looping a stray curl over one ear. 'And you?'

'Glad to be home,' he said, looking towards the house.

'Then you had best be into it,' she said briskly. 'Perhaps you can persuade your mother to come down into her own hall occasionally.'

He gave her an anxious glance. 'Is my mother not well?'

Rachel ran one hand over Valiant's trembling flank. 'How would I know? I have had no word with her since I arrived.'

Hal considered her, and the horse. Rachel, he thought, looked strong and vivid and healthy, the animal the reverse. 'How is Valiant?'

'No better, I believe. But no worse.' She led the great creature gently over the lush green ground. All her movements were gentle, Hal thought objectively, yet full of vigour. During his ride from Hampton to Kew he had found himself thinking of his last conversation with the Queen. The phrase he had translated for her was significant to him in some way he could not understand. His interpretation had not been the orthodox, yet he had chosen to describe it so. Why? Was there in it some relevance to his own life to prompt this? Not his relationship with Katherine, he thought, for that was over now. Had it ever truly begun? he wondered now. When she had conveyed to him that she had transferred her affections to Piers, what had he really felt? Nothing, was the answer to that question, at least as far as she was concerned. Piers was a different matter, for his friend of so many years should not have so trespassed. Hal raised his blue eyes to the sky now and wondered at himself. He had truly fallen in love with Katherine, yet had felt little more than a pang when she had forsaken him. Far more was the hurt Piers Roxburgh had inflicted. It was a mystery, he thought.

Rachel drew the rein over Valiant's bowed head and gave him a gentle slap to encourage him to walk a little on his own. He made for the shade of one of the old trees just inside the railings and stood patiently. Rachel sighed and began to turn down her sleeves. She glanced at Hal, who was again staring at the house. Was it her place to invite him to refreshment after his ride? He turned his head and said, 'It is a beautiful day.'

'Yes. It is my birthday,' she added suddenly. He smiled.

'Indeed? We must celebrate.'

'It has not been celebrated since I left Spain.' She thought involuntarily of a sheer white gown, embroidered with lemon yellow flowers, that she had worn to receive the warm congratulations and gifts from the *castillo* tenants who had come throughout the day to pay homage to their little *señorita*.

'Then it is time to begin again,' Hal said. He reached for her hand and tucked it under his arm. 'Let us start with a glass of wine.'

'I must first ask Wat to take Valiant into his stall,' she said, flushing at his touch.

'Let him enjoy the sunshine for a while. He will come to no harm under the old apple tree.'

When they were in the hall and Hal had asked for cakes and wine, she asked, 'Is all well at Hampton?'

Hal loosened his collar. He was more casually dressed than she had yet seen him, in shabby breeches and a white linen shirt over which he wore a soft leather jerkin. He was hatless and his fingers and ears were unadorned by their usual glitter. He had the impulse to tell her exactly how things were, and knew suddenly why he had come home. Instead, he reached into his jerkin and took a square of card out. 'A gift after all for your special day.' He put it into her hand and she studied it. It was a playing card. 'Turn it over—Nick Hilliard asked me to give it to you.' She turned it over and flushed brilliantly. It was her own image but not how she had ever seen herself. The features were hers, but the expression and sophisticated hairdressing and jewellery were not.

'It is...beautiful.'

'Yes, Nick has a shining talent.' Nicholas Hilliard was the only English-born painter recognised at this time. His work was of the highest quality and he had a penchant for painting miniatures on the backs of playing cards.

'But...' she frowned '...I wonder why he should paint me; I had no idea he had—I have never sat for him. Also, I have never looked like this in my life.'

'Artistic licence, perhaps—that is obviously how he sees you.' He took the picture from her and examined it, turned it over. 'The Queen of Hearts...'

'Why, Hal!' Bess was on the stairs. 'Two visits in a week!' She came to kiss him.

'You'll be tired of me, Mother.' He got up and put her into his chair. Rachel rose, too, and curtsyed, but Bess did not look at her.

'Never! What have you there, my dear?' She took the card, looked at it briefly, then at Rachel. 'Your likeness to your grandmother grows more striking each day,' she said coldly. She looked more carefully, then handed it, not to Hal, but to Rachel. 'It is Hilliard's work, is it not? You must keep it safely when you leave here—he is an artist already famous.'

When you leave here, Rachel thought desolately.

'Rachel cannot leave until the Tribunal is satisfied she has no case to answer,' Hal said coolly. 'She is in my custody.'

What has that to do with us? Bess Latimar's expression plainly said. But she rose without speaking and made the excuse she must be about her duties.

'Do I still have a case to answer?' Rachel asked fearfully when the kitchen door had closed.

'I think not—but one must be prepared and 'tis better you are safe here where I can be informed of any statement your accusers might make.' He made a dismissive gesture with his hand and went on, 'However, it is your birthday today, let us not think of anything unpleasant. What would you like to do?'

'Do?' She had no idea, no one asked her such a question these days.

'Whilst riding here, I noticed various spring affairs being assembled in the villages—would you like to attend some of those?'

'But…should you not spend the day with your mother…or your brother? When do you have to return to Hampton?'

'Her Majesty intends visiting Maiden Court soon—I am at liberty until then. We can call upon George at the lodge on our way to the villages.'

'Then I will change into riding clothes.'

Hal rose when she did and pushed open the door to the kitchens. Bess was not there, but he was greeted with pleasure by the staff. Smilingly he listened to their news and made appreciative comments about the food under preparation. He leaned over the cook, an old friend, as she sat in her chair directing operations. Margery was old and immensely fat and her interest in and loyalty to the Latimar family legendary. 'What is amiss with my mother, Margery? Why does she not eat in her hall these days?'

'She doesn't like the young lady guest.'

'Did she say so?'

Margery's face crinkled in a smile. 'No, she would never do that, but I know, and I know why.'

Hal straightened up. He patted her shoulder and went out. In the hall he paced about, thinking. Probably it had been a bad idea to bring Rachel here, but where else could he have taken her? He paused by the hearth where the sunlight, slanting down through the coloured panes of the high windows opposite, cast a vivid pattern of gold and violet on to his face and hair. These windows depicted the Latimar arms and scenes from the life of a family who had striven for peace throughout England's troubled history. Hal wondered how to find a peaceable solution to the problem on hand, how to protect Rachel without making his mother miserable.

Wheeling, he ran lightly up the stairs and tapped on the door of his mother's bedroom. She was inside, carefully lifting clothes out of a trunk and shaking them. A sharp scent Hal associated with his father rose from the velvet and silk and linen.

'Come in, my dear,' Bess said cheerfully. 'I am just airing some of your father's clothes. Most I have stored safely, but these were favourites with him.'

'A sad task on such a lovely day,' Hal said gently.

'Oh, I don't find it so.' She held up an old-fashioned doublet, grey slashed with silver. 'Look—he wore this the first time we danced together.' She hugged it to her breast. 'I was so impressed by all his costumes.'

'He was a dandy.' Hal smiled. 'I inherited that, I think.'

Carefully, Bess laid back the garments, sprinkled more lavendar sprigs, closed the lid of the trunk. 'Not only that, which is why you must be careful not to let other, more destructive, traits overcome the virtues you also share.' She got up and Hal followed her to the door, opened it for her, then pushed it softly shut again before she could pass through.

'What do you mean?'

She sighed and looked up at him. 'Oh, you know what I mean! Why did you bring that girl here? You know how I feel about her.'

'I know what you felt about her grandmother, but here is a completely different person. Come, be fair, this is not like you, Mother.'

She clasped her hands before her. 'It is! And your behaviour is exactly like your father's and George's and Anne's—all the Latimars, they cannot bear anyone to mistreat those they love!'

'Are you suggesting I love Rachel?' Hal stared at her.

'I don't know. Do you?' Bess shot back. Silence fell in the sun-filled room. She walked to the bed and sank onto it. 'Oh, I have seen it coming—seen history repeat itself. The way that girl walks and talks and—looks at you! Madrilene looked just like that over three decades ago, and I cannot bear to see it happening again.'

'I am simply trying to be kind to her,' Hal said helplessly. 'I am sorry for her.'

'Oh, yes, indeed! That is how it starts!' Bess was incoherent in her distress. 'Then it ends with her coming to your room at night, and…and…' That was how it had been nearly four decades ago— Madrilene do Santos had tried to seduce Harry Latimar. But Hal had never heard that story—he looked horrified.

'What are you saying? Why, Rachel would die of shame to know that anyone should hear—let alone say—such words of her! In fact, I will not hear them!' A second away from losing his temper with the person he adored, Hal wrenched open the door and slammed it violently behind him. Bess looked disconsolately at the stout oak door. Now she had committed the cardinal sin for all parents— she had made the unsuitable appear desirable by showing her opposition.

In the hall below Rachel heard the door slam and saw Hal running down the stairs, his blue eyes shining with rage, every muscle in his body taut with fury. She looked at him with wide eyes. 'What is wrong?'

'Wrong?' Hal took a deep controlling breath. 'Why, nothing—I see you are ready. Shall we go?'

'You have quarrelled with your mother,' she said bluntly. 'Over me?'

He passed a hand over his hair. 'Well, yes…at least, I'm not sure if it was over you. Or over me.' He gave her a rueful glance. 'Howsoever it was, it was unpleasant.'

'Perhaps we shouldn't go,' she said doubtfully.

'Nonsense! Your birthday must be celebrated.'

George was surprised to see his brother ride in with Rachel, but greeted them warmly. Judith, who was looking after two of her little grandchildren for the day, made Rachel very welcome. Hal told of their intention to visit the spring fairs. 'Naturally, we will avoid any excessive gaiety out of respect for Father, but I felt the day should be marked.'

'Yes, indeed,' Judith agree, removing a chubby hand from her string of pearls. 'And my father-in-law would have been the first to say enjoy the day! He showed a fondness for Rachel even after so short an acquaintance.'

Rachel flushed with pleasure. Her eyes, which had been troubled since leaving Maiden Court, shone a clear amber in the direct sun pouring into the bright parlour.

'I would ask you and George to join us, but suspect you have your hands full,' Hal said, shaking an admonishing finger at little Robert, who was determined to demolish the necklace. He rose and swung the child up on his shoulders. Robert crowed delightedly, Hal was a great favourite with all the family youngsters. Rachel sat back in her chair, watching him and enjoying the warm atmosphere, feeling she would be happy to stay forever. But soon Hal set down his great-nephew.

'Well, let us be off before the sun loses its power. It will be cooler later.'

It was much cooler later as they made their way home. It was a clear night and in the moonlight a frosting of white could be plainly seen on the hedgerows and fields. Rachel shivered in her thin cloak.

'You must ask Katherine for your property back,' Hal remarked as they rode abreast in the quiet lanes.

'Oh…I can scarcely do that. It was far too grand for me anyway. Also, I would hesitate to anger her in view of your association with her.'

'My—? Ah, well, that is over. Katherine and I are no longer contemplating marriage.'

Rachel pulled up her horse. 'What? Oh, but why?' Hal examined her face in the pale light. With a tug at his heart he realised that she had been a different person all afternoon, so gay and happy. Now the familiar look of insecurity and diffidence was back. 'Please say it had nothing to do with your championship of me, Hal; I know it annoyed her very much.'

'It was nothing to do with that,' he said dutifully, 'at least only indirectly. The fact is, while I was concerning myself with that business, Piers apparently made advances to Katherine and she has decided he is the one for her.'

'Oh, no! I cannot believe Piers would do that!' I

would have thought he had more sense, she thought inwardly. 'Have you spoken to him?'

'I have, and insulted him, so he has challenged me to a duel of honour.'

Her first reaction that it was a good thing Katherine had decided to release Hal from their tentative contract was swept aside by this statement. Hal and Piers! Lifelong friends, to meet on the field of honour! It must not happen. 'When?' she demanded.

'As soon as I agree on a date,' Hal returned casually.

'That is why you came home,' she said painfully. 'To speak with your family…'

Was it? He had said no word to his mother or brother on the subject. But he had to Rachel Monterey. His horse, disliking to stand idle in the wind and in such close proximity to another animal in a narrow space, lowered its head and pawed at the ground. Hal gripped the reins. 'Let us move on, Rachel, we can talk at home.'

She went with him to the stables, warm with the breath of those not lucky enough to have been out that day. Hal paused at each stall with a word and a caress for the animals. Rachel unsaddled and watered Belle, rubbed her down and led her into her stall for the night. She found Hal outside, leaning against the railings and looking at the sky. She joined him, saying, 'You often gaze at the sky, Hal. What do you look for?'

'Look for? I'm not sure. But don't all men like

to think there is a larger pattern than the one they struggle with?'

'In my experience,' she said ironically, 'most men like to think they exist in the largest pattern available and that they are critical to its existence.'

He laughed, turned and spread his arms along the rails. 'You are a cynic, Rachel.'

'A realist,' she corrected him.

'Maybe. But I like to think of larger worlds, or of a society with more vision.'

'So speaks a privileged gentleman, one who has never had to grapple at all for the basics of life— food, warmth, a future.'

'I know I have a privileged life, and a pleasant one.' He sighed.

'Yet would give it up for a very dubious principle,' she observed. 'Whatever possessed you to tangle with Piers?'

'He tangled with me,' he returned mildly. 'I really had no choice.'

'So could at least six men say if they could sit up in their shrouds,' she said with asperity. 'You must get out of it. After all, what is it about? Not Katherine—you seem quite resigned about her.'

'Perhaps that's because I have never yet finished anything worthwhile in my life so far. It comes as no great surprise to me I could not see a betrothal through to its conclusion.'

She frowned. 'That cannot be so. You saw your page and squireship years through in splendid fashion. George told me only today that you were the youngest in many years to be awarded your knight's spurs.'

'An easy task for me,' he said without conceit. 'Had I been an impoverished hunchback, 'twould have been a challenge.'

She laughed. Rachel so seldom did so that the transformation was startling; the contours of her face changed and her very hair seemed to vibrate. Looking into her shining eyes, Hal thought: I would like to be responsible for producing this effect every hour of every day for the rest of her life. The thought was so unsettling he stared at her.

Mistaking his expression, she said hastily, 'I am not laughing at what you said, for I understand it. And I am not trying to interfere in your business, but it seems such a waste.' She paused, then went on, 'This afternoon, when we had such a good time at the fairs? You made all those people so happy just by being there... Think how sorely you would be missed were you not to be there next spring.'

'I have never thought of myself as indispensable,' he remarked. 'Except, of course, to my immediate family.'

There was an odd pause. The wind had dropped, the stars appeared even more defined in the stillness. Hal's dogs, which had come out of the house at a gallop when he returned, and fussed about the stables until he was finished there, stood silently as if carved of stone, their tails drooping, their muzzles pointing at the sky.

'I am not your immediate family,' Rachel said.

'but you are indispensable to me.' Her voice sounded breathless, as if she had been running. Perhaps she had, mentally, to get to this place where she could say such unconsidered words. Were they unconsidered, or had they been in her heart for weeks now? Whatever the truth was, they both knew they had tentatively set their feet on a path away from the one they had been travelling since they met. Hal was prepared to put this knowledge down to her responding quite naturally to the interest he had shown in her, where no one lately had. Rachel, more instinctive, thought she knew better. The wild blood of her Spanish grandmother clamoured that she had always known.

Madrilene de Santos had come to English shores nearly forty years ago, set her eyes on Harry Latimar and known what Rachel acknowledged now. The difference between them was that Madrilene had not cared that Harry was committed elsewhere, but Rachel, accepting that Hal had in the first instance chosen elsewhere, had not attempted to further any play of her own. But now Hal was free by his own admission and—under the diamond-pricked sky—Rachel allowed herself to hope. Before he could answer the kitchen door across the yard opened and a butter-coloured slice of light illuminated the cobblestones. Margery's bulk filled the doorway.

'Master Hal? You out there? Your lady mother is asking for you.'

Hal looked towards the light, then took Rachel's

arm, saying lightly, 'I thank you for that, Rachel. We'd best go in now, it's late.' As they crossed the yard, he added, 'I would be grateful if you would speak no word to my mother, or anyone else, of what I told you concerning Piers and me.'

The moment shattered, she said curtly, 'Naturally I will not.' His asking that puts our relationship back on its rightful footing, she thought disconsolately.

Hal, not giving her a helping hand over the rough ground because he knew if he touched her the feeling which had been growing for some time might be ignited, allowed her to think that. What else could he do? All his life he had, within set boundaries, gone his own way, but, whilst it was acceptable for him to take a stand with his mother over helping Rachel Monterey in her role as family connection, it would be unforgivable if he fell in love with her.

# Chapter Thirteen

April, an unusually dry month that year, was drawing to a close when Elizabeth Tudor made good her promise to visit Maiden Court. Hal was to ride to Hampton to join her escort to Kew; after two weeks she would leave for a short tour to inspect her sea ports. As the Queen would not be returning to the palace before her journey, her personal retinue—and their luggage—would be larger than usual and Bess was concerned as to where the manpower and trunks would be accommodated. George offered to house her gentlemen and store her effects, but Maiden Court would have to find bed space for her ladies and their trunks. She and Margery held long conferences as to meals; the maids were at fever pitch to turn out the manor so it appear even more trim than usual. Rachel wanted to help in the enterprise, but had no wish to be snubbed.

'And I am actually quite efficient,' she said wistfully to Hal as he watched her groom Valiant in the grassy paddock the evening before leaving for Hampton Court.

'I am sure you are,' he said soothingly, 'but my lady mother likes everything her way. It is not personal, you know.'

'Isn't it?' Rachel turned with the curry brush in her hand. 'If you think that, you are less observant than usual. When in the last week has she taken a meal with us? When, if she wishes conversation with you, has she not sought you out when I am absent? She hates me, Hal, and I cannot live in her house knowing that.' She turned back to the animal, before the tears that filled her eyes could fall.

'It is not her house,' Hal remarked, affected by her distress. 'It is my brother's.'

'Oh, that…' Rachel dismissed the technicality. 'I really feel I should leave here.'

'And go where?' he asked practically. Word had come that John Monterey had succumbed to a fit and was in a deep coma. Katherine had sent word from Hampton that all but his personal rooms were to be closed and a skeleton staff only retained until further notice.

'I don't know…' She faltered.

'Also, you have your charge here,' Hal said gently, 'or would you carry Valiant on your back on your travels?'

She half smiled and ran a hand over Prince Valiant's velvet face. 'Ah, no, poor old fellow—he would have to stay here until—'

'Until,' Hal repeated relentlessly, 'he reached the

state Jack envisaged when he left you in charge of his old friend. Would you let both of them down?'

Now she allowed the threatened tears to spill out of her eyes and course down her cheeks. 'You are unfair,' she choked out. 'Perhaps I am the kind of person you once described—one unable to see the task through.'

'Not at all,' he stated calmly, resisting the impulse to take her in his arms. 'Come, Rachel, what are a few uncomfortable moments with my mother, compared to—?' She turned, trying to remove the tears with her gloved fingertips.

'Doing your duty,' he returned lightly.

'Oh…' She continued with her task a moment, then threw down the brush abruptly. 'And that is to wait here for an old horse to die, or for a few religious fanatics to decide to allow the axe to fall on my neck!'

'You look quite different when you're in a rage,' he remarked detachedly. 'Or when you are happy.'

She stripped off her gloves and threw them after the brush. 'There has been little of either emotion for me in the last years.'

'Feeling sorry for yourself again?' he asked teasingly. The desire to comfort her was now almost a physical pain. What was he doing? What was he feeling? He knew it was a matter he should not contemplate, but where Rachel Monterey was, was where he belonged.

In a real temper now, she whipped off the linen enveloping her head and shook out her hair. The crimson rays of the sun settling into the tinted horizon struck the blue sheen on its shining length. She faced him, her eyes dark in the gathering dusk. 'You are swift to tell me my duty: what, pray, is yours?'

He considered her a moment—the dust and chaff of the stable yard clung to her clothes, her skirts and stout shoes were beaded with the mire of the paddock—then said gently, 'Mine is quite clear to me. 'Tis to deny Piers his inclinations and to admit to myself the real reason for my lack of enthusiasm to meet him.'

'You have realised what it will mean to your family, and your larger family here on the estate?'

'No, darling, it is because I am aware of a greater challenge than dancing about, rapier in hand, in a field at dawn. That of making you understand that I love you, am in love with you and probably have been since the moment we met.'

She took a faltering breath. 'You are jesting, of course.'

'Jesting? Is it amusing, then?'

'No—no, it is not amusing, but—'

'But what? Really, Rachel, you are always quoting your grandmother. What would Madrilene have said to your girlish hesitation?' His tone was teasing still, but she was not deceived; this conversation was of crucial importance to him. Behind him the sun had finally disappeared, leaving a suffused light of rose and violet. She looked distractedly up at the navy sky where a skylark, late to his nest that evening, paused in flight as if in sympathy.

Hal stepped forward, took her in his arms, and kissed her. She smelled of the stables, the new-mown hay, the liniment she had been applying to Valiant's aching legs, the exotic scent she wore, and of…joy. Hal, who had kissed his first girl at the age of eleven and been an enthusiastic participant in the art ever since, experienced a variety of emotions: sensual delight in her response, tenderness for her inexperience and the desire to protect—something he had never before felt for any girl.

Rachel broke the embrace first, standing back with wide eyes. He said, 'Now do you believe me?'

Unable to think clearly, she looked over her shoulder at the house, the windows ablaze in the afterglow. At any one of them Bess Latimar could be looking out on a sight which would distress her immeasurably.

'Your mother…she would never permit…'

'Permit?' he echoed. 'I am not an unbreeched child, I may marry whom I choose.'

'M-marry?'

'Certainly.' Darkness was falling swiftly now, the sunlight no more than a streak of fire in the west. 'Did you think otherwise? Or perhaps I presume too much. Perhaps you don't care to cast in your lot with me?'

She pressed her hands together. Before she could answer—if, indeed, she could think of anything coherent to say—from the house came the faint peal of the supper bell. Grooms and workmen were crisscrossing the yard as they hastened their duties to get to their own meal. They had not seen the embrace but glanced curiously at the two in the paddock. She said breathlessly, 'You must go in, Hal, 'tis time for supper.' She was trembling, her one desire to get away from the proximity of his dangerous charm to think. If their kiss had proved something to him, so it had to her.

Hal hesitated, reluctant to leave her. Last week he had been engaged to marry with her cousin, now he veered around and asked her for the honour. Perhaps she was thinking of that, and doubting—

'Go on, Hal,' she said with her rare smile. 'I will not run away; after all, where could I go?'

Hal found his mother in the parlour, sitting by the hearth with her feet up on an embroidered stool. She gave him a smile of welcome and indicated the wine jug. When he had poured his glass, she said, 'Supper will be on directly. Well, you are off tomorrow to bring Elizabeth for her visit.'

He sighed. 'Yes…I think perhaps you could have done without the resulting havoc.'

'Ah, no,' she said reprovingly, 'it is a pleasure, as always, to welcome Her Majesty. Your father was very fond of her in his way. Also—' Bess assumed a maternal expression '—it is a good thing for you. To have the patronage of one's monarch is flattering to a young man making his way.'

'Hmm.' Hal turned his glass in his hands, stared

out of the window, went to examine the climbing rose showing its buds early above the sill of the open window.

'Do sit down, darling, and stop pacing about. By the way, I have not asked how the affair with Katherine is progressing.'

'To tell you the truth, Mother, that is all over. We have decided, mutually, we are not suited.'

Bess was taken aback. She had not particularly liked the arrangement, but had been resigned to it. 'But surely...this is a change of ideas? I hardly know what to say.'

Hal dropped into the chair opposite—his father's chair. 'Then say nothing, darling. For I know my own business best.'

'But do you? Forgive me for saying—how many times have you begun something, then abandoned it? Shown preference for one girl or another, and changed your mind in all too short a time?' It was a criticism long in the voicing, and Hal could have wished Bess had not made it at this particular time.

He gave her the straight, blue Latimar look. 'I assure you, once again, I know what I am doing,' he said deliberately.

Bess sat more upright in her chair. 'But coming directly on top of her grandfather's turn for the worse—it will not look well for you to abandon her. Poor girl, she went to court betrothed and now is discarded.'

'Not so. She discarded me for she had another gallant waiting in the wings: Piers Roxburgh.'

'Piers?' Bess was astonished. 'Surely not? Fond as we all are of Piers, he is scarcely eligible enough.'

'Rich enough, you mean?' Hal put in. 'Well, Mother, you are out of touch with court news. Piers has recently come into a fortune—his father finally claimed him before shaking off this mortal coil and leaving his son heir to all.'

'But—surely Katherine did not, did not—'

'I am afraid she did.' Hal tossed off his wine and poured another. 'This time it was not I who proved fickle.'

Bess's blue eyes clouded. 'Oh, my poor boy. You must be terribly upset.'

'I am surviving.'

'You have not quarrelled with Piers?' she asked anxiously.

Hal hesitated. 'Nothing that cannot be resolved,' he said evasively. Between gentlemen, he could have added, but knew that would put his mother on the scent. He rose. 'Let me give you my arm to the board, then we must get to bed. It will be a long day tomorrow—Her Majesty is no more inclined to keep country hours than ever she was.'

Bess got up. There was obviously more to this tale than she was hearing, but Hal had no intention of telling her and she could not press him. He had grown up in some particular way lately, she thought, puzzled. From being a precocious boy, he was now a man intent on keeping his own secrets.

Later Hal went to his own room, after taking

Bess to hers. He lay down on the bed, but did not sleep. He was waiting to hear Rachel go to her room. She had not come in for the evening meal and he had no intention of seeking her company again tonight, but he listened intently for her quick light step in the passage and lay quite still until he heard her door softly close. Then he linked his hands behind his head and stared up at the embroidered hangings of the bed; mythical images of rioting cupids, hardly inducive of sleep to a man who knew himself to be finally in love.

Hal brought the Queen to Maiden Court in the late afternoon of the following day. In her entourage was Katherine Monterey, which was expected by Hal, her family being close to the family Elizabeth was honouring. Also, amongst her gentlemen, was Piers Roxburgh, Her Majesty as eager as ever to keep the riches of England under her eye. Both rode at the end of the column, however, whilst Hal accompanied his sovereign at the head. Outside the manor, he lifted her down and she looked around with a satisfied air.

'Ah, my Maiden Court…nothing changes here, I am happy to see.'

Bess came hurrying out and the two women embraced. As she took the Queen into the hall there was confusion in the yard, the chaos swiftly taken in hand by George Latimar and his wife Judith. George carried some of the gentlemen off to the lodge to stow their gear and take refreshment; Judith performed a similar service for the ladies, ushering them in, overseeing the taking of their luggage up to the bedrooms, offering cups of wine and honey cakes. Hal, seeing Katherine and Piers standing about uncertainly, went to them.

'Katherine, Piers—welcome to Maiden Court.' He kissed Katherine's hand and inclined his head to Piers.

Katherine was embarrassed, she had not wished to come here, but the Queen had commanded it, making it clear she was not included for the future tour which would have been an honour.

Piers had received the summons to escort Her Majesty to the place where he had for so many years been almost one of the family with mixed feelings. He, too, was embarrassed. To cover this, he said with forced aggression, 'Well, Latimar, you have not yet answered the pleas of my seconds to name a time and place. Perhaps you do not intend to do so?'

'Perhaps I don't,' Hal agreed equably. 'Shall we go in?'

In the hall Katherine went to take her place beside the Queen and her ladies. Hal and Piers stood just inside the door.

'What kind of answer is that?' Piers demanded.

'The kind of answer you would expect from a host to a guest, I suppose.'

With a spark of temper in his eyes to be reminded of his manners, Piers said, 'You insult me again!'

'But there is nothing new there, is there? We have been insulting each other for two decades now.' He looked unconcernedly into his friend's eyes. 'But let us leave this for now—my mother needs all our support at this time.' He moved away into the throng. Piers gulped his wine, perplexed. Hal was hard to provoke, but even he must know he could not put off a confrontation forever.

Rachel was up in her room at that moment, making up her mind to go down. Once again, Lady Bess had made it clear she wanted no help with the upheaval. The servants, each with their appointed task, had brushed her offers of assistance aside. Even George's wife, Lady Judith, who had been here all day ensuring all was ready for the royal visitors and her attendants, had given Rachel a kind smile, saying,

'There is nothing for you to do, Rachel, except make yourself beautiful and prepare to enjoy yourself.'

*I forget how!* Rachel could have informed her. Years of servitude had stripped away the feeling of excitement before a party of any kind. Once again she was part of a household with no part to play. As she washed and changed into one of her court gowns she thought of her passage with Hal the night before with dispassion.

'On the rebound' was a bleak expression, but the one which sprang to her mind. Another, more disagreeable one, also came to her: 'Another woman's leavings.' The other woman was her cousin Katherine. She had thrust Hal aside, so he had turned to her to salve his pride. A tap on the door interrupted these miserable thoughts. Hal stood in the passage-way.

'Are you ready to go down? You look very lovely.'

'I'm not sure I want to go down.'

'Don't be silly.' He took her hand in one of his and closed the door behind her with the other.

At the head of the stairs she said, hanging back, 'I shall just be out of place as usual.'

He turned her around to face him. 'What is this? I thought, last night in the paddock, we had reached an understanding. What has changed since then?'

She removed her hand from his and placed it flat against his chest. 'You don't love me, Hal. You are just sore-hearted about Katherine.'

'You didn't believe what I told you last night?'

'I didn't…disbelieve it. It is just that you are al-ways changing your mind. Tomorrow, maybe, 'twill be yet another different story.' He made no attempt to touch her again and her hand fell away. 'I am sorry if that sounds unfeeling.'

He laughed harshly. 'Unfeeling? Yes, it does rather. But I suppose it is no more than I deserve.' He had been totally honest with her the previous evening. He never remembered being so candid with a woman before. This was his reward.

Bess, hurrying up the stairs, said, 'Hal, my dear, you must come down. The Queen is waiting to be taken to the table.'

'I am just coming, Mother.' He looked at Rachel. 'Oh…Rachel, are you joining us?' Bess said vaguely.

The plain lack of invitation in her voice stiffened Rachel's spine. 'I had thought to, my lady,' she said. She and Hal descended the stairs with Bess between them.

The hall was aglow with candlelight and the dazzle of jewels. Elizabeth wore diamonds and pearls, her ladies rubies, emeralds, opals and sapphires, her gentlemen amethysts, lapiz lazuli, turquoise—Rachel could not identify all the gems of the universe which were on display tonight. She, of course, had no jewellery save her shining amber eyes and the translucent shimmer of her skin.

At the foot of the stairs they separated. Hal led the Queen to the head of the table, her senior gentleman took Bess on his arm. Another gentleman rose from the table and came towards Rachel; she saw it was Hal's brother George. He held out his hand.

'Rachel, we are supper companions, I believe.' Cursing the usual colour flushing into her face, she took her place beside him.

'How kind of you, sir,' she murmured. Surely Lady Bess, who always supervised the seating, had not suggested this?

'Hal arranged who sat where tonight,' George said, as if reading her mind. 'Being more *au fait* with court circles and our guests being mainly courtiers tonight.' He helped her to various dishes.

'We sat together when you first came to Maiden Court,' he observed when a few moments had passed. 'You have changed a great deal since then.'

'I have?' she asked, surprised.

'Yes, indeed.' George smiled. 'Are you not aware of it?'

'You mean—inside myself?' she asked hesitantly. She had heard that George Latimar had 'the sight'.

He laughed. 'No, I mean on the outside. Don't you have a glass in your chamber?'

'Well, of course, clothes do make a difference.'

'I am not speaking of clothes, but of manner. Confidence of manner, I suppose I mean. Do you not feel that yourself?'

I suppose I do, she thought, startled. All the years of feeling second-best had left their mark on her soul, but apparently she was learning to compensate outwardly, where it showed. Impulsively she reached into her belt and took out the little portrait Hilliard had made of her. She showed it to George.

'Mmm, yes, a very excellent portrayal.'

'When it was first given to me, I could not see it so, but now I feel I could be like it. The way Nick saw me.'

George smiled. 'That is a start, then.' He poured wine for her.

'Is it true,' she asked suddenly, 'that you have the sight? I mean, can you really…see that which others can't?'

George tried his own wine. He looked up the

table and saw that the Queen was much entertained by something his brother was saying. If Rachel was showing signs of a rebirth of confidence, Hal showed the reverse. It would not be obvious to those who did not know him well, and it would do him no harm to let what was inside come out for once, George thought. Elizabeth laughed again and George was glad, for she had a very personal problem weighing on her mind at the moment.

Robert Dudley, the Earl of Leicester, was to go with English troops to Holland shortly. He was a trifle elderly for such an exercise and Elizabeth was worried about him, although reluctant to question his going. For himself, George had bid farewell to his old friend with resignation. He had, with his peculiar facility, seen death for Robert in the near future, in the same way he saw vivid happy life for the vibrant girl beside him this candlelit night. He could speak of neither vision, because this was the code he lived by. He said slowly, 'Who told you that? Hal?'

She was putting away her picture. 'No, it was Piers.'

'Ah, yes, the recent inheritor of vast wealth and…our Lady Katherine. Hal doesn't seem particularly put out by events.'

Rachel was silent. No, Hal showed nothing tonight. The courtier's mask was firmly in place, he was as charming and urbane as ever, flattering the Queen and being the perfect son of the manor.

\* \* \*

Much later the company rose from the table and, it being a fine night, drifted out into the gardens, drinks in hand. Rachel was in the hall, replacing candle stubs, when Piers came in search of her.

'Rachel, here you are! Everyone has repaired to the summer house, or the Queen's Rest as it is quaintly known.'

Rachel started. She jammed the last tall church-white candle in place. 'Oh…do they wish for more wine? Shall I—?'

'No, no. They have plenty. I came to ask you to join us.'

Rachel set down the silver snuffer. She came across the polished boards and looked up into his face. 'I have not yet congratulated you on your good fortune.'

He smiled down at her. 'Thank you. A little luck has been long in coming, but much appreciated.'

'What a shame you must spoil it by falling out with your best friend. Your friend from all the years you were less fortunate.'

His face sobered. 'It was not of my choosing,' he said stiffly. 'I really cannot account for Hal's remarks to me those days ago.'

'Can you not? Set your acute mind to the facts— I find myself in difficult—nay, desperate!—straits. Hal hurries to my aid, and while he is so engaged you take advantage of the situation and lure his love away.'

'What—?' Truly astounded, Piers stared at her. 'I have lured his love away? Katherine, mean you?

Why, 'twas not that way at all. Katherine came to me and told me he no longer cared for her, had actually cast her off! Knowing Hal, I was not surprised... Anyway, that is the extent of our relationship so far, Katherine's and mine.' As she turned away he grasped her arm, turning her about. 'What! You don't believe me?'

'But you challenged him!' she said passionately.

'On the rough words he used to me—for no other reason!'

'It is a misunderstanding, then,' she said doubtfully.

'On his part, not on mine,' Piers countered. 'However, he is tardy taking up my challenge, and that suits me well, my dear.'

In the silence which followed the sounds of the old house could be clearly heard. Bess had gathered all the blooms her garden could offer to deck the hall and, knowing of Elizabeth's fear of cold, had lit a vast fire in the house, which produced a great heat. In self-defence the flowers were dropping their petals now. They fell in whispers, which gentle sound vied with the old floorboards settling back into place with protesting creaks after so many feet had trod upon them.

'I seem,' said Rachel, 'to have got the wrong end of the stick, and am guilty of meddling in matters which do not concern me.'

'Do not concern you?' Piers asked softly. 'I think you are very much concerned—with Katherine, with myself and with...Hal.'

Rachel had chosen a snuff-brown dress of heavy
silk to wear this night. Its subdued colour, relieved
by a caramel-coloured ruff at the neck, allowed her
face to rise creamy pale and flower-like in its perfection from a dark mass, the only brightness supplied by her gleaming eyes. Those eyes flashed
now. Had Hal been talking her over with Piers, in
his usual casually irreverent way? 'I may be poor,
Piers, and of little account,' she said, 'but I will not
be made mock of, by you or by Hal.'

'There was no such intention,' Piers replied, distressed. 'It was just a chance remark, I assure you.
What is this about, Rachel?'

'It is about me. For once. Me.'

They were standing some yards from the darkened hall door. It opened and closed now and Hal
stood in the starlight piercing the high windows. He
had come up from the Queen's Rest, curious to
know where Piers was. Now he stood completely
still, watching and listening, unobserved by the two
in the circle of light by the table.

'Well, well...' Piers said soothingly. He had
known Rachel for some time, but never seen her in
such a rage. Whatever he had said, it had upset her.
'I have offended you somehow, please tell me
why.' He put an arm around her.

'Oh, I can't! I am being foolish... It is just that
I...that Hal—'

Hal stepped forward. In one graceful movement
he swung off the light silk cloak he wore and hung
it on one of the pegs provided. Sweeping off his

gay cap, he put it on another and advanced towards them. 'Did I hear my name?' he enquired genially.

A very fine entrance, thought Piers admiringly. Hal had always had a talent for them.

Rachel turned away to hide her brimming eyes. She blinked determinedly, then turned back and asked calmly, 'Is it me you are seeking? Am I needed?'

Hal thought about it, then said, 'Yes. To both questions.' She blushed, her heart thumping wildly, for she heard the unmistakable meaning in his voice.

Once more the door opened and Katherine came in. Hal thought of his first impression of her—that she had brought all the sunlight into the room with her. This time it was moonlight, but just as dazzling. This time, however, it had no effect on him.

Katherine said, 'Oh, is there a private party in here? Rather impolite to Her Majesty, I would have thought.'

'It is indeed,' Rachel said. 'Let us go back to her, shall we?' Before the amused and surprised eyes of the two men she crossed the floor, seized a cloak and her cousin's arm in what appeared to be one movement, opened the door, pushed Katherine through and slammed it behind them. Piers and Hal were left alone.

# Chapter Fourteen

'Well...' Piers let out his breath. 'What do you make of that? What will happen now?'

Hal lifted a wine jug and set it down on the table between two chairs. 'Whatever, I will bet she comes out first.' He sat. Piers took the seat next to him.

'I'll not take that bet, my friend, if the "she" in your challenge be Rachel.' They both chuckled. Hal poured wine.

'So?' Piers continued. 'What of the challenge between us?'

Hal drank. 'It is abandoned. If you agree. We were both astray in our reasoning.'

'So Rachel told me earlier.' Piers tipped back the oak chair, regarding his friend seriously. 'How could you believe that of me?'

'I was mad,' Hal said cheerfully. He put an arm back and righted the chair with a thump. 'It weakens the legs, my mother always says.'

'Don't change the subject,' Piers said sternly. 'You were outrageous that day and fully deserved what I intended giving you. However, what of Katherine now?'

'She's all yours,' Hal said laconically.

Piers raised his eyebrows. 'This is so sudden, as they say.' Hal turned to him.

'Is it? She gave me to understand that she and you—that you and she—'

'She neglected to tell me before she spoke to you,' Piers replied wryly, the whole matter suddenly clear to him. 'But, you know, Hal, a few short weeks ago you were willing to die for her smile.' He could not resist the jibe.

'I know,' Hal admitted. 'But now I know what is actually worth dying for.'

'Rachel?' With an intuition born of twenty years' experience, Piers had arrived at the right answer. He knew his best friend very well.

'Yes. She is the one, Piers. I see no other now.'

'I see,' Piers said enviously. 'And how thinks she to this?'

Hal tapped one long finger on the rim of his wineglass. 'She does not believe my good intentions.'

'And who can blame her? You have been changeable, to say the least, in the past. Still… Katherine and me…? I do not mislike the idea, she is a beautiful girl, after all, and if she has a fancy for me—'

'It may be she has a fancy for any man who roves into her vision—providing he is well-heeled enough,' Hal said quietly.

'Frank talk,' Piers said, 'but received in the spirit it is no doubt offered. I like a challenge, as you know.'

'You might find yourself issuing—and receiving—any number of those if you pursue this,' Hal said gravely.

Piers shrugged. 'We'll see. But enough of that, tell me about you and Rachel.'

Hal cast Katherine and her affairs out into the dark beyond the hall. 'What can I say. Except to say again she is the one I want. And intend getting.'

'It will not be easy,' Piers said judicially.

'Why? I think if you want something enough, it happens.'

Piers glanced at his friend's handsome profile. Yes, that had been true in the past for golden Hal, but times had changed; his father, who had always paid the debts, smoothed the path for his younger son, maintained the ties with whichever Tudor monarch was in power to consolidate Hal's place at the royal court, was dead. His older brother, George, was his own man, and had a large family of his own to consider. And yet, Piers also thought, Hal had shown unexpected fortitude in the last months—standing by Rachel Monterey in her life-threatening illness, saving her from an equally desperate brush with the law. The Latimar family might be breaking up in the natural course of things, but he would not underestimate his friend's ability to breast the turning tide and float into a safe beach. Hadn't the Latimars always done that? The one rock he might wreck his hopes on was very personal—his mother, Bess Latimar. He sighed.

'You will have storms ahead,' he observed. 'Your mother will not like this new course you are bound to.'

'No. But my father liked Rachel greatly. Before he…died, he made that very clear.'

'Hmm. But he was an exceptionally worldly man.'

Rachel had pushed her cousin out into the night air on impulse. Halfway along the path to the Queen's Rest, Katherine turned and said, 'Really, Rachel, you are quite impertinent tonight! I believe Hal's attention to you has quite turned your head.'

Very true, thought Rachel. My head is in a complete whirl. She stood quite still for a moment, then said, 'He has said he wishes to marry me.'

Katherine turned up the collar of her fur cloak. 'Oh, indeed, I am sure he has. But remember back to our time at Greenwich before…well…before you left. How many of the ladies we knew had he said similar to?'

'I recall no one claiming that Latimar had ever spoken those words to her,' Rachel said stoutly.

'Apart from myself, you mean?' Katherine asked sweetly. She put a slim white hand on the other girl's arm. 'Dear Rachel, we have not been good friends in the past, I know, but I do have regard for you and you may wish to learn from my mistakes.' Bright moonlight shone down on this blatant lie, then she went on. 'Hal Latimar is, by all accounts, very fervent at the beginning of the chase, but swiftly cools.' Katherine raised innocent eyes to the heavens. 'I was taken in by this. I believed him, to my sorrow. But fortunately I have been saved from embarrassment by another gentleman…' She allowed a sentimental sigh to escape her. 'But, I do think,' she continued, unblushing, 'it will all be for the best.'

Does she really believe what she is saying? wondered Rachel incredulously. From what Piers had said earlier, he had no notion that Katherine thought herself now betrothed to him. She said nothing and after a moment Katherine shivered again and said, 'Well, let us continue to the Queen's Rest, shall we?'

'Before we do—' Rachel caught her cousin's arm '—I think Hal is sincere in his intentions towards me.' How prim that sounded.

Katherine gave her a look that showed she thought the same. She patted the hand resting on her velvet arm.

'I understand, Rachel. You have been taken in as much as I was. But, you know, now you are out in the world you must be more clever about the people you meet. Particularly the men.' Having delivered this homily, she swept away and Rachel had no choice but to follow her.

The following day, another sunny and lovely day, Bess woke early and was in her kitchens arranging the day's food. Margery was inclined to be hysterical and out of sorts, but Bess calmed her and all went ahead. Bess had arranged, after breakfast, a morning to please the Queen. Her Majesty would ride out into the countryside on a mettlesome horse, inspect the outlying farms, then be entertained by a number of rustic plays and dances. Bess had been organising this for some weeks and was confident that Elizabeth would enjoy meeting 'her people' as she always did. After that her escort—the gentlemen she had brought from court and her ladies— would be accommodated by George at the lodge. The Queen would be at Maiden Court for the midday meal.

The morning went well, Her Majesty was lavish in her interest and praise, but lunch was a subdued affair. Looking around her table, Bess was a little annoyed with the members of the gathering. Hal had been monosyllabic on the ride, and at the entertainments—the Queen had frequently drawn his attention to what was happening and been rebuffed with a shrug, or a muttered reply, although Bess had noticed he had a sharp eye to her well-being and safety. On returning to the manor, he had been distantly respectful, but little more. Now Katherine Monterey and Piers seemed to have caught the contagion and sat in silence during the many courses. It was altogether too bad, decided Lady Bess. Of Rachel—who had not been included in the forenoon expedition—she expected nothing and received it: the girl sat at table with flushed cheeks and angry dark eyes which she seldom raised from her plate. Time, definitely, thought Bess, that she go home. That home might be closed, her elderly relative dying, but arrangements must be made by her cousin. She would speak to Katherine that very day! Bess rose from the table and invited the Queen to sit in the parlour awhile.

'I do apologise for my son's and my other young guests' lack of animation today,' she said when the two women were comfortably seated, with a dish of strawberries and ground sugar conveniently to Elizabeth's hand.

Elizabeth popped a succulent red fruit, well tossed in the costly sugar, into her mouth, savoured it and said through the sweetness, 'Ah, the young...always so selfish. I was myself.'

'Never!' declared Bess. 'You always performed your duty, however arduous. As Harry and I always have.'

'A compliment indeed,' Elizabeth said drily.

'Not,' Bess added hastily, 'that entertaining Your Majesty could be described as arduous.'

'Dear Bess,' Elizabeth said, smiling, 'surely no explanation is needed between such old friends as you and I. No...the young people have their own concerns.' She took up another strawberry and looked at its perfection with delight, sniffing its fragrance and dropping it into the sugar. 'One of the compensations of being old in experience is to observe the machinations of others less well set. It is an amusement, if you like... For instance: the Lady

Katherine—a singularly cold girl, if you will forgive me saying—has thrown over your son in favour of young Roxburgh. She thinks, no doubt, that Lord Piers will be grateful for the honour and heap his new riches at her feet.' She chuckled. 'I know, from the experience I spoke of, that she will have to earn every coin— And I see that golden Hal Latimar has fallen in love at last, truly in love, I mean, with that prickly Spanish girl.'

'She is not Spanish,' Bess murmured, unconsciously echoing her son's oft-spoken words.

'Hmm…and she with him. A great love, we would have called it in our youth, Bess. A veritable force.'

Bess got up and went restlessly to the window. She might not like what the Queen had said, and be frustrated because she could not say so, but she could not deny the statement—she had too often been witness to Elizabeth's peculiar facility for seeing such things. Harry had had that facility, too, and he had said the same… She pushed open her window and touched one of the newly opened buds of the climbing rose which grew beneath it. On impulse she snapped it off and, turning, offered it to the Queen. Elizabeth put out a graceful arm and took the striped flower, twirling it between one white finger and thumb.

'Very beautiful,' she said thoughtfully. 'The Tudor rose! My grandfather took it as his emblem and all over England its likeness is carved in wood and stone to honour our dynasty. But the real thing is

ten times more lovely than those soul-less copies.
But less enduring, like the love I just spoke of.
Even a lifetime of love is—poof!' She snapped her
long fingers. 'No more than a star's wink. Over so
quickly, it would seem sensible to take advantage
of it while it lasts.' She glanced up at her hostess.
'My dear,' she said softly, 'you must make the best
of it.'

Bess said painfully, 'Hal was my Harry's favourite son. Madrilene was my mortal enemy. Now
her granddaughter comes and takes our boy. The
Spanish girl...' she added scornfully. 'Your own
words, madam.'

'Ah, but,' Elizabeth said, 'Madrilene's Spanish
blood is tempered in the Lady Rachel with our good
English blood. Her father was a stalwart soldier.
However...' she got up with difficulty '...I am tired
now and must rest a little before the evening.'

Bess accompanied her to her room and saw her
safely under the covers, her ladies hovering in attendance. Then she went slowly back to the hall.
Piers and Hal, Katherine and Rachel were still
seated at the table. The two young men rose courteously as she approached and bowed. The two girls
remained seated and looked up at her.

Bess compressed her lips. 'I am not pleased with
any of you,' she said gravely. 'I will not have Her
Majesty treated to such a show of ill manners beneath my roof.'

Piers said awkwardly, 'I apologise most sin-

cerely, my lady, on my behalf and that of Katherine.'

'Pray don't apologise for me,' Katherine said
sulkily.

'And why not, miss?' Bess rounded on her. 'You
need such apology to be made! Let me tell you, if
you have not been told before, a lady of breeding
rises to the occasion on hand no matter what her
personal trials!'

Rachel got up.

'And where do you go, lady?' Bess demanded.
'My observation was intended for you also.'

Rachel flushed brilliantly. 'I was in no way involved in this occasion, my lady. I was not included
in the riding party, and no one—least of all Her
Majesty—addressed a word to me at board.'

'Then you should know enough to at least act the
part of the lady and make pleasant overture.'

Rachel lifted stormy eyes to Bess's face. 'My
parents did not raise a mummer, madam!' she said
with quiet dignity.

'Your parents did not raise you at all, I believe.
That was the task of a woman singularly unfitted to
the task of any decent lady.'

The bright colour drained from Rachel's face,
leaving it deathly white. 'You mean…my grandmother?'

'Indeed. Madrilene!'

Hal, who had remained standing during this
exchange, leaned forward and refilled his glass. The
ruby liquid bobbled into the glass, catching and

holding the light. This confrontation had always been on the cards, awaiting a suitable time. Better it was here and now, where he could look on and support both the women he loved. At the moment, he felt, neither needed his help.

Rachel, who had risen still holding her glass, now set it down with a crash. For a moment she was speechless, then she said, 'How dare you say that to me? What do you know of the woman you abuse? My grandmother was not yet twenty when she came to your cold and horrible English court! She was spoiled and rich and had no friend or advisor to tell her she was to deal with a race as alien to her warm nature as fire is to ice… So she dared to fall in love with your husband. I am surprised you did not understand that, you who judge all books by their covers! That is what you have done with me, have you not? When did you ever look at me and not see some phantom rival? So it was,' she continued at white heat, 'when I came here and my dear cousin—' she gave Katherine a scornful glance '—saw only an impoverished orphan whom she could treat as less than the dirt beneath her feet! And so Madrilene,' she concluded triumphantly, 'looked at Sir Harry Latimar, with his air of having no attachments! Well, who could blame her—and me, with any regard at all for the truth?'

As Rachel had been earlier, Bess was now speechless. For it was all true. Harry, her darling, her most beloved husband, had always maintained an air of independence of anything so inconvenient as a wife and children... She said slowly, 'But...she lied...your grandmother. She lied most grievously when it suited.'

Rachel laughed derisively. 'Lied? Well, perhaps she was swifter than I to learn English ways. For that is what you do, is it not? That is the English way. From the highest to the lowest, you all do it! The soft word and the knife in the back—as deadly as any Spanish stiletto in a dark alley. But without the honesty.'

There was a brief, silent pause. Those in the hall, listening to the impassioned voices of the two women, were now aware of a concerted knocking on the outer door. Bess spun around. 'Oh, what now?' She went to the door and, shooting the bolt, flung it open. 'Oh...George.' Her older son stood there, behind him another man, soberly clad, and two others in uniform.

George stepped into the hall. 'Mother, we could not make ourselves heard—' He stepped back and allowed the three others to enter. The two soldiers removed their headgear.

'What is this?' Bess asked.

George drew her aside and said quietly, 'This gentleman...' he indicated the plainly dressed man '...is Thomas Carstairs, who has a warrant for the arrest of Rachel Monterey on the charge of treachery to the Crown. I have examined the warrant and found it to be in order. I think it best if Rachel collect a few belongings and go with the escorting officers.'

Unobserved by any but Hal, Katherine got to her feet and, crossing the floor swiftly, sped up the stairs.

Hal, who also had acute hearing, had heard every word. He moved away from the table and came to the door. He said calmly, 'Rachel does not leave this house this day.'

'Hal…' George gave his brother a cautionary look '…the warrant is in order, and signed by the Queen herself.'

'How fortunate,' Hal returned genially, 'for that lady is upstairs at this very moment and can be asked to confirm it.'

Bess gasped. Elizabeth must have signed this warrant before she left Hampton. She would not have forgotten that the girl was a house guest at Maiden Court—how she loved to test her loyal subjects in this way. 'My dear, don't be foolish! You will see us all in the Tower with your mad ways.'

'If that is what it takes, Mother, so be it.'

George gave his brother another long look, then turned to the three silent strangers. 'Whilst we arrange things, please come into the parlour and take a glass against the coming night.' The men followed him.

Hal and Bess looked at each other. The three officials seemed to have brought dusk in with them; a storm was brewing outside, dark clouds rolled across the sky. Rachel, who had not moved since hearing those dreaded words again, sank back into her chair.

Bess said, 'Hal, you must not think of going to the Queen about this. We must just accept it...do what we can, naturally, but accept it.'

'You don't understand, Mother,' Hal said quietly. 'I promised Her Majesty I would produce Rachel at any court she chose. I will do that, but I cannot allow her to be removed from my custody until I have had sight of the charges which face her, and have prepared some necessary defence.' A white flash of lightning, followed by a growl of thunder, greeted these words. Rachel turned her head and looked at the two by the door. Her eyes, wide and frightened, met Hal's cool blue gaze. 'So...' he came to her and held out his hand '...let us confront the lions in their den.' By sheer force of personality he got her out of the chair and they went to the parlour door. Bess watched them go, recalling Elizabeth Tudor's words about a great love. Never in her life had she seen such a look of trust in anyone's face as was in Rachel's at this moment.

Hal pushed open the door and led Rachel in. Thomas Carstairs was seated in the window, a glass in his hand. The soldiers stood awkwardly by the hearth with beakers of ale; George Latimar, elegantly thin and pale and dressed in the latest of court fashions, held a jug of ruby wine. He looked his brother over with affection and held up the jug. Hal nodded, then ostentatiously escorted Rachel to a chair and set her in it, looking reassuringly down into her face. Glasses were filled and George and Hal found seats.

'Now, Carstairs,' Hal said, 'I would like to see the warrant you have for the Lady Rachel's arrest.'

'By what right?' Carstairs demanded.

'I am her betrothed,' Hal supplied smoothly. 'And as such responsible for her welfare. May I see it?' He held out an exquisitely manicured hand. He did not rise and, after a moment, Thomas Carstairs got up and gave him the paper. Hal unrolled it slowly and read it carefully. It was the bare bones of a serious charge. Hal, a quick study, absorbed it in seconds. He refolded it thoughtfully, then said, 'By happy chance we have the main complainant here in this house. The Lady Katherine Monterey.'

'Do you suggest we hold a court of enquiry here, sir?' Carstairs asked sarcastically.

'What a good idea!' Hal said cheerfully. 'For we also have you to act with fervour for the Crown and my brother George, who among his other talents is a qualified lawyer, may be for the defence, so to speak. I myself can be a character witness, and—' he waved a hand at the two soldiers '—we also have the means to keep the peace should we all become unduly riotous.'

Thomas Carstairs's already florid complexion became enpurpled. For a moment he could not speak, then he ground out, 'You may make mock of the law, you insolent puppy, but I have too much respect for it to listen to your ramblings.' He turned to George. 'My lord Earl, I look to you to control your foolish young brother.'

George sipped his wine. 'Yes…well…and yet it

is not beyond reason what my brother suggests, or without precedent.'

Thomas rearranged his ruff—a very fine one, gleaming white and painstakingly starched—to give himself countenance while he thought, What can you do with these people! Since rising in the ranks of petty clerks, Thomas was constantly coming up against the damned smiling arrogance of the English nobility. 'Surely you do not suggest—? The Lady Rachel is required to stand before the tribunal!'

'Which you represent,' George pointed out. 'And the majority of the evidence comes from Lady Katherine, who can be summoned in a moment. I will undertake to represent Lady Rachel.'

'We have no justice present,' Thomas blustered. Why am I even discussing this? he thought, bemused.

'We have the greatest English justice of all to call upon,' Hal said. 'Her Majesty.'

Thomas pulled again at his ruff. 'I—surely you would not—to even contemplate calling upon Her Majesty in this affair!'

'Who calls upon us?' Elizabeth, who had awoken refreshed from one of her short naps, had wandered down and, curious to know the cause of the raised voices from the parlour, appeared at the door. Everyone seated sprang to their feet. The two soldiers, who had been transfixed by the scene played out before them, stood to attention.

Thomas got out, ''Tis nothing at all, madam. A dispute…'

Elizabeth continued regally into the room. 'A dispute my lord Latimar suggests I preside over.'

'Not at all, your Grace,' Thomas said, visibly sweating. 'It was no serious suggestion, I assure you.'

Elizabeth sat on the window seat, spreading her wide skirts. George gave her a glass and filled it. After trying the wine, she said musingly, 'I have known the Earl for many years and have come to know that all his suggestions are serious.' She looked around at the others in the room, all standing as if children engaged in a game of Grandmother's Footsteps—quite still in the attitudes they held when she entered. How amusing, she chuckled inwardly, 'Now, tell me all.'

The situation has taken her fancy, thought George, so half the battle is won. He said, 'If it please Your Majesty, it is not my suggestion at all but my brother's, and he has all the relevant details. May he give them?'

Elizabeth inclined her head graciously, and Hal stepped forward and began in brief succinct sentences to give Elizabeth the picture. Seeing her begin to frown, he put in, 'As you will remember, I promised to produce the Lady Rachel at any time requested in the future.'

'And any place requested,' she reminded him. He gave his flashing smile and bowed.

'It is such attention to detail which makes you

such a superb statesman, and an ideal adjudicator
in this affair.'

She half laughed. Hal pleased her in this mood;
so tall and straight and vibrating confidence and
suppressed passion. There had been times when the
Queen had sat in rooms with all three Latimar
males and Hal had been, in spite of his golden
looks, much less a presence than the others. She
thought, were those occasions to be repeated—impossible, of course—such would not now be the
case. But he must not have this all his own way.
She turned on Rachel. 'What say you, lady, to this
effort on your behalf?'

Rachel, who had returned to her seat twisting her
hands in her lap, got up and curtsied. 'I have asked
for no effort to be made for me, Your Majesty,' she
said quietly. 'I am prepared to answer the charges
at an official tribunal and have no fear of doing so,
innocence being the best defence.'

Not always, thought George regretfully, and if
you take that combative tone with the Queen you
might shortly find that out.

Hal took gentle hold of one of Rachel's hands.
'As Lady Rachel's future husband—' he began.

'I beg your pardon,' Rachel interrupted. 'That is
the second time you have said that this night.'

'Because it has bearing,' Elizabeth said shortly.
A betrothal, especially involving anyone of noble
blood, was almost equal to a marriage and, like a
marriage, it gave the male the power to oversee all

his future wife's affairs. 'As you must have known when you agreed to it.'

'But I have not agreed to it!' Rachel said angrily.

'You mean it has not been formalised?' Elizabeth asked, knowing full well it had not. 'But a private arrangement, before witnesses, with a ring or some such symbol of intent has taken place, I assume?'

'No…' Rachel said. Hal took a firmer grip on her hand and turned her to face him.

'Then what were we speaking of at sunset those days ago?' She tried to think, to turn, but he slid his hands up her arms and grasped her shoulders so she could not. She looked at the floor and shook her head. He put a hand under her chin so she must meet his eyes. 'I ask you again, Rachel. What were we speaking of? If you have forgotten, I have not.'

'I have not forgotten,' she said huskily, 'nor have I forgotten that I said at that time: It is impossible!'

'Why impossible?' Elizabeth demanded. 'Is there some let?' Blonde and black head turned to look at her.

'It is a family matter, madam,' Hal said. What he had wanted to know he had read a second ago in Rachel Monterey's eyes, and knew she had read the same in his. She loved him as he did her, and if they could just get over this hurdle—

The Queen smacked one hand down on a silk-clad knee. 'If it is a family matter, where is Lady Bess? George, I notice, is keeping uncommon quiet at present.'

George rose then and inclined his head. Out of

the corner of his eye he saw his mother enter the room. 'I do not have the full facts, Majesty; as my brother has said, 'tis a family matter.'

'Then—Lady Bess?' The Queen turned to look at her hostess. 'Are this young man and woman betrothed, or not?'

Rachel looked fearfully at Bess and there was a hushed silence. Hal passed a hand over his gleaming head and sent a long look into his mother's eyes. Thomas Carstairs yet again rearranged his neckgear, wondering when they would get to the business of the day; the two guards were like figures of stone.

Bess, who had been listening from the hall and doing internal battle with herself, looked to George for support and received only an ironic smile. The moment seemed endless for Hal. Nothing could prevent his having Rachel, but what happened now would make a difference to her immediate wellbeing. Thinking of this, he unconsciously turned the sapphire ring in his left ear and Bess started. This gesture more than any other had been peculiar to her husband Harry. She had never seen her son practise it before. She said firmly, 'Yes, they are informally betrothed. I have here a ring, and, if Your Majesty so pleases, they could declare their vows before you now.'